FOR BETTER AND FOR WORSE

What a fool she had been! Clarice angrily told herself. She had let Julian back into her life, listening to his argument that they still were legally man and wife. She had let him back into her arms, listening to the fierce beating of her own heart.

But now she would listen to the voice of reason. She would take heed of the evidence of her eyes that Julian already had taken a new mistress. She would believe the shattering proof she had discovered: not only was he an unfaithful husband, but a traitor to his country as well.

She had given Julian her best. Now she would do her worst. . . .

Broken Vows

Broken Vows

By

Elizabeth Hewitt

A SIGNET BOOK
NEW AMERICAN LIBRARY

Publisher's Note

This book is a work of fiction. Names, characters, places, and incidents are either the product of the author's imagination or are used fictitiously, and any resemblance to actual persons, living or dead, events, or locales is entirely coincidental.

SIGNET TRADEMARK REG. U.S. PAT. OFF. AND FOREIGN COUNTRIES
REGISTERED TRADEMARK—MARCA REGISTRADA
HECHO EN CHICAGO, U.S.A.

SIGNET, SIGNET CLASSIC, MENTOR, ONYX, PLUME, MERIDIAN AND NAL BOOKS are published by NAL PENGUIN INC., 1633 Broadway, New York, New York 10019

First Printing, May, 1982

3 4 5 6 7 8 9 10 11

PRINTED IN THE UNITED STATES OF AMERICA

For Jim

1

Lord Ardane walked down Grosvenor Square with something very like a lilt in his step. He was convivial by nature and had spent an agreeable afternoon loitering about his clubs, and was looking forward to an equally agreeable evening in the company of a few cronies of similar tastes in dissipation. With his wife and sons visiting relatives in the country, he was a temporary bachelor and not minding it in the least.

Peter Ardane, sixth Earl of Ardane, was a very tall, fair young man of thirty-two who had inherited his father's dignities at the unlikely age of twelve. He had married, at the age of nineteen and in the face of great opposition, a very young, very pretty girl of good family and small fortune. This circumstance had very naturally horrified his family, for his inheritance, no more than genteel to begin with, became little more than a competence after his mother's jointure and his sisters' dowries had been set aside; but anyone who came to know Peter Ardane at all well was very much aware that it was a mistake to oppose him when he set his mind to something, and his mind had been very much set on Lydia Bastow.

Despite the voices of gloom that proclaimed that he would be wretched and a victim of his folly within a twelvemonth, Lord Ardane was a reasonably contented man. It had not always been easy to attain the style of life to which his wife had insisted on becoming accustomed, but one way or the other he had managed well enough.

As he reached his home, a trim Georgian town house on Half Moon Street, he frowned slightly. Just before his wife had left that morning she had mentioned, not for the first time, that the house was becoming impossibly small and cramped. She had been more than pleased with it when he had recklessly purchased it—at her instigation and to the horror of his man of business—during the first year of their marriage. The sale of his father's aged and crumbling mansion, in what the new Lady Ardane did not hesitate to condemn as an impossible section of town, had much defrayed the cost, and for a time they had been comfortable enough. It was only much later, when they had had occasion to visit his younger sister, who had married a man of great wealth, in her elegant and spacious mansion in Curzon Street, that the complaints had begun.

But Lord Ardane shrugged these thoughts off, for purchasing another house at this time was out of the question, whatever Lydia might insist, and with an impulsive start, he skipped nimbly up the front steps. He greeted his permanently impassive butler, who let him in, cheerfully.

Stevens took his lordship's hat, gloves, and cane and then looked up to Lord Ardane's superior height to address him. "My lord," he began as he placed his lordship's things on the receptacle by the door, "there is a gentleman waiting to see you. I have placed him in the bookroom."

Lord Ardane glanced up from his perusal of the silver tray that held the visiting cards left that day. "Well, Stevens, which is it, Mr. Tomlin or Lord Beach?" he asked with a rueful sigh. "Which shall I steel myself for, charities or politics?"

"As to that, my lord," replied the correct Stevens, "I cannot say. But I can say that this man is neither of those gentlemen."

"No?" queried his lordship. "Then who is he, pray? The only other card belongs to my Aunt Tabitha, and you can't have taken her for a gentleman, unless perhaps you've been tippling in the cellar?"

Stevens did not hold with this kind of levity and he did not permit himself so much as a conciliatory smile at this sally. He said stiffly, "I cannot say who he is, my lord. He did not give his name."

Ardane viewed his servitor with a mixture of amusement and annoyance. "Did you by any chance bother to ask him his name?" he enquired sweetly.

Stevens looked hurt. "Yes, my lord," said this august personage in an even stiffer (if possible) voice. "The gentleman declined to say."

"Did he, now? Then what the devil is he doing in my bookroom?" thundered the earl, not unreasonably.

"He claims a connexion to Lady Rown, my lord, and as her ladyship is your lordship's sister, and he had the look of a gentleman, I did not care to gainsay him," replied Stevens, unruffled.

Or his purse, thought Ardane, but he was curious, so he said, "Oh, very well. I suppose I might as well see the fellow."

He strode purposefully up the stairs toward his library, muttering to himself on the pity that servants were not immune to the lure of gold. But in this he did his henchman an injustice. It was not gold that had got the stranger past the earl's generally close-guarded portals, but a certain something familiar about him, in a family sort of way. So as the man was obviously well-bred and well-dressed and gave no appearance of being one of those dirty dishes that all families possess, Stevens complied with the stranger's request to await the earl's return. Besides, though Stevens might not have admitted it, there was a forceful quality in the man, an air of command, that had made it difficult to refuse him.

Lord Ardane opened the door to the bookroom and was amazed to discover it almost in darkness; the fire had died down and an approaching storm had brought about an early gloom. He perceived the gentleman in question silhouetted against one of the windows facing the garden. His back was to Lord Ardane, and in any event he was too far away in the darkened room for the earl to make him out. He began at once to apologize for such inhospitality.

"I beg your pardon. I can't imagine what the servants were about not to bring you candles." He started toward the bell-pull, but halfway there he was (as he later described it) struck by a thunderbolt: the shadowy figure spoke.

"It's quite all right, Peter. They did bring candles, but I've put them out. I don't believe surprises should come all at once."

Words with nothing too startling in their content, but the voice that spoke them made the small hairs on the back of the earl's neck stand up in a most unpleasant manner. A gasping "Good God!" was all of which that startled nobleman was momentarily capable, for there was no mistaking that soft, distinctive voice.

Taking advantage of this lapse of good breeding on the part of the earl, the shadowy man moved from the window to the mantle, and discovering a tinderbox, lit several candles in a holder. The light outside had all but gone now, and a heavy rain that had just begun obliterated that little bit. The candles, the only light, flared brightly, casting grotesque shadows about the room.

Lord Ardane was a prosaic man, and asked if he believed in ghosts, would have scoffed hotly at the idea; but that did not prevent him now from feeling ice cold in a somewhat stuffy room. "Good God!" he repeated, scarcely aware of doing so.

The dark figure of the man moved forward, the shadows playing eerily on his face. He was an attractive man of above average height, fine-boned, and his features, sharply relieved by the candlelight, were patrician. His hair and eyes, both very dark, caught the glow of the flickering flames and took on, to Ardane's mind, an unnatural glitter. The man walked over to the earl, and placing the candles on a table, held out his hand.

"I'm not a ghost, Peter. I am quite real." He looked up through dark lashes at the taller man. "Touch me if it will reassure you."

Lord Ardane, unconsciously doing as he was bid, momentarily grasped the hand held out to him and then abruptly sank into the nearest chair. The apparition, or so he had at first thought it, was indeed real. "Good God!" he exclaimed yet a third time. "You're dead!"

The man responsible for his lordship's agitation laughed softly, seeming amused by Ardane's discomfiture, and sat down in a chair opposite him. "You have just seen otherwise, haven't you, Peter," he said. "I've never yet heard that ghosts have substance."

Ardane was by no means a stupid or inarticulate man, but his generally excellent brain was refusing to focus properly on this untoward event. "I don't understand . . . How can this be . . ." He faltered. "They said you had been killed. They said . . ."

"They lied." On the table next to the candles were a decanter of wine and two glasses, and the man poured out the pale golden liquid and handed one of the glasses to Ardane.

The earl thanked him absently. He was aware that he was babbling and made an effort to compose himself. "But how is this possible?" he asked slowly. "We were told—by the government, mind—that you and Mme. Rouane were passengers on the *Spider*, sailing for Canada when it was taken down by a French privateer. It went down with all hands on the open seas and was witnessed by a man-of-war. They claimed there were no survivors. No one could have made a mistake like that." He paused to drink deeply from his glass. "Are you asking me to believe that they deliberately lied to your wife and family?" he added suspiciously.

The man bowed his head and stared at the flickers of candlelight reflected in his glass. "Are you wondering, Peter, if I am an impostor?" He sighed. "I wish you will not waste our time forcing me to prove that I am not. I can, you know. It would be the easiest thing in the world, but time-consuming, for we go back almost to infancy, you and I, dear cousin, do we not?"

Peter hesitated. He would dearly have loved to believe this man a clever impostor, but he did not. "I suppose it must be you," he admitted grudgingly. "No one else would have the audacity to disappear for four years and then just show up again without a blush." He got up and began to pace restlessly about the room, but he was composed now and his voice was firm. "Where were you, Julian? I suppose Therese Rouane wasn't on the *Spider* either. Is she still with you?"

"No, she isn't," Julian replied without elaborating. "I was mostly in Canada, ironically enough, though I never set eyes on the *Spider*." He paused for a long moment and then went on thoughtfully, "Do you know, I would wake up in the middle of the night to a silence so complete that you could hear the snow fall, and I'd miss England and my family"—he spread his hands in a gallic gesture—"all of it, so much that it was almost past bearing. In the end, with the war over, or nearly over as it happened, and my usefulness in America at an end, I gave up resisting its siren's call. But why don't you sit down, dear boy, before you knock over some unfortunate table, and I'll see if I can piece my adventure together for you."

Ardane sat down reluctantly, for he was the type of man who needed to move about when anything troubled him; his cousin, a man of calmer mien, put his head against the back of the chair and half-closed his eyes. "The government did lie to you," he said, "they had to. These things are so very delicate, you see. As to Therese, she may, for all I know, have been on the *Spider*. But if she was, she didn't mind it going down. The last time I saw her, the night I left London, she was quite dead."

"The devil she was!" exclaimed Ardane, his brow creased with puzzlement and surprise. "Do you know how she died?"

"Yes," replied Julian, flashing him a quick mordant smile. "At least I know what killed her. A difference of opinion with a long sharp knife. Don't think me callous, Peter; she was thoroughly bad. I believe even her own people had come to doubt her loyalties. I don't believe she had any. Beautiful woman, though. Pity."

"What do you mean 'her people'?" asked Peter.

"The French."

"The French! Julian, were you involved in some sort of intrigue?" asked Peter in a puzzled voice. "What the devil were you, a spy?" he added in a tone that might have been inquiring if Julian were a leper.

Julian smiled broadly at this, showing perfect teeth. "How sordid you make it sound! But the assumption is essentially accurate."

"English?"

"Of course," Julian murmured. "Now, why would you suppose otherwise?"

"Oh, I didn't mean anything by it," Ardane assured him. "It isn't beyond the realm of possibility, is it? You speak the language like a born *frog*; and intrigue, at least intrigue of another sort, is hardly foreign to you. And," he added as the crowning point to his argument, "your great-grandmother was French."

"The great-grandmother that we share," Julian reminded him. "I'm afraid I'm not following your logic, Peter."

"Well, I'd heard it said that Boney was offering fair remuneration to émigrés or their descendants in return for a little . . . ah . . . assistance."

Julian raised his eyebrows. "Is that for my benefit? What a charming picture you paint of my character. But surely you will not accuse *me* of selling myself for a fortune?"

"No," agreed Peter with a trace of bitterness as he recalled his wife's complaints earlier that day about the size of their house, "you would never need do it for money."

There was a faint stress on the word "money," but Julian let the implications of this pass. "In a way, though," he said, "it was that very offer of Boney's that brought me into it. In certain quarters it was thought that my background and fluency in French might make a useful cover, enable me to pick up bits and pieces of information about who was being recruited by the French and by whom. It was even hoped that I might be attractive to them, which it turned out I was; hence the lovely Therese."

"Are you going to tell me that your relationship with La Rouane was purely business?" sneered Ardane. "I won't believe you."

"No, I know you would not," agreed his cousin with perfect amiability.

"I still don't see what any of this has to do with why you played dead for four years," said Peter. "It can't be because you feared being blamed for her death. No one believed her dead until the sinking of the *Spider*. Certainly no body was ever found that I ever heard of. Do you know what became of her?"

"I haven't the least idea. They dispatched me without a trace, so I suppose they did the same with her body," replied Julian.

"And you have no idea who killed her?" Peter persisted.

"Not really. I've thought about it, certainly. The French, because they believed her false, is a likely explanation. Who knows?" He shrugged slightly. "But there was another possibility. I had reason to believe that there was someone who used her as a courier, a go-between with the French, and of whom she was afraid."

"An émigré?"

"Possibly, but I don't think so," Julian replied thoughtfully. "Therese was just a tool. Her beauty and charm made her useful in attracting young men to the French cause, and that and the information she passed on for this man—shall we call him Mr. Smith, as anonymous as he no doubt wished to be—were her sole tasks as far as I could discover. I believe she was used this way because the man himself had to be above suspicion. He couldn't afford to be seen in a normal way with any known or suspected agent, but Therese's lineage was impeccable, and her conduct, though reprehensible, was always discreet. She was accepted in society; one met her everywhere. Such settings must surely be above reproach, or Prinny himself would be suspect."

"Are you suggesting that he was an Englishman, and one of us?" asked Peter, incredulous.

"Almost certainly. I never had any proof; I was close, but never quite close enough. In the beginning, when I first became aware of his existence, I thought it was someone in the government itself; then I realized that it just as likely could be someone who only had contacts with such people. It absolutely amazed me how careless some people were with privileged information. If one had the right name, went to the right schools, behaved oneself, and thought as one ought, why then of course one could be trusted. What damnable rot!" Julian paused, then added, "He was clever. I don't believe they ever found him out. But then, he wouldn't take chances; he had too much to lose."

"So you think he killed Therese?"

"It's just my opinion. It doesn't matter anymore."

Peter shifted uncomfortably in his chair. Out of deference to his guest he remaind seated, but he itched to move about while he digested the story Julian was telling him.

"The night that I left London," Julian continued, "she was expecting me, and I wasn't at all pleased about it. I had every reason to believe that one moment of stupid carelessness—never mind what it was—had undone me. I unintentionally betrayed myself in a way that the rawest recruit wouldn't have been fool enough to do. Far worse, I wasn't sure how constant her contact with other French agents was, or whether this was the sort of thing she would pass along to Mr. Smith. Think about it. If you were he, would you be comfortable with the discovery that your primary contact, the one person who could betray you, was the mistress of an English agent? If she told this man her suspicions about me, our little rendezvous could have been a trap. But an intimate knowledge of La Rouane told me that she would most likely try to sell her information to the highest bidder, and I am a very rich man, or at least my father is, which is much the same thing.

"However," he went on, "I never had the gratification of learning that I was right. I don't know what happened that night, but I can guess. Either she decided to approach him first, offering the information of my existence for sale, or perhaps she threatened to betray him to me in order to gain a greater hold over him. Whatever, she badly miscalculated his

reaction. Then again, her death could have been the result of her own dealings and nothing whatever to do with me. How distressing not to know for certain!"

Julian poured wine for Lord Ardane and himself. "I won't say finding her like that wasn't a shock to my sensibilities, for it was. How opportune and yet how inopportune! If only I had known. Was I safe, or had she betrayed me? I hadn't a notion, of course, but it seemed to me that I ought to do something, so I went through her desk and any other place she was likely to keep papers. A foolish enterprise, you might say, for someone had patently been there before me. Still, I persevered. Fruitless, of course, and dangerous. There was always the possibility that the person who had murdered her was still about, perhaps waiting to discover my identity if he had not managed to get it out of her before he killed her."

Peter chewed throughtfully at a fingertip. "Did you put something in writing, a letter perhaps, that might have exposed you to him?"

"I hope I'm not such a fool!" retorted Julian. "I was hoping to find something that would give me proof of Mr. Smith's existence, perhaps even his identity. But of course, I should have known better," he added with self-mockery. "And with no tangible proof to bring him to account, Mr. Smith had nothing to fear but me and my suspicions. He had already killed once to protect himself; if he was as sure of me as I was unsure of him, my life wasn't worth a farthing."

Ardane nodded slowly. "Yes, I can see that. But why didn't you just leave the country?"

"A known agent in a clandestine operation is utterly useless, and the government had decided—heaven knows why—that I would be an asset to them in America," Julian replied. "You might say that my misadventure was quite timely for them; in different circumstances I might not have so willingly fell in with their plans. As it was, they believed that it would better serve the task I was assigned to do there, and my personal safety as well, if I were believed dead. At the time it suited me to agree with them."

Peter considered this. "But if Mr. Smith did kill Therese he must have known that she couldn't have drowned on the *Spider*," he said slowly. "When the list of casualties was published, mightn't he have wondered whether your name was simply planted there as well as hers?"

"How astute of you!" said his cousin in a congratulatory tone. "I have no doubt that he had a bad time of it in the beginning. He must have been in a sad state when I disappeared and Therese's body was never found. I am vindictive enough to hope that he was positively tormented with worry and fear. Then when he heard of my death he probably vacillated between overwhelming relief and nagging doubt. It was certainly just possible that I *was* on that ship. I sincerely hope he was miserable.

"But naturally, as time went on and I did not reappear, and, most importantly, as no action was taken against him, he must have relaxed considerably. Pity.

"When my search of Therese's rooms discovered nothing," Julian continued, returning to the main thread of his story, "I went to my contact and was persuaded to leave matters in his hands. He took my plight to those to whose tune we danced, and returned with their instructions. At first I was inclined to look askance at the suggestion that I take an active part in my own funeral, however spurious, and there was a fallback plan should I refuse, but in the end, as I've said, it suited me well enough.

"He told me that he had booked passage for me on a ship sailing for the West Indies, and things not being what they might with our neighbors to the west, I had my doubts about the soundness of their course, but one is trained not to cavil at the decisions of one's superiors. Quite a basic tenet of the spy trade, I believe.

"I did as I was told, and after a perfectly ghastly crossing, ended up in Barbados. From there I went to New Orleans, passing myself off very credibly as a French émigré—one does not, after all, dine out on nothing—and from there eventually to Montreal, where I spent the greater part of the last few years. I had money when I left, or rather that which is easily converted to money, and I lived tolerably well.

"Then the war was over," he continued, "and I received the message that my usefulness was yet again at an end and I could return home or not as I pleased. I did please, so I booked passage, the only qualms I had about returning being personal ones."

"You must have had many," interrupted Peter tartly.

Julian lifted the corners of his mouth just perceptibly. "To be quite open with you, Peter, I wasn't at all sure that I

ought to come back. I wondered if it mightn't be best to leave things as they were. But I would have spent the rest of my life wondering what would have happened if I had, and a life of fruitless conjecture did not appeal to me. So, the prodigal returns."

Ardane snorted. "I must say that puts it exactly! Have you seen your family?"

Julian looked down at the glass in his hands. "No. Is my father in London, do you know?"

"He was at Creeley last I heard. I thought you might have written to him."

Julian shook his head. "No. In fact, you are the first person I've honored with my interesting adventures."

"I'm flattered," said Peter sarcastically. "Does the government know you've returned?"

"Does that matter anymore?" Julian replied noncommittally. "Is everyone well? Information of England was necessarily rather scant. It generally is, I've been told, even without a war to hinder it."

"Everyone is well, Julie," answered Peter. He rose impatiently. "What made you come to me first? I would have thought that I'd be the last person you'd come to."

Julian looked up at him. "I came to see you first because you were the last person I saw before I left town, the last person of my family, that is. Call it sentiment."

Ardane laughed mirthlessly. "You are the last person in the world I would credit with an excess of sentiment."

"Do you think so?" asked Julian with a sigh. "Well, then, I will admit there is another reason—a rather obvious one, I should think."

"Clare," said Peter succinctly.

Julian nodded and looked down at his hands. "How is she?" he asked.

"Quite well."

"Have you seen her recently?"

"Last evening."

"I see. Then she is in town. In Curzon Street?"

"No, that has been let. She's with Anne."

Julian put his glass on the table, rose, and walked past Ardane into the shadows of the room, beyond the light of the candles. Once again his tall, slim figure was wreathed in the darkness. "I find this difficult to ask," he said slowly, "but of course I must. Is she married?"

"To you, it would seem."

"You know what I'm asking."

"There'll be a devil of a coil now if she has remarried. Did you think of that when you left?" Peter demanded.

"Of course I thought of it," Julian replied in an expressionless voice. "You needn't think I mean to ruin her life a second time if she has."

"No?" asked Ardane sarcastically. "And just what *do* you mean to do?"

"I mean to put the past behind me. I'm tired of living a life that isn't mine. I suppose what I want most is peace; if I can find it. If Clare is still mine, then I mean to win her back to me; if she has remarried . . ." He shrugged. "So much for what I want."

"What will you do if she has?"

"Go back, most likely. At least I'll know and won't spend the rest of my life wondering."

"Would you leave without letting her know you're alive?"

"Yes. What else could I do? If she has remarried, the marriage is illegal and any children of it illegitimate. I won't do that to her."

Peter shook his head slowly. "The thing that amazes me is that you couldn't send her some word or sign in four years. At least to let her know you were alive. Did you think her so little to be trusted? Didn't you care at all?"

"It was more than a simple matter of trust." Julian moved to the window facing out on the garden again and turned his back on the room.

"What, then? Loyalties?" pursued the earl. "Damn misguided ones, if you ask me."

"I wouldn't dream of asking you, Peter." Julian turned again and faced him. "There were other considerations. I might have been lost at sea, captured by the Americans, or even accidentally caught up in that unlikely war we were waging there. It would have been to no purpose for her to believe me alive, only to discover that I was not after all. I was not known by my own name, of course, and if anything had happened to me, no one here would have ever known. I think it was better this way."

"Better!" Peter exclaimed, his voice filled with disgust.

"Better, by God! Better for a wife to suffer the humiliation of believing her husband had run off with another woman? Better for her to grieve and mourn for you?"

"Did she indeed grieve?" asked Julian, a shade caustically. "You will give me leave to doubt it. She made it abundantly clear the last time I saw her that she considered me the mistake of her life and would have given a deal to be out of our farce of a marriage. I wouldn't be terribly surprised if you told me she'd married again before she was out of black." He stopped and then said in a quite different voice, "But you may believe this, Peter: I never meant to hurt her."

This was too much for Ardane; his bubbling wrath exploded. "Hurt her!" he stormed. "Dammit! How dare you say so to me, of all people. You did nothing but give her pain from the very beginning."

"No, I was not a pattern-card husband," Julian agreed, "but some things couldn't be helped."

"I see," Peter said sourly. "Your 'mission in life' again. Bad, but tempered with nobility. Very pretty eight years later. No doubt all those barques of frailty you threw in her face were part of your 'great work'?"

"No."

Ardane peered into the darkness but could not make out the expression on his cousin's face. Giving it up, he abandoned his pacing and cast himself into a chair. "Did you by any chance know that Clare was breeding when you left?" he asked.

"Yes."

" 'Yes,' " Peter mimicked. "That's all? Just like that? 'Yes'?"

Julian said nothing.

"Are you even interested in the outcome?"

"I feel sure you'll tell me."

"It was a girl, called Julia. After you." Peter threw up his hands in a gesture that might have been disgust or defeat and was in fact a little of both. "What do you mean to do now? See her?"

"That depends, doesn't it? You still haven't told me if she has married again."

Peter pursed his lips and didn't answer at once. Then he said resignedly, "The temptation to tell you that she has is almost overwhelming, but I suspect you'd be able to discover the truth in some other quarter. No, she has not married again. She's happy now; I'll be sorry to see that change."

Julian did not rise to this bait. "Then of course I must see her; but I'd like your help. I don't want to startle her any more than is necessary."

"I hope she takes a heavy object and throws it at you," Peter said flatly. "Well, what is it you want me to do?"

"Send for her," Julian said. "Ask her to come here. Then tell her, as gently as you can, that I am back and want to see her . . . if she wishes it."

"I rather think she will wish it."

"I hope you may be right. I'd prefer to risk injury than not see her at all. I'm sorry for the things I said to her the night before I left; I'd like to make it up to her if I can."

"How noble!"

Julian walked back into the small pool of light and stood looking down at his cousin. "You may sneer at me if you wish, Peter. I was a shockingly bad husband." He sat down carefully, as if he were very tired. "For the last four years I have had time to think a great deal about Clare, myself, and our marriage. That's really why I had to come back. I want to make right, if she'll let me, what was so very wrong between us."

Lord Ardane crossed to the bell pull, and presently Stevens arrived in answer to his lordship's summons. Though no hint of it appeared in his face, Stevens was avid with curiosity. It was soon clear, though, that the earl had no intention of enlightening him with any explanation. Instead Lord Ardane merely remarked on the dampness of the room and desired that the fire be relit and the candles rekindled, and almost as an afterthought, that a footman be sent in shortly to carry a message. Stevens, a temporarily disappointed man, retired to give his orders to his underlings.

The first part of the earl's commands having been carried out, the room gave up its last traces of melodrama. Lord Ardane sat down at the broad desk at one end of the room, and taking a piece of foolscap, a pen, and a standish, began to write. When he had finished, he took it over to Julian, who was standing before the mantel staring into the fire. Julian read it and handed it back to him with a slight nod.

Several moments later a lanky, loose-limbed footman

dressed in the earl's green-and-brown livery entered the room and stood obediently at the foot of the desk to await Lord Ardane's commands. Ardane looked up, handed him the note, and directed him to take it to Lady Rown. The footman bowed and left.

The earl sat where he was, at his desk, frowning pensively at nothing in particular. Julian, Viscount Rown, gazed on into the fire, awaiting events.

2

Lady Rown picked a piece of chocolate out of the frilly box and frowned at it. Clarice cared little for sweets, but the candy was a present from Mr. Prescott, and as he was the type of man who liked his gifts to be enjoyed and was apt to comment on them, she thought it better to nibble at the confections than to offend him. She grimaced at the sugary taste, and then with a short sigh picked up the novel she had tossed aside earlier in the day and began to read. It was a diverting, if improbable tale, relying largely on amazing coincidences. Clarice thought the heroine a silly chit possessed of an excess of sensibility, and the hero, untouched by base instinct or vice, nauseatingly perfect. Not, she thought, like any man *I* ever knew. As a matter of fact, she was beginning to root unabashedly for the villain.

She had just reached the part in the story where the villain lures the unsuspecting heroine to his gloomy castle on a barren rock (which one would probably later discover he had no right to own, having cheated the rightful heir, who would probably turn out to be the hero) to carry out his base designs, when the door opened and Clarice's sister, Lady Fowle, breezed in.

Lady Fowle was a plump, attractive young matron who had just reached her thirty-seventh birthday, and although in a world that glorified beautiful youth she might have found this depressing, she did not. Her childbearing days having been completed (she hoped), she was now settled down with her doting husband and lively young family into a complacent domesticity. Anne Fowle was a born mother.

As she crossed the room to her sister's couch, a disinterested observer would have been hard put to recognize them as sisters, for a greater contrast could hardly have been imagined. Where Anne was fair, a bit plain, short and plump, Clarice was possessed of rich chestnut-colored hair, was quite tall and fashionably slim, and reckoned by many a beauty. She had large doelike brown eyes, and full, slightly pouting lips that gave her a sensual quality. Anne was a friend to the men she knew; Clarice was coveted.

But the observer would have been deceived, as anyone who knew Clarice might have told him, for Lady Rown, the mother of two young boys aged seven and five, and a little girl just three and a half, was every bit as devoted and domesticated a parent as her older sister.

Anne sat down on the sofa next to her sister. "I wish you would change your mind, Clare, and come with us," she said coaxingly. "With Mr. Prescott in Hampshire and the children in bed, you'll be moped to death by yourself."

Clarice put aside her book and smiled at her sister. "After last night's celebrations, I don't crave excitement. A dull evening of comfortable repose will suit me exactly, Anne. Besides, I believe there is a storm brewing. It's not even seven, and becoming quite dark already."

"As if that signified!" retorted Lady Fowle. "Do you suppose we mean to walk to the Patchers'? Sir Thomas will be quite put out if you don't come, you know."

Clarice's ready laughter bubbled. "Oh, dear, he will have no one to wink at or pinch, I expect."

"Wretched girl!" said her sister sternly, but with laughter lurking in her eyes. "If you aren't kinder, you'll have no flirts left to you. And serve you right, too!"

"Well, as for that," returned the unrepentant Clarice, "it doesn't matter anymore, does it? In a few months I will cease to be a 'dashing widow' and become a stodgy married lady again."

Anne regarded her earnestly. "Are you happy, Clare?" she asked abruptly.

"Happy?" said Clarice, surprised. "Why, what an absurd question, Anne. Why shouldn't I be happy?"

"Are you quite sure . . ." Anne stopped. "I mean," she tried again, "if you aren't . . . if you don't quite like . . ." She faltered, gave it up, and then rushed on, "You know you are welcome here for as long as you wish to stay. For good, if you like."

Clarice got up from the sofa. "What nonsense you talk, Anne. Of course I am sure."

"I wish I might believe it."

"Well, you may," snapped Clarice.

"Oh, I'm sorry, Clare. Don't be angry," cried Anne. "I don't know what I'm talking about. A fit of the doldrums, I expect."

"Oh!" Clarice exclaimed in feigned outrage. "What a bouncer! I don't believe you know what the doldrums are. You are the sunniest creature dear, dear Anne, and I am a beast to take offence." She reached down and hugged her sister. "There, I will beg your pardon and we may be friends again."

Anne did not reply but only smiled a little sadly.

Clarice walked over to the window and leaned over the low sill. She watched the raindrops that were just beginning to fall for a few moments and then turned and faced Anne, who was watching her somewhat anxiously. "I know what is troubling you, Anne," she said, "but you can't expect me to go on forever in the same way. I must put the past behind me; all the more so because much of it was unpleasant. I made a great many mistakes with Julian, but I hope I have learned from them and will do better with John. No, don't tease me," said Clarice hastily, seeing the retort forming on Anne's lips. "You know it was so. I know you object because John is so very different from the way that Julian was, but surely that is only for the best. You think I can't be happy with him, but you are mistaken; I shall be.

"I know how fond you were of Rown, but even you cannot say that he was a model husband or our marriage a happy one. Dashing, romantic men in the Byronic image may do very well for an unseasoned girl's fantasies, but they make abominable husbands in real life. I know." She attempted a laugh. "You always did deal with him better than I could. I wonder you didn't marry him yourself."

Anne smiled. "Now who's talking nonsense? When I married Fowle, Rown was scarcely out of short coats, and by the time he was, he was chasing after that redheaded creature who caused such a stir and eventually married Sir Edmund Trotter." Then, realizing that this was not the most propitious memory (Lady Trotter having made a second appearance in Lord Rown's life some years later), she said hastily, "The trouble was that you took it all so to heart. He was always a little wild; you knew that when you married him, and it wasn't reasonable to expect him to drop all his fast friends and change his ways overnight. If only you had let it alone for a bit, I'm certain he would have settled down and become a good husband. I know he loved you, Clare. But no man likes to be wept on and harped at constantly; it was bound to make him feel stifled." She paused and sighed in recollection. "Well, never mind, it is, as you say, the past and best forgotten. If you are content with the course you are taking, if you are certain that you will be happy with Mr. Prescott, you know there is no one who will wish you greater joy than I do."

Clarice took her sister's hand in hers and smiled. "You really don't have to worry about me, you know. My eyes are wide open this time, and I promise you I won't let my possessiveness override my judgment again."

By tacit consent the subject was changed, and shortly thereafter Anne took herself off, exclaiming that she was dreadfully late and must dress for dinner at once. Clarice, who was to take a tray in her room, did not bother with this nicety, but went back to her book and her chocolates.

A few minutes after eight, Lady Fowle bustled back into the room, pecked her sister on the cheek, and said that they were off now, and that Fowle was in a dreadful pet because they were late. With a whisk of silk and a trail of scent, she hurried back through the door she had left open, and nearly collided with the footman who had come to remove Clarice's dinner tray. However, instead of going directly to the table that held this, he surprised Clarice by stopping before her. He bowed and proffered a silver tray holding a sealed piece of paper. Clarice waited until he had taken up the tray and left the room before she broke the seal of the note. She recognized the seal, of course, and was mildly curious as to why her brother would be sending her a message at this hour of the evening, when it might be supposed that she was about to go out. With a little impatient sigh she settled herself comfortably in her chair and read the short missive. It was simple and to the point, but vague for all that. She read it over again to see if she might discover some clue to the reason he summoned her so urgently, but it was too short, and held, as far as she could see, no hidden meanings. "Provoking creature!" she exclaimed aloud. How like Peter to demand her presence with no explanation. Most likely, she surmised, he was in some sort of domestic scrape and needed extricating before Lyddy returned to discover it.

Her first impulse was to send him an equally cryptic note, presenting her compliments and informing him that she would call upon him in the morning. But on reflection, her curiosity urged her to go. She really had nothing to keep her at home but her book, and if he *did* need her . . . She gave an exasperated sigh and got up to pull the bell for her maid.

Less than half an hour later she was in her town carriage, rattling through the wet streets, preparing a scold for her brother. As Lady Fowle's house was not far from Lord Ardane's, it was a short drive, but the rain, which had grown steadily harder, made it anything but pleasant. Her destination arrived at, not the best efforts of her groom, nor of Stevens, who had personally opened the door at the sound of the carriage, could prevent her skirts from becoming slightly damp, and it was in no good humor that Clarice followed Stevens to the saloon at the back of the house where her brother was waiting for her.

"Well," said Ardane testily as his sister was announced, "you took your own damn time about it." His humor, too, was sadly put out by the events of this night. The pleasant anticipation with which he had looked forward to the evening had long since been banished.

Clarice waited until her brother had nodded a frigid dismissal to the interested Stevens before answering. "My dear Ardane," she said haughtily, "I do not possess wings, nor am I yours to command!" She cast herself tomboyishly into a chair before the fire. "Well, what mess have you gotten yourself into? Has Mrs. Higgens given notice or the kitchen staff walked out *en masse*? I promise you, Peter, it had better be good!"

"Oh, it's good, all right," said Ardane. "But it's nothing like you're thinking. And," he added indignantly, "you needn't assume because I want to see you it's to get me out of some scrape."

Clarice smiled at her brother. "If it's true that you aren't in any scrape, I beg your pardon. But it's so late, Peter! What would you have me think? What could be so important that it couldn't wait until tomorrow?

"Well?" she asked when she received no reply. "Do you mean to tell me what it is that you want?"

Peter continued to just look at her for a moment, and then said, "Let me tell you, my girl, this is by no means easy. If I'd even guessed it would be so hard, he could have done it himself. Not, of course, that I'm doing it for him. He said he wanted me to make it easier for you, and so I wish I might, if I only knew how." He placed his hand on the mantel and stared into the fire. "The thing of it is," he continued, absently kicking a stray coal back into the fire, "is that it's bound to be a shock to you, no matter how I say it. Stands to reason."

Clarice's heart was beating just a little faster. The thought that came to her as she heard him speak was that John Prescott for some reason or another had changed his mind about marrying her and was using Peter as the means of telling her so. She got up and went over to him. "If it is something as startling as all that, I think you had just better tell me at once." She put her hand on his shoulder. "You must know that my imagination is running quite wild, and the truth is bound to be easier."

"You think so, do you?" he asked gloomily.

"Yes, I do," she replied firmly, but she was aware of an unpleasant feeling of rising alarm.

"It's Julian," he said in funereal accents.

"Julian!" exclaimed Clarice, startled. Relief flooded over her. It was the last thing in the world she had expected him to say.

"He's back. Here, that is to say. In my bookroom."

Clarice stood very still and stared at him in amazement. Then she hit upon the obvious explanation. "You're foxed!"

"I am not!" Peter exclaimed, injured.

"Then this is a very poor joke, especially after last night." She took her hand off his shoulder.

"Clare," Peter said earnestly, "this isn't a joke. Believe me, it *is* the truth. Julian is here in this house."

Clarice gazed at him critically for a moment and then decided that he at least believed he was telling the truth. She said slowly, as if to a dim-witted child, "Peter, Julian is dead. He died four years ago."

He took her hands in his and pressed them firmly. "Clare, please, just listen. I know how this sounds to you, but I truly have not lost my senses. Early this evening I came home and Stevens told me there was a man waiting to see me in the bookroom. I went in, and there he was—not a ghost, nor an impostor, but Julian, very much alive."

"Peter, you know that can't be true," she said, incredulous. "You know when he died, and how."

"It was all lies, apparently," he said gently. "It's a long, involved story, but the sum of it is that Julian was never on that damned ship. He was in America, lording it as an émigré or some such thing. But he's back now, and he wants to see you."

Clarice stared at him, her eyes very wide. She fought hard with herself to accept what he was saying. For such a long while now she had believed herself a widow—the husband she had loved so deeply, and at times so passionately hated, dead—that it was almost impossible for her to grasp the idea that he was still alive. "I don't know what to think," she said, her voice tremulous. "I must believe you, I suppose, but . . . Oh, Peter, it is too incredible! It cannot be!"

"I'm sorry, love, it is."

"Sorry? Ought I to be sorry or glad? I just don't know. I don't know what I feel. Oh, Lord!"

Peter put his arms around her and brought her close to him. "You don't have to see him tonight if it's too much for you. He's used you abominably, and if you want him to go to the devil, you may safely leave me to tell him so."

Clarice raised her head. "No, of course not. I must see him. Only, I must have a few moments; I must think."

She put her fingers to her flushed cheeks in an effort to cool them. She had never felt so stupid or unable to think straight. She had to see him, if it were indeed Julian; some part of her still doubted this. But what then? For the second time in her life her whole world had been turned upside down in the space of a few moments. She looked up at her brother, her lovely eyes glistening with unshed tears caused by emotions that were too confused to define.

"What am I to do now, Peter? What on earth am I to do?"

Peter compressed his lips and shook his head sadly.

Lord Ardane's bookroom was just down the corridor from the room where they had been speaking, but with each step she took, Clarice was more and more aware of a sense of unreality. The hall seemed endless and yet too short, like that of a dream; or a nightmare.

Just as her brother was about to reach for the handle of the bookroom door, she put out her hand to stop him. She took a deep breath and bit at her lower lip. He reached around her, opened the door, and pushed her in ahead of him.

When she entered the room she saw him at once, standing before a bookcase, thumbing through one of the books. He turned when he heard them come in, and instantly all of her doubts, all of her half-formed thoughts about impostors and hoaxes, vanished. Her lips parted but she discovered that she could not speak. The space of the room yawned between them like a chasm, and once again she had the feeling of being in a dream. If he speaks, she thought wildly, I'll wake up and discover this was all caused by too many chocolates. For what seemed an interminable time, no one spoke. Then Peter, seeing his sister sway slightly, and fearing she was about to faint, took hold of her from behind, and broke the spell.

Clarice spoke his name so softly it was scarcely audible, and two large tears welled up in her eyes and spilled over onto her pale cheeks. In a moment she was in her husband's arms, her head buried in his shoulder, sobbing uncontrollably and repeating his name over and over. Julian bent his head over her and murmured softly in her ear.

Ardane stepped back a bit to watch this affecting scene, his lips curling sardonically. He thought that women, not excluding his sister, who had good reason to know better, were fools where Julian Rown was concerned, and he felt a contempt not untinged with envy. He stood there for a few more moments and then quietly let himself out of the room.

Clarice took a deep, shaky breath and brought her tears to an end. She took a step back from him and searched his face. There was not the slightest doubt that he was her husband; she knew this man so well. Every movement, every expression, every plane of his face were so familiar to her, and once had been so dear. It was as though the past four years had never been; as though she had seen him only a day ago, an hour ago, he was so unchanged. Somehow this seemed wrong to her. There ought to be something to show the years that had passed—new lines in his face, perhaps, or something in his eyes. She reached up to touch his cheek with the back of her hand, as though to assure herself again that he was not an illusion. He took her hand away from his face and held it tightly in his own. His dark eyes were unusually bright and slightly misty. "My poor, lovely Clare," he said softly in a voice he was just able to control, "I don't deserve that you should know me." He brought her hand to his lips and reverently kissed her palm.

Clarice withdrew her hand from his, and breaking from his embrace, resolutely turned her back on him. This effectively dispelled the magic of the moment, precisely what she wished to do. In spite of her husband's miraculous return, she could not allow herself to be beguiled into softness toward him. He was, after all, the man who had abandoned her for another woman; the man who had allowed her to believe him dead, to mourn for him, to be alone through the longest four years she could remember. She could not permit herself to bury these facts in a rush of sentiment. She crossed her arms over her breast and took another deep breath. "I don't know what to say to you, Julian," she said over her shoulder.

"Then don't say anything just yet," he said gently.

She turned again to face him, all the softness gone from her eyes. "It is not I who have anything to say."

He regarded her for a moment. "No, I suppose not," he agreed, and turned and walked over to the chairs at the opposite end of the room, where he had earlier sat with her brother. Clarice followed and settled herself in the chair near his. She folded her hands primly in her lap, and prepared to listen.

"Did Peter tell you anything other than that I was alive and here?" he asked.

"No. No doubt he felt it was better left to you."

Julian nodded. "I wish there were easy words to explain, something that would make you blame me less for what I've done to you, but there aren't any," he began. "I was an agent, Clare, for the government. An intelligence gatherer, a spy, if you like. Mostly unimportant nonsense, tattlemongering. I was an eavesdropper, an insinuator. In the course of this not very pretty gossip-gathering, I stumbled on something that was important, very important—important enough to result in one death and to threaten my life and possibly others. It was deemed best for me to disappear, not haphazardly, but permanently. So I 'died.'" He went on, telling her the same story he had told to her brother, only in greater detail, and avoiding mention of Therese Rouane as much as possible.

There was obviously to be no immediate forgiveness in the overwhelming miracle of his return, but then, he had not expected it, so he was not disappointed. He was sensible enough to realize that what he had to say this night, and Clarice's reaction to it, would go a long way toward deciding his future, so he chose his words with care.

Clarice sat silently, listening to him and watching his face. When he was done, she questioned him on several points she had not completely comprehended or about which she wanted more information.

"What I don't understand," she said after a short silence had fallen between them, "is how, if this man, Mr. Smith as you call him, was so clever and careful to cover his tracks, how it was that you came to be so sure of his existence and became a danger to him, and thus endangered yourself. Unless it was through your intimate knowledge of that Frenchwoman and his connexion with her."

"Yes, it was; but I thought it better not to go into that," he replied candidly. "I am sorry, Clare. I don't wish to upset you any more than I have to."

Clarice gave a short, bitter laugh. "You can't suppose that that would still have the power to upset me. I certainly knew all about the vivacious Therese. As you doubtless recall, our last conversation, or more accurately, battle, concerned her in detail. It is more lowering still to reflect that you preferred her to me even though you knew you shared her with a traitor." She had meant to say more, but stopped abruptly. Tears of anger at the memories her words evoked stung her eyes, but she would be damned before she would shed another tear for this man.

"I won't say that that is unjust," he said when it was clear that she did not mean to go on. "Lord knows, I gave you cause enough to distrust me. But you know now that I did not leave you for Mme. Rouane. I never would have, Clare. I'm sorry you were forced to think that I had for such a long time."

"Ought I to thank you?" she asked bitterly. "Oh, I understand what you have been explaining; all the things that it was necessary for you to do. What was not necessary was that I be told the truth."

"I had no hand in any of the arrangements that were made after I left." He paused. Nothing in her face encouraged him to believe that she heard him at all favorably, so he decided to be brutally honest with her now, and get the worst over with at once. "I am not trying to excuse myself, Clare," he went on. "Then it seemed the right and only thing to do. In retrospect, I am no longer certain that it was. It is true my life was in grave danger, and that the government wished to employ me elsewhere, but those weren't the only reasons I agreed to the plan to 'die.' I had reached a point in my life, in our marriage, where I was coming to detest it about as fast as we were coming to detest each other. You know that's true. If none of this had happened, we would no more be sitting here talking to each other tonight than if I had in reality gone down in that ship. We would be one of those so-called 'fashionably married' couples who never meet except by accident, and certainly never *tête-à-tête* if they can help it. I took what I believed was the simplest and best solution. My intention was to free us both; I never meant to come back. I have, though. Right or wrong."

Clarice let out her breath, unaware that she had been holding it. "I see. Then, stripped of the melodrama, it comes to this: you left me. Damn you, Julian!" she cried. "Damn you!" As soon as she could trust her voice again, she went on bitingly, "At least you have rediscovered your courage long enough to admit it to me. Now it is even less forgivable that I was never told that you were alive. What if I had remarried, Julian? This is the most damnable thing you have ever done to me."

"Having decided to do it, I had to do it properly," he said calmly, though beneath the surface he was as upset as his wife. "In order for me to be 'dead,' everyone, including you, had to believe it. You couldn't simply look the part of the, I trust, grieving widow; you had to be one. If anything, if any one thing did not ring true, well, then the whole of it would have been impossible to carry off."

Clarice looked down at her hands in her lap. "Yet it was possible for me to believe you had eloped with another woman, and oh, dear God, such a woman! Was that really necessary? Couldn't I have been the perfect widow just as well if you had been killed travelling on family business or . . . or anything else? You might have spared me some of the agonies of my grief if I had not believed on top of it all that you had left me for that creature."

"It was necessary to account for her disappearance as well as mine, and in such a way that no bodies would be involved. But your solicitude is quite touching, my love," he said with a touch of asperity. "I had flattered myself that any grief you might feel would stem from your regard for me, not just the hurt your pride suffered at being deserted. But," he added with a slight smile, "it would be most unjust of me to blame you for that, would it not?"

"It would!" she said hotly, and got up and began to pace about the room as her brother had done earlier; like him, she could not bear inaction when she was upset. The heavy rain caused the fire to smoke periodically, and she found the room stuffy and oppressive. "Oh, Julie," she said sadly, "so much time, so much waste! You have a daughter you've never seen; the boys are half-grown knowing no man's guidance but what your brother and Peter have supplied in odd moments; or Fowle, and though it is bad of me to say so, for he and Anne have been very good to us, he is such a fussbudget and a dull dog, that I can hardly wish for that. Our Perry will be at school next spring, it is already arranged, but I've been dreading it. Not just because he'll be away from me so much, but because I knew it would just be a matter of time before he learned the truth about you. Children can be so cruel to each other! We tried to keep the scandal to a minimum at the time, but it was all but impossible to stop the talk completely. The two of you disappearing at the same time; both of your names on the list of those who went down on that wretched ship." Her voice choked a little, but she continued. "I've wondered if perhaps I should tell him the truth myself. It might be better if he heard it from me . . ." Her voice trailed off and she sighed. "It seems forever that I've been alone."

As she spoke, she watched the firelight playing in the facets of the betrothal ring John Prescott had given her on the night before. Beneath it she still wore the wedding band that Julian had given her eight years ago. By rights she should have taken it off when John gave her his ring, but wearing it had been so much a part of her life for so long that this morning when she had put on her rings she had slipped on the band as well, purely out of habit. As she looked at it now, she decided that the time to make her position clear was now, before Julian could formulate any thoughts or ideas concerning their future together. She came to a standstill before the fire, with her back to her husband, and said abruptly, "Are you acquainted with John Prescott, a cousin of Lydia's?"

"No. At least, I don't recall the name," he said carefully, instinct making him wary.

"That's not too surprising; he resides mostly in the country, and is very involved with the management of his estates," she said in a low voice. "I only met him myself about a year ago."

Julian said nothing. He waited.

"He has been in town more frequently lately. I have seen him quite often." She was rushing her words to get it over with. "Last night I said I would be his wife. He's gone to Hampshire to tell his mother about us."

"A signally unprofitable journey," Julian said dryly.

"I love him, Julian," Clarice said baldly, turning to face him. "He makes me very happy. Perry, all the children, are fond of him. He . . . we plan to make a real home for the children. It's time, after all. Julia and Augustus can't even remember ever having one. I said these years alone have been hard on me, but it's been far worse for them, shunted from the house of one relative to another, never being able to go home, because there wasn't one."

"Very touching," drawled Julian, "but I think you have forgotten the fact that I left you with not just one home, but two. And Creeley. It may be my father's, but it will be Perry's one day, and certainly is now and always will be his home. You may have many just complaints to make of me, Clare, but not that I left you a pauper."

"How would you know how things were? Were you here?" she asked bitterly. "Kerrton reverted to your father, along with the lease on the house in Curzon Street. Perry, as your heir, of course, had almost everything else, except for the provisions in the marriage settlement for the others."

"Among which, as I recall, was a substantial and unconditional jointure for you," he pointed out. "And you will not make me believe that my father put you out of Kerrton or refused to renew the lease of the London house."

"Thank you!" she said sharply. "But I do not care to subsist on your father's charity."

"Doing it rather too brown, aren't you, Clare?" he asked caustically. "What you had was scarcely niggardly. You might have set yourself up in some style if you chose."

"A young widow, alone with three infants?" she asked in mock surprise. "Now who does it too brown? You know well what is said of such arrangements. I would have a 'suitable,' preferably elderly, and not too bright companion, and visits, I make no doubt, from an occasional 'uncle' or 'cousin,' or no male company at all. If you have no regard for my reputation, I have."

He sighed. "To think I wondered what we'd talk about! Do you feel that somehow the years have receded, and allowing for a slight rearrangement in the furniture, we are once again the 'loving' couple spending a quiet evening in the pleasure of one another's company, tearing each other to bits?"

"That is just it, Julian. You had the opportunity of wondering. I hardly know what I am saying or doing. I'm still not even sure this isn't just a nightmare." She hesitated, realizing how nasty that sounded, and added, "Of course I am glad, for your sake, that you are alive, but . . . I don't know what to think for myself. What did you expect? Did you think that four years of believing you dead would erase everything that had come between us? Did you think that I would cast myself into your embrace and we would suddenly live happily ever after? Do you even want that?"

"I want . . . No, I hope that we can take it one day at a time," he replied. "We can neither of us change the past, Clare, however much we may regret it. The only thing to do now is to see if we can begin again."

"You can't be serious!" Claire stared at him in amazement. "Not even you could be so vain that you would suppose that you could suddenly reappear, literally from the dead, and our lives would go on as if nothing had ever happened. The time to begin again, Julian, was four years ago, only you weren't here, and I was in black."

"I'm sorry for it, Clare," he said gently. "I am sorry you were forced to grieve for me; I am sorry you were left to raise the children alone; I am sorry for any and all unhappiness that I have caused you. I can't turn back the clock, and I can't undo it. The only thing either of us can do now is to try to salvage whatever is left."

"That isn't possible now," she said emphatically, "even if there were anything left, which I doubt. I told you that I am in love with someone else, which is no doubt inconsiderate of me, but I hadn't your knowledge that we would one day be together again. I am sorry, too, but there are no days for us to put together again, Julian, no future at all to salvage."

Julian regarded her for a moment and then said softly, "Yet you are, nevertheless, still my wife. Have you forgotten that? Perhaps we haven't the future that I'd hoped for, but you must admit that that fact makes for a future of some kind. Or were you thinking of an annulment or divorce? On what grounds? Desertion would be difficult now, with me here; I am not impotent; and the marriage has, most visibly, been consummated. Do you suppose that I will be noble and divorce you? That wouldn't be much of a favor to you, would it? Do you think he'd have you then? A ruined woman? A social outcast? Don't imagine that I would let you have the children. When Perry begins school, you would have considerably more to worry about than old gossip about his father. You know well what divorce means."

"Stop!" she cried, pressing her hands to her head. "I know that everything is on your side. I know that you may abandon me for four wretched years and then return and I am supposed to go back to you as though nothing has happened. Well, I won't. I will not go back to a marriage that was a travesty before you even left." She sank wearily into a chair. "Please, Julie, I have to go home. I can't say or do another thing until I have time to think."

He obediently summoned a footman and requested her carriage. Neither spoke for several minutes after the footman had left. At last he said, "There is one other thing, Clare. Like it or not, I will eventually have to show myself to the world. I can't stay in hiding until we sort everything out. I'll leave for Creeley tomorrow to see my family, and that will give you the time you need to think for a few days; but when I come back, I will have to go into society, and that will inevitably be as your husband. I think it would be a good idea if you were to follow me there and stay for a time as well. I want very much to see my children, and perhaps there we will be able to talk more calmly and decide what we are to do."

Clarice wanted to snap back at him that there was nothing to decide, but she held her tongue. She knew well that when she had said that everything was on his side, her words had not been idle. If there was any sensible solution to her difficulties, it would not be achieved by headstrong obstinacy. Julian was not a man to be pushed. "If I decide to come, I'll send you word," she said instead.

"Very well," he replied. "We'll leave it at that."

3

As the carriage made its way through the dripping streets, Clarice rested her head against the velvet squabs and closed her eyes tightly. What a difference twenty-four hours made! What she had wanted most at this point in her life was peace and order. Last night at this time, all she had believed the future held for her was a placid existence on the Prescott estates in Hampshire, but now order, peace, and certainly placidity were the last things that she could look forward to.

The irony of the situation, she thought, was that even if Julian had not chosen this most inauspicious time to return to her, it wouldn't have made any difference. As long as he was alive, he was her husband, as he had so clearly pointed out to her, and the devastating consequences that that could have caused had she remarried were beyond forgiveness. How dare he do such a thing to her!

Well, she thought grimly, he might return after abandoning her and believe that he would have the ordering of her future, but he would soon discover his mistake. Divorce might be difficult, but it wasn't unheard of, and he might say now that he would never agree to it, but that was no more than she could expect; he would hardly give in at their first meeting. But he would have to in the end. In the end he would realize that she loved John Prescott and would never, ever go back to Julian as his wife.

What would John say and do when he discovered that he was not, as he thought, betrothed to a widow, but to a married woman? Was Julian right? Would he want her then, another man's cast-off wife with her reputation in shreds? John had little use for society or town life, but a divorced woman was an outcast wherever she went. Would John love her enough to share her disgrace?

The carriage at last rolled to a stop before Fowle House

and Clarice gratefully brought her unpleasant thoughts to an end. She was thankful and relieved that the Fowles were out for the evening. Anne would know the moment she set eyes on her that something momentous had happened, and Clarice wanted, needed, time to sort out her own thoughts and emotions before discussing the events of this night with anyone. In fact, she told herself as she descended to the wet street, the only thing she wanted tonight was a hot bath and her bed; tomorrow would take care of itself.

Entering the hall, she permitted the footman who had opened the door to remove her damp travelling cloak. He had just opened his mouth to speak to her when a door slammed behind them and they both turned to observe a sandy-haired man in his mid-thirties with a pleasing if not striking countenance, striding toward them.

"John!" exclaimed Clarice in dramatic accents that would not have disgraced a Siddons, "what are *you* doing here?"

"As I was just about to tell you, my lady," said the footman, casting a slightly offended glance in the direction of the man approaching them, "Mr. Prescott called and is, was, awaiting you in the green saloon."

Mr. Prescott started to speak, but Clarice placed her hand on his arm and thanked the footman in a louder-than-necessary voice to forestall him. She meant to keep the inevitable gossip to a minimum, as far as she was able, and anything she and Mr. Prescott had to say to one another tonight, she wanted to be for their ears alone. With this in mind, she voiced only absent pleasantries as she led him back to the room he had just quitted.

It was her favorite room in Fowle House, decorated in varying shades of green and tastefully trimmed with complementary colors, and small enough to allow for comfortable conversation, though comfortable conversation was not what she was expecting. She toyed with the idea of not telling him now, of simply discovering what had brought him here when he was supposed to be with his mother in Hampshire, and then getting rid of him as quickly as she might, so that she could be alone with her thoughts. But she realized that this wouldn't answer; he would be justifiably angry if he discovered that she had not confided to him at once something which so closely affected his future as well as hers.

Prescott closed the door of the green saloon at Clarice's request. "Is something the matter, my love?" he asked. "You don't seem pleased to see me."

"Don't be silly, John," Clarice chided, "I am just tired." She tossed her bonnet on a small table and nearly upset a small ormolu clock. As she reached out to save it from falling, Prescott crossed the room and deposited himself in a comfortable wing chair and stretched out his legs. He had the look of a man sure of his welcome and intent on a long visit.

"Why are you here, John?" she asked as she seated herself near him. "I thought you left this morning for a visit with your mother." She forced a laugh. "Did she forbid the banns and you've come to break the news to me?" This effort at lightness fell sadly flat, but Prescott didn't seem to notice.

"Very much the contrary," he replied, smiling. "I arrived at home this morning, and as soon as Mother wished us happy, I barely stopped to bait the horses before posting back to town to tell you."

"I see," said Clarice coolly. "Our future happiness depended on your mother's consent. Shall I pen her a note expressing my gratitude?"

Prescott looked bewildered. "No, of course not," he said carefully. "I'm of age and all that." He paused, and then, as if enlightened, smiled knowingly. "I see what it is," he said. "Not feeling quite the thing."

"I am quite well," she snapped at him.

His smile faded at the sharpness of her tone, and a hint of apprehension came into his voice. "Are you having second thoughts about marrying me?" he asked.

Clarice saw the concern in his face and was instantly contrite. She went over to his chair, and kneeling before him, rested her head in his lap. "I'm sorry, dearest. Of course I haven't any doubts. We will be together no matter who or what tries to come between us. I don't know whether I'm on my head or my heels tonight, but I have no right to take it out on you."

"What is it, Clare?" he asked, assisting her to rise and sit on his lap. "Is it some family matter? Did Ardane have something unpleasant to tell you?"

"How did you know I was with Peter? Oh, yes, of course, the servants told you," she added as she realized how it must have been.

She was nestled comfortably in his arms with her head

resting on his shoulder. They might have been an old married couple lounging comfortably after a peaceful day of attending to their family and domestic routine. Clarice closed her eyes, almost willing it to be so. But it wouldn't do, of course. Reality was not so easily banished.

"Tell me what it is, Clare," Prescott said gently. "If anything has upset you, tell me and I'll put it to rights."

Clarice smiled sadly. "I wish you could. I want you to understand, dearest, that what I am about to tell you changes nothing with me. If you still wish it, we will find a way to be together."

Genuinely anxious now, he sat up straight and thus forced her to do so as well. "Don't be absurd, Clare," he said sternly. "Nothing could possibly come between us."

Clarice laughed bitterly. "No? Well, something has; something neither of us would have thought could happen in a thousand years." She got up off his lap and moved nervously about the room. Before the stunned Prescott could speak, she said, "It's Julian. Julian is back."

"Julian?"

"My husband."

"What utter nonsense!" exclaimed Prescott. "Rown's dead. How could he possibly have anything to do with us?"

"He isn't dead," she replied. "I know everyone believed that he was, including me, but it wasn't true. He is very much alive, and he is here. He—"

"Where?" Prescott interrupted. "In this house?"

"No, of course not," said Clarice with a trace of exasperation. "I meant in England. At Peter's, more precisely."

"Nonsense!" he said stoutly. "It's a hoax or some such thing. Thing is, you were surprised, and that made it easy to take you in. I'll see this fellow calling himself Rown in the morning, and you may depend upon it, we'll hear no more such gammon."

"John," Clarice said slowly and carefully, "it is not a hoax. I have seen him and spoken with him. It is unquestionably Rown." His expression was still mulish, and she quickly told him the basic facts of her husband's story before he could interrupt her again.

"Nonsense," repeated Prescott when she had finished. "Even if all of that were true, they'd tell *you* he was still alive. You were his wife, dammit! Couldn't keep you in the dark about a thing like that."

"Well, they did," said Clarice in growing irritation. She was beginning to appreciate the difficulties Peter had met when he had tried to tell her about Julian's return. "And it is Julian, and he is here. And I am still his wife."

"No!" Prescott exploded. "That I will not accept. If this man you saw is Rown back from the grave, and I by no means concede it, his conduct toward you surely relinquishes any claim he had on you. To treat you so is inhuman, and he deserves to be sent back to wherever he came from without so much as seeing you again, let alone claiming you as his wife!"

Although her own feelings on this coincided exactly with his, Clarice felt an uncheckable desire to defend her husband. "I know his conduct has been unforgivable, but it wasn't entirely his fault. His life was in danger and . . . and there were other considerations."

"What about his running off with that Frenchwoman? I'll never believe the government made him do that!"

"He didn't run off with her." Clarice pressed her fingers to her temples. "Please, John. I'm getting the migraine. I can't go into it all tonight."

"Didn't run off with her, eh?" snorted Prescott. "Is that what he's saying now? Well, if he is telling the truth, it's been several years. Why didn't he manage to get word to you that he was alive in all that time? Didn't think you'd betray him, did he?" He shook his head ponderously. "No, Clare, this story just doesn't wash. If it isn't a hoax, it's still a pack of nonsense anyway. Got bored with the life he was living, wherever, and needed an excuse to come home on."

"It isn't nonsense!" Clarice said, more sharply than she meant to. "Julian would not be such a fool. He will have to tell basically the same story to all the world. To make up such a thing would be madness, it could too easily be disproved." She didn't know if that were so, but it sounded reasonable.

"He still could have let you know he was alive."

"He said it was impossible."

"I don't believe it!"

"Does that signify?" she retorted. "The thing that is important, important to us, is that I know now that he is alive. He is here, and whether or not he deserves to have me for his wife, I am still married to him."

"Surely something can be done about that," cried Prescott angrily. "A man can't simply leave, abandoning his family, whatever the reason, and expect to come back as if nothing had happened."

"Oh, but he can," said Clarice dryly. "What would you suggest we do? I told him about us, and he made it quite clear that divorce was impossible."

"I don't see that. Happens every day."

"It does not, and you know it!"

"Well, perhaps not," he conceded, "but it isn't impossible."

"Isn't it, John?" she asked earnestly. "I cannot divorce him, and he has said he will not divorce me. Would it be such a good thing if he did? You know I would be ruined by it. And he said he would not let me have the children, damn him! I couldn't bear that, John, I couldn't. Everything is on his side. I think there is even something in the law that says a divorced woman may not remarry unless a dispensation is granted along with the bill of divorce. Bill of divorce! Do you know what that would mean? It would be before Parliament, John, a veritable circus of a scandal. Would you even want to marry me then, a social pariah?"

"Pooh!" he exclaimed airily. "It wouldn't be as black as you paint it."

"It would, and worse," she said firmly. She was inwardly determined that she would, somehow, overcome all these difficulties, but she wanted them spoken aloud, laid down and dealt with. She wanted his assurance and backing that however impossible it might seem, they would some way prevail and be together. "Divorce is not impossible, but it is unthinkable. One may do as one pleases, so long as one never, never airs one's behavior in public. If we were lovers, and reasonably discreet, that would be acceptable. But to go through the public spectacle of a divorce so that we could be honorably married, that we would be damned for."

He stared at her in surprise. His breeding was impeccable, but he lived mostly in the country and his acquaintance with the ton and its ways was severely limited. "No one in their right senses would blame or ostracize you," he said, and believed it. "He is the one they would condemn."

"Go back to Hampshire, John," said Clarice sardonically,

"and ask your mother if she would bestow her blessings as gladly on your marriage to a divorced woman."

"I told you Mother has nothing to say to it," he asserted. "In fact, no one does. If the fools that make up what is called society choose to take so absurd an attitude, to hell with them. What matters is us." He went over to her and put his arms around her. "Don't tease your poor head with this tonight," he said gently. "Rown must and will be made to see that he has to let you go. I daresay he thinks that if he makes things difficult for you, you'll give up and go back to him. We must stick to our guns until he comes around. Then we'll be together and damn the world."

Clarice rested her head gratefully on his shoulder. Now that she knew that he meant to stand by her and still wanted her, she could face Julian and whatever barriers he tried to throw in her way. She and John would prevail.

"I don't want you to go," he said for at least the fifth time.

"It is settled, John, and I have explained to you why I must go," Clarice said in a tired but patient voice. "I wish you would try to understand and not continue to tease me so."

Mr. Prescott paced the length of the room angrily. "There is no reason for you to go at all."

"He wishes to see his children, and you must admit he has a right to do so."

"But not to see you," Prescott argued. "Send the children to Creeley, then, if you insist, but don't go yourself."

"Don't be absurd, John. They are little more than infants; I can't pack them off for so long a journey with no one but servants to care for them," she said reasonably.

"Then let Ardane escort them by himself. Surely you trust them to him?"

Clarice laughed. "Yes, but not him to them. Picture, if you can, a man on a journey of three days with three nursery children under his sole care and only servants to help. The poor man would be fit for Bedlam by the time they reached the first change."

Prescott did not smile. "It is just excuses. Whatever I say, you have an answer. I think what it really is, is that you want to go to Creeley."

She put off packing things into her dressing case and pondered this for a moment. "You may be right. I shall have to face him and his family eventually. I think I'd as soon it was over and done."

"At Creeley? To their advantage?"

"Nonsense," she retorted. "This isn't a battle with lines to be drawn."

"They'll be at you the entire time to go back to him," he insisted. "You aren't being realistic if you don't realize that. And to top it, there's Rown himself. Do you really expect him to sit back and discuss this at a purely intellectual level?"

Having completed the packing of her dressing case to her satisfaction, Clarice hurried across the room to rifle through the cloakbag she meant to have with her inside the travelling carriage, to make sure she had not forgotten anything. Though she was trying very hard to be patient with Prescott, it was becoming increasingly difficult. "I don't know what you mean," she said shortly.

"Yes you do," he said doggedly. "You told me yourself how it was between you. He'll appeal to your emotions; he'll make love to you if he can." He turned her away from her work and took her hands in his. "Clare," he said earnestly, "I love you and I trust you, but he is your husband and you were in love with him once. You can't expect him not to use that to his advantage. I am not so naive that I imagine my addresses are superior to his; he is a man of the world and I am not. He'll use any means he can to get you back to him."

Clarice met his gaze, but she was not really listening to him. Her mind was on the hundred different things necessary to a long journey with three small children, and in any event, she had already heard his arguments a half-dozen times over the last few days.

A footman came into the room to collect the last of her baggage, and Lady Fowle's voice could be heard in the hall admonishing her nephews for getting chocolate on their travelling clothes. Mixed with her soprano were childish voices, the hustle and bustle of the servants, and the clatter of hooves from outside as the carriages were brought to the door.

Clarice released herself from his grasp and said absently, "It will be all right, John. I'll be gone only a fortnight."

She began directing Eddly, her dresser, who had come into the room in the wake of the footman, and Prescott sighed, half in disgust, half in despair. He knew from experience that Clarice was not biddable, but he had dared to hope that his pleas would be to some effect. Up until now, the very last moment, he had still tried to dissuade her. But with the chaises at the door, even he had to admit that he had failed.

He glumly followed the remainder of the bustling party down the stairs, trying vainly to form a last-minute argument. They reached the hall just as Lord Ardane entered it from the street.

"Everyone ready?" Peter asked briskly. "Still determined, are you, Clare?"

"Does it look as though I am not?" said Clarice as she dutifully kissed his cheek.

"No."

"Well, I think you are doing the right thing," said Anne, casting a frown at her brother. "It's not only the best thing for you to do, it is the only thing."

"Yes," laughed Clarice, "and your reasons were the one thing that nearly put me off it. Where is Fowle?" she asked, looking about her. "I wouldn't want to start off without taking leave of him."

As if on cue, the tardy Lord Fowle entered the hall at that moment and all private conversation was lost in a round of affectionate good-byes and last-minute instructions. As the impressive retinue of carriages at last disappeared around the corner of the street, Mr. Prescott came out of the abstraction that had held him since the chaise door had shut Clarice off from him, to find Lady Fowle regarding him fixedly.

"I suppose I'd better be going," he said lamely.

"Why, of course, Mr. Prescott, we wouldn't wish to keep you from any appointment." With this, Lady Fowle ushered her children and the various servants who had seen the travelers off back into the house.

Mr. Prescott descended the front stairs and began to walk down the street, but stopped and turned back, only to face a door being firmly shut to the street. He made a brief disgruntled sound in his throat and went on to his club.

Thank heavens, thought Clarice as she watched the ostlers bring up the fresh team. By dinnertime or even before, they would reach Creeley. The weather, always changeable at this time of year, had miraculously held for their journey, and was even unseasonably warm. But this had proved no boon in travelling with three lively children, who quite rightly resented being shut up in a stuffy chaise.

One of the most difficult things of all, Clarice had found, was telling the children that the father they had believed dead was in reality alive after all. Julia, born after he had left, and Augustus, just fourteen months at the time, had no memory of their father, but Peregrine did, and wise at seven, was frankly sceptical. People who died, he pointed out to his mother, never came back again, hadn't she taught him that? Clarice explained in as much detail as she dared, or as she thought they could comprehend, but it had been one of the hardest things she could remember doing. Perversely, she was furious with her husband for the difficulty in explaining. She had wanted him to go to Creeley to give her time to think, and would, in fact, have resented any attempt on his part to see their children before she had had time to prepare them, yet at the same time she longed for his help and support in this difficult task and marked it down as a grievance against him that here again was another situation she had had to deal with on her own.

She and Julian had agreed, by post, that the children should not be told that their visit to Creeley would include meeting their father, lest they become too excitable on the long journey. But Perry was a clever child, who easily saw around his mother's evasions and had figured out for himself what this rare visit to his ancestral home portended. He had informed his brother and sister of his opinion, with the result that Clarice was virtually pelted with questions both before and during the trip; added to this were sibling disagreements, necessary stops, and naturally high spirits. Miss Minnie Poll, their very capable governess, had been a great help, but it was exhausting nevertheless.

Still, she had to admit that her motherly duties had precluded any time for being closeted alone with Peter. He had said nothing to her about her decision to go to Creeley since his comment in the hall at Fowle House, but Mr. Prescott had found in him an unexpected ally, and Clarice had listened to at least as many arguments from her brother as she had from Prescott.

Clarice had heard him patiently, but with surprise. True, Peter had not hesitated to revile Julian in no uncertain terms four years ago, and had cursed the day that he had given them his blessing on their marriage, but that was hardly surprising in view of the circumstances. Now, as a member of the family, it might have been supposed that Peter would lend his voice to those urging Clarice to return to her husband posthaste, to avoid the inevitable scandal if for no other reason.

It was certainly not as if Peter were mad for Prescott; the earl had never concealed his mild contempt for him. He clearly thought Prescott a dull dog and hinted that he suspected him of being more than mildly interested in Clarice's handsome jointure, which continued even if she remarried. But Ardane held that Clarice had suffered enough at her husband's hands, and told her in no uncertain terms that he would consider her foolish beyond redemption should she put herself at his mercy yet again. The world might believe that returning to Julian and avoiding scandal was the lesser of two evils, but let the harpies be damned and say what they would, he, at least, would stand by her.

He had then very generously offered to escort her and the children, over the vociferous opposition of his wife, who had had her own schemes for a family visit to her sister disrupted by his generosity. Clarice had insisted that this was hardly necessary, as she was to travel with a positive army of servants, both her own and the Fowles', but Ardane had remained adamant and determined to overcome all her objections.

"What will servants avail you once you get there?" he had asked. "It will be best if Julian knows you are not without protection."

"Protection!" Clarice exclaimed, laughing. "Why, what do you suppose, Peter? That he'll ravish me the moment I walk through the door?"

"I wouldn't put it past him."

Clarice had laughed at his absurdities, but in the end she had agreed that she would be more comfortable knowing that there was at least one at Creeley who would be on her side and not her husband's.

Anne, of course, on learning and finally being made to believe that Rown was really alive and that Clarice was not simply suffering from a distemper, had urged her at once to go to Creeley. But it was not the support of her sister and her sister's husband (who suffered private horrors at the thought of scandal touching any member of his family), but rather the opposition of Peter and Prescott that had strengthened her resolve to go there. Not, of course, she told herself, that she intended to go back to Julian in the least. That had certainly been decided; but Julian was right when he said that something had to be resolved upon and, badly as she felt he had treated her, she believed the very fact that he was her husband and the father of her children entitled him to some consideration.

She gazed at the front of the inn; it was the last change of horses before reaching Creeley Lodge, and she and Julian had stopped there many times on their way to or from the sprawling, chiefly Jacobean manor which was nestled in the hollow of a beautiful rolling parkland. There, away from the gaiety and pursuits of London, some of the happiest moments of their married life together had taken place. She knew a sudden wish to go back to the peace and comfort of those days, and quickly took herself in hand. She could not afford the luxury of sentiment.

Clarice put her head out of the window and looked about for Miss Poll, who had taken the boys inside for refreshments. She was about to call to one of the men in the yard to fetch them so that they might be under way, when her brother entered the chaise and pulled the door shut. Julia, resting against her mother, stirred in her sleep, and Clarice bent to brush hair from the child's eyes. "Are the children ready?" she asked her brother. "I'd like to be off."

"We are," he replied, and at that moment they started with a slight jolt.

"But where are Minnie and the boys?"

"In the carriage behind us with Eddly. I wanted a chance to talk to you before we reach Creeley."

"Peter—" she began plaintively.

"No, no, love," he interrupted. "I've promised not to tease you again on that head, and I shan't. I just want you to know that I'm here; if you need me, I'll be with you, no matter what."

Clarice smiled. "I know. Whatever else, I know I can count on you. But really, I don't expect it will be too bad. I could wish that I didn't have to face the whole of his family at once, but that can't be helped. In other ways, though, I'm glad that they'll be there; there is comfort in numbers, after all. I wouldn't care to be alone with him."

"No, that would facilitate things," said Peter caustically. "For him."

"I won't pretend to misunderstand you; but you are mistaken. He may have had the power to attract me once, but that was over even before he left, and now is gone altogether. I feel nothing for him."

"Perhaps," granted Ardane, "but your first meeting was hardly a normal situation. The assault on your sensibilities at discovering him alive very likely left little room for other emotions."

"No," Clarice mused. "I don't think so. In the past, my emotions seemed to have little to do with it. I could be furious with him, almost hate him, but then he'd smile at me in that way that he has, and take me in his arms and . . . Well, it could hardly be so now. I am no longer in love with him."

Peter opened his mouth to reply, but thought better of it and turned the subject.

4

Clarice gently dabbed scent behind her ears, on her wrists, and as an afterthought, between her breasts. She reflected on her arrival at Creeley and decided that it had passed off better than she had dared to hope. The ninth Earl of Creeley, gray now, but still trim and dashing, had taken care that any moments which might have proved awkward were easily glossed over. Her mother-in-law, Lady Creeley, had been all kindness and had treated the occasion of their arrival with no more fuss than had it indeed been a simple family visit of former days. Clarice could not but feel a little guilty that she had made so little effort to seek them out in the last few years. They were, after all, dear, kind people, and to take out on them the unhappiness caused by their eldest son was unjust.

Clarice had so far been spared any private conversation with her husband. As they had agreed, he had not been there to greet them, lest his sudden presence startle the children. But shortly afterward he had come up to the nursery sitting room, where Clarice and his mother were waiting for him as Miss Poll settled the children into the nursery. He came in without knocking, and after absently greeting his wife, said something to his mother in a quiet voice that Clarice could not make out. Childish laughter could be heard through the open door into the nursery, and Perry was informing his brother of the evils that would befall him if he did not immediately give back a wooden soldier. Lady Creeley took her son's hand and pressed it, and he returned the pressure, but he wasn't looking at her, he was staring straight ahead of him at the open door of the children's room.

He's frightened, unsure of himself, thought Clarice,

amazed. But she brushed this off as the product of her own imagination. She had never known him to be either.

The scene in the nursery then had been very touching, bringing tears to the eyes of the three women observers. Perry, whose memory of his father was dimmer than he admitted, saw him first, but hesitated. Julia, following the direction of her brother's gaze, turned and saw the tall man standing on the threshold. With the instincts of a three-year-old, she cried out "Papa" and cast herself in his arms with abandon. Julian went down on one knee to her level, and Augustus, too, ran over to him, followed by the more shy Perry. Soon they were all laughing and hugging him and asking him a thousand questions at once. Lady Creeley and Clarice had followed Julian into the room, and after a short time Lady Creeley motioned to Clarice and Miss Poll to follow her into the sitting room. "I think," she said as she closed the nursery door, "that it would be best to give them time alone. Both women agreed, and shortly afterward Clarice had left to see to her unpacking.

Clarice put down the small crystal scent bottle and went over to the bed and removed a beaded reticule from beneath a pile of dresses. She informed Eddly that she would ring for her when she wished to undress, and went out into the hall.

She was halfway down the main staircase when she was hailed by a cheery baritone. She turned and saw her brother-in-law, Peregrine, coming toward her.

"Come to face the dragons, have you?" he asked.

He possessed himself of her hand and whistled softly under his breath. "Lord, but you're lovely." He bent to kiss her lightly on the lips. "And you smell good, too," he added with a wide boyish grin.

"One of these days, Perry, you're going to have to grow up and stop saying outrageous things," laughed Clarice. "You are totally reprehensible. That man at the bottom of the stairs is not a statue." She nodded toward the footman, who was giving an excellent imitation of a man deaf and dumb to his surroundings.

"The devil fly away with him for spying on his betters," said Peregrine airily.

"He is not spying, he is doing his job, and you had best do yours."

"Which is?"

"Take me down to the Great Hall, of course, you hopeless rattle!" laughed Clarice.

The Great Hall, which was neither great nor, strictly speaking, a hall, but more of an armaments and trophy room, was the place where the Rowns had met before dinner at Creeley Lodge for countless generations; the reason for which was beyond the memory of anyone now living there.

It was a decidedly cheerless room hung with the trappings of forgotten wars and the heads and stuffed carcasses of even less-memorable hunts. It was Peregrine who maintained that the custom had begun with the ancestor he was named for, one Sir Peregrine de Rowne, who was remembered chiefly in family histories for his inability to pick a side and stick to it during the Lancaster and York hostilities. Sir Peregrine, claimed Mr. Rown, was a shocking nip-cheese who had started the tradition in order to spoil or at least dampen the appetites of his guests and dependents, and thus cut down on expenses.

The maligned man's present namesake, however, was well known for his generosity and even temper. Clarice had more than once wished that she could combine the best attributes of both brothers into one perfect man. That was not to say that her husband was niggardly or distempered, but his nature had more reserve. He was a man who brooked no nonsense, and while not afraid to say what he thought if he deemed it suitable, he had not Peregrine's openness of manner. Peregrine, on the other hand, could be, and occasionally was, put upon through his desire to avoid any fuss. His character was less firm than that of his older brother, and he was definitely given to the outrageous, or as some said, the vulgar.

Both brothers were well-bred, possessed of exquisite manners, winning smiles, and a charm so engaging that even their occasional detractors were inclined to forgive their slight lapses from the norms of society; and Peregrine, though not generally counted as handsome as his brother, had caused many a female heart to flutter in his own right.

They entered the Great Hall just as Lord Ardane came in through an opposite door. The two men exchanged greetings and Clarice moved away to sit next to her mother-in-law. All of Julian's family were assembled there except his sister Lady

Augusta, who was recovering from a recent confinement and had not been able to travel to Creeley. Clarice joined in the usual desultory pre-dinner conversation.

Julian had not come down yet, and to her annoyance, Clarice found herself glancing at the doors from time to time in anticipation of his arrival. The butler came in to announce dinner, and as Lord Creeley said there was no need to wait for Julian, who would be down any minute, they were all rising to quit the room when he finally came in.

Clarice involuntarily caught her breath. She had always believed him the most beautiful man she had ever seen, and nothing in his appearance tonight changed that opinion. His evening dress was impeccable and in the first stare of fashion, if somewhat conservatively so. He was what her sister Anne's dresser, Mary O'Reilly, would have called a fine figure of a man. No stays or padding were necessary to improve on his fine athletic build, nor were the rich, dark, windswept curls that crisply framed his face the result of his valet's art with a curling iron. Either American tailors were more capable than they were generally given credit to be, or Julian had managed to outfit himself superbly in the short time that he had been back. How like him to manage it either way, she reflected.

She waited while he kissed his mother for him to greet her. "Good evening, Clare," he said simply, and immediately turned to speak to his father. Clarice felt let down. She supposed she had expected something more dramatic for their first meeting before the whole of his family. Lady Creeley called everyone to order, and taking the arm of her elder son, led the procession in to dinner.

After dinner, when Lady Creeley rose to leave the men to their wine, Clarice meekly followed her, but not without misgiving. She could hardly excuse herself and go immediately to bed on her first night with them, though she was very tired, and she rather dreaded the *tête-à-tête* with Lady Creeley that would follow. To her surprise, Lady Creeley, though she did mention him in her conversation, did not discuss Julian's miraculous return nor in any manner, subtly or otherwise, plead his cause. Clarice felt it was almost unnatural, but could not bring herself to introduce the subject. They were vapidly discussing the merits of various fabrics for draperies when

Peregrine and Peter entered the room, laughing heartily at something one of them had said.

Peter went over to make himself pleasant to Lady Creeley, and Peregrine sat down beside Clarice. He followed her eyes toward the door as Julian entered with his father.

"Why so troubled, pet?" Peregrine asked sympathetically.

"I'm not."

"No? You look ready to leap up and flee the room at a moment's notice."

Clarice relaxed into a smile. "Not quite, but I admit I am a trifle vaporish tonight."

"Tired?"

"Yes, but it isn't only that." She paused and then asked, "Tell me, Perry, is it my imagination or is everyone purposely avoiding the topic of Julian's return?"

He gave her a crooked smile. "Damme, Clare, you know how to throw a fellow into confusion. I am under strict orders, from the very top, mind, to discuss inanities tonight, and here you are asking me things like that."

"Why?"

"Because we decided that whatever is between you and Julie should stay that way, for now at least. We aren't blind, after all," he added reasonably. "We've been wondering for some time about you and that Prescott fellow."

Clarice looked away from him. "The night before Julian returned, Mr. Prescott asked me to become his wife, and I accepted him."

Peregrine let out his breath in a quiet whistle.

"I love John and want to be his wife." Clarice continued, "You *must* know how things were between Julian and me before he left."

"I can guess," he replied. "Julie doesn't talk much about personal things."

"What am I to do, Perry?"

Peregrine smiled sadly. "I'm the wrong person to ask that, Clare. My answer would be very predictable."

Clarice turned sideways to look directly into his face. "You think that I should take Julian back, don't you? Put the past behind me, forget that he abandoned me for four years, and go on as if nothing had happened."

"I think," he replied gently, "that you should not damn

him without a hearing. Perhaps he used the time to mend his manners."

Clarice looked away from him and studied the pattern of the Aubusson carpet. "What did he tell you?" she asked.

"About what?"

"About us."

"Not much. He wouldn't, though. He said that you were greatly unsettled by his return; that you were angry, confused, and in short, not ready to fall into his arms and exclaim 'All is forgiven.' To his credit, I don't think he expected it. He never said a word about Prescott, if that is what you mean. Does he know?"

"Yes, he knows," she said shortly, and looked up to discover her husband watching them. He did not look away, but returned her gaze; Clarice was the one to drop her eyes.

"Well, well," said Peregrine with a devilish smile. "This ought to prove interesting. Julie won't much like being cut out by a gentleman farmer."

"I'm pleased our difficulties afford you so much amusement," Clarice said sarcastically.

Peregrine was not abashed. "But think of it, Clare," he said eagerly. "If you were going about with a regular dasher like he is himself, he might not like it, but he'd understand it. Prescott may be the devil of a fellow and all that—I don't know him much except through you—but he's hardly up to Julie's weight." He saw by her expression that he had gone too far and quickly changed the subject in the interest of harmony.

Shortly afterward Clarice excused herself and went up to her room, still not having exchanged one word of private conversation with her husband. Perhaps, she decided as she lit several candles on her dressing table, it was better left until tomorrow. The journey had left her tired and dispirited.

She removed her necklet and earrings and instead of ringing at once for Eddly, she opened the French doors leading out onto the raised terrace at the far end of her room and looked out over the familiar view of parkland. It was quite warm for the time of year, and the night air was just cool enough to be refreshing. She heard a door open behind her and turned. It was Julian.

"What do you want?" she asked sharply, surprised into brusqueness.

"To talk to you," he replied in his usual soft-spoken manner.

"You had the entire evening to do so."

"I prefer to be private with you."

"You might have tried being civil," she retorted. "You scarcely spoke a word to me tonight."

"I couldn't say what I wanted to then."

"Well, whatever it is, I wish you will say it in the morning. I'm tired and I'm going to sleep."

He smiled. "Julia has your eyes; she is very like you, I think."

"I hope she may have better judgment than I've had," said Clarice crisply.

"In the choosing of a mate?" He laughed. "Well put, madam wife."

She turned her back on him and went out onto the terrace.

"You don't like that, do you?" he asked, following her into the cool night air. "For me to call you wife. But you are my wife."

"As you so kindly insist on reminding me," she said tartly. He was close enough to her for her to feel his presence beside her. She moved quickly away, not caring for the sudden feeling of impending excitement that came over her. Nor did she wish to define it.

He smiled again, this time sardonically, and sat down on the balustrade. "Conforming to old patterns, Clare? At loggerheads from the start?"

"I don't want to argue with you; I am tired."

"I know. I'll let you sleep now, but we will have to talk tomorrow. We can't avoid it forever."

"I have no wish to avoid it."

He looked away from her to the park on his right. "It will unquestionably be difficult for a while for us, but with a little practice we'll jog along, I expect."

"I don't want practice," she said abruptly.

"Yet you came," he said, turning back to her.

"I came so that you could be with your children."

"Thank you," he said simply, and meant it.

He still made no move to leave. "What were you and Perry talking about so earnestly when I came into the drawing room?" he asked after a few moments of silence.

"You, us. What else?" she said with a shrug. "You mustn't blame him, though. I brought up the subject."

"What did he say?"

"Exactly what you'd expect; he thinks I ought to forgive and forget."

"Truly? I thought he might advise you against such a course, for the sport of it."

"You do him an injustice!"

"Not really," he said, and sighed slowly. "I wasn't serious. I don't want them to pester you, though. We must resolve this between us without interference. If I hadn't their promise on that, I wouldn't have let you come here."

"Is there any resolving this, Julie?" she asked wearily. "I have tried and tried to think of some answer but come out at nothing. There has been so much unhappiness between us, and not just for me. I know I smothered you—clinging to you one moment and telling you I hated you the next. I must have made you almost as miserable as your infidelities made me." She paused and sighed. "I can't think why you would even want us to be together again."

"I love you," he said very, very softly, but distinctly. Clarice was startled into staring at him. Whatever she had expected him to say, it was not this. What she saw in his eyes by the dim reflection of a starlit night convinced her that he meant it. There was no mask now.

She looked away from him. Unexpected and unwanted tears stung her eyes. "I'm sorry," she said gently. "In spite of everything, I have no wish to wound you, but I won't lie to you; I am no longer in love with you."

"I know. You've made no secret of it," he said, still very quietly, even for him.

Clarice made an attempt to laugh. "I'm not even sure I believe you. We have been apart for so long."

"I thought of you. Endlessly. It didn't take me a month to realize the mess I'd made of our lives. I could hardly believe it was possible to miss someone the way that I missed you." He stopped abruptly, as though he had to.

"You left me, Julian, not I you," she deliberately snapped at him. Even fighting would be better than the emotions his vulnerability aroused in her. Was this a different man she saw now and earlier in the nursery, or had he always been so?

Beneath that cool, cynical, controlled exterior, had he always possessed a full complement of human frailties, and had she been too blind and caught up in her own troubles to see? Had he changed, or was it her ability to perceive him that had done so? She didn't really want to know, feeling matters were complicated enough.

He got up and stood in front of her. Clarice suddenly became aware of the stillness and darkness about them, broken only occasionally by the scurrying sound or fleeting cry of some night creature. She took a step backward, away from him, and found herself against the stone railing. She could have pushed past him; she didn't believe he'd stop her, but she refused to give him the satisfaction of knowing how uneasy she was made by his closeness.

"Can't we put aside our differences and remember, if only for tonight, the good that was between us?" he said. "There was good, Clare, a great deal of it, if you will just choose to remember it."

She looked into his eyes and felt something inside herself soften. Almost in spite of herself, there came to her a picture of days spent laughing, in happy companionship, of nights that had held a poignancy that had been with her even through the long years of loneliness.

To her dismay he rested his hands lightly on her shoulders. She made a movement away from him, and his grip on her tightened.

"Please, Clare, don't push me away," he said, almost pleading. "I promise not to make love to you; I just want to touch you, if only for a moment."

She didn't believe his promise, but perversely made no move to free herself. He took her face in both his hands, and she knew he was going to kiss her. As his lips met hers, the melting feeling grew stronger within her, so strong that it frightened her and gave her the will to pull away from him. She pushed past him into the room, aware of the sound of her heart beating wildly. As she heard his footsteps behind her, she went to the bell pull and tugged it sharply. She turned, half-expecting him to be behind her, but he was at the door, his hand on the handle. "Good night, Clare," he said softly, and was gone.

Clarice sighed with relief, but could not quite shake off the aura of disappointment that permeated her. So, Peter was right, she thought grimly, it has not entirely died within me; I still feel something.

She did not at all like what she felt.

5

A welcoming gleam of sunshine greeted the brothers as they passed from the tree-shaded and therefore dimmer breakfast room into the morning room. They were followed closely by Lord Ardane, carrying a morning mug of ale, which he sipped from time to time as he walked. He cast himself into the nearest chair and said, "Damned if I don't envy you, after all. Good morning for a ride."

"Well, then, why don't you come with us?" asked Peregrine. "You're used to playing benevolent lord of the manor; more than I."

"What's this?" said Julian with a grin. "Jealous of my patrimony, Per? Does it surface at last?"

Perry gave him an answering grin. "I should say not! I'm well enough set up without the headaches. I can smile and be sympathetic, and they all touch their forelocks to me, but when it comes to repairing their bridges, or supplying new roofs or fencing, I don't have to lay out the blunt."

"Nor do I. Don't be too quick to set me in our father's shoes."

"So I don't, dear brother, but neither do I envy you. As heir, you have nearly the same responsibilities without even the power. You may sleep easy at night; I don't scheme for your position," answered Peregrine.

Lord Ardane chuckled. "Small good it would do you! You've two nevvies between you and those 'responsibilities.' "

"Poor mites," said Peregrine with mock sorrow.

"Dear Perry," asked Julian, curious, "did you spare such sympathy for me when we were, ah, mites?"

"Of course not!" exclaimed Peregrine. "I thought it served you right for having the effrontery to be born first."

Julian laughed at his nonsense, and Peter, finishing the last of his ale, rose. "I think I will join you," he said. "It won't take me a moment to change," he added, and left.

There was silence for a time, and then Julian, aware of his brother's earnest gaze, said at last, "Well, what is it, Perry?"

Peregrine made a self-mocking grimace. "No card player, eh? You're right, of course. Something has been preying on my mind."

"Then, dear boy, be rid of it," invited Julian.

"I mean to." Peregrine sat down in the chair vacated by Lord Ardane. "What really happened four years ago, Julie?" he asked baldly.

If Julian was surprised, he didn't show it. "Do you really think I could have made that nonsense up?" he asked. "I should be flattered by your opinion of my imagination."

"Oh, I daresay it is the truth. Basically."

Julian raised his eyebrows. "But not entirely? Well, perhaps I did omit a few minor details," he admitted. "Does it signify now?"

"I think so. *We* might have calmly accepted the story of your running off with Mme. Rouane and both of you being lost at sea, but if he killed her, Mr. Smith would have had to know it was a lie."

"That's true," agreed Julian, "but I think that while Mr. Smith knew part of the story was invented, he eventually allowed himself to believe that I was dead. He'd want to so very much, don't you think?"

"Could he afford to take the chance?"

"No, he couldn't," Julian said amiably, smiling slightly at his brother's earnestness. "Not at first, but my family obviously believed it; my will was probated; the succession devolved upon Perry; everything legal and emotional pointed to that belief. All of you carried on as if you never expected to set eyes on me again, as you truly didn't. You may depend upon it he is a clever man; if anything had struck a wrong chord, he would have picked up on it, damnably quick."

"Has it occurred to you that you might have been followed to the coast?" persisted Peregrine. "Suppose he knew you never boarded the *Spider*?"

Julian shook his head. "The only thing anyone would have discovered was that I went into a stinking little inn and never came out. I promise you, Per, you would have been horrified to see me in my guise as 'old salt'; no one, not even Clare, would have known me." He laughed. "I had trouble myself."

"*I* don't think this is such a light matter," said Peregrine with unaccustomed severity.

"It isn't, of course," replied Julian, still smiling.

"To listen to you, you'd think it was," snapped Peregrine.

Julian was too surprised to be offended at his brother's tone. Ill temper was not common to Peregrine's nature. "I lived it, Perry," he said gently. "Very seriously."

"I know. I'm sorry." Peregrine put his head down and rubbed his eyes with a thumb and forefinger. "But . . ."

"But . . . ?"

"Dammit! I'm worried about you."

Julian was astonished. "Why on earth?"

Peregrine raised his head and looked directly at him. "For the same reason you should be worried. What's going to happen when Mr. Smith discovers that you are alive and here in England?"

"Nothing, I suppose."

"Nothing!" exclaimed Peregrine loudly. "You can't be any less dangerous to him now than you were then!"

"I don't agree," said Julian calmly. "If anything, my return should make him rest all the easier."

"Dear Lord! Why?"

"Because, dear unnecessarily concerned brother, from that night until this, he has remained unmolested. I might have disappeared, but if I'd had sufficient evidence to hang him, I certainly could have told others. Surely he would not still be free? He may now sit back and assure himself that he overrated me."

"And did he?"

"Obviously."

"I wonder." Peregrine's voice was caustic. "*Is* he still free, Julian?"

"I assume so. *I* never heard that he was found out."

"Perhaps he was privately taken care of."

"Perhaps he was."

"Then you'd have nothing to worry about."

"I'm not worried."

"I don't believe you, Julian. I think . . . it is just intuition, mind, but I think you know full well who Mr. Smith is."

Julian smiled slowly. "Now why, if I did, would I have let

it go? I could have saved myself a great deal of difficulty if I had told the right people at the time."

"I don't know. No doubt you had your reasons."

"Such as a lack of patriotism."

"Hardly that. But if I ask you one straight question, will you give me a straight answer?" Peregrine persevered.

"What is the question?" asked Julian noncommittally.

"Are you not telling me the truth because you honestly don't know, or because you don't choose to voice what is only a suspicion?"

"Perhaps both," answered Julian, and that was as much as he would say.

When Clarice awoke to the bright sunshine, she stretched luxuriously. From the evening Julian had returned until the day before she had left London it had rained almost continuously, and these rare, gorgeous early-spring days that held the promise of summer were a wonderful contrast. She stretched out a hand for the morning chocolate Eddly had left on a tray beside the bed.

Rested now, she was in better frame to take stock of her surroundings. She was in the beautiful garden room at the back of the house, which had always been given to her and Julian in happier times. She wondered, vaguely, what room he was in. She turned and looked to the opposite end of the room at the closed French doors leading out to the raised terrace. She got out of bed, and throwing on a wrapper, went over and opened them.

The day was brilliant, and everything, the rolling parkland, the woods behind, the formal garden to her right, from which the room got its name, stood out sharply. All the emotions Clarice had felt last night standing on this terrace vanished, dissolved in the sunlight. Had Julian truly dared to make love to her? And had she nearly, so very nearly, responded to him? She had been tired, yes, but that was not sufficient excuse. She knew her weakness now and would guard against it. Mere physical attraction would not come between her and her resolve.

Her attraction to him had certainly long been her weakness. It wasn't as if their marriage had been arranged. Their union was the fond wish of both his family and hers since they had been in their cradles, but no pressure would have been brought to bear on either of them had they been disinclined toward each other. That they had been very much inclined, there had been no doubt. Cousins, and friends since childhood, the six-year discrepancy in their ages had prevented them from forming the brother-and-sister attachment that so often did in the carefully laid plans of fond parents.

By the time she was a schoolroom miss of fifteen, chafing at the bonds of convention that kept her tied to the tutelage of a careful governess, he had become the object of all her romantic fantasies. That was not very surprising; at one and twenty he had been dashing, handsome, well-formed, and personable; she had thought him perfect in every way.

When eighteen and properly presented, she had found herself queen of her own little court. Her birth, her beauty, her dowry, and not least, the pleasant disposition that all the Ardanes were noted for, made her much sought-after. But she had eyes for one man, and one man only: her darkly handsome cousin, Julian Rown. Spiteful mamas and their daughters alike smiled behind their fans and said that her interest was in vain. Though no one would have gone so far as to name him a heartless libertine, his reputation for being very much in the petticoat line was already well established, and though many a prize far greater than his pretty cousin had been laid at the feet of Lord Rown, it was widely believed that his interest in marriage was nonexistent. Many confident matchmakers had come a cropper at the hands of that eligible bachelor, and many doting mothers with daughters still in the nursery were content to bide their time, waiting until greater age and wider experience made him, as it did so many young men, willing and even eager to settle down.

But by some marvelous, magical miracle, her cousin's attraction to her had matched her own. It was almost a matter of course that four months after her presentation she had been betrothed, and two months after that married. Lady Rown! Viscountess Rown! She had marvelled at bearing his name, and her joy had known no bounds when shortly after their wedding she had found herself with child. She thought them the most glorious days of her life, had enjoyed more than a full year of bliss before disillusionment had rudely shattered her dreams.

Had Julian ever truly loved her? She supposed he must

have, but he had never displayed that gentle vulnerability he had shown her last night. His love then had been bold, assured, mostly physical. Would it be so again, if she permitted it?

She walked out in her bare feet onto the sun-warmed stone. If it hadn't been impossible, unthinkable for them to be together any other way, would marriage have been his choice? In all fairness, it might have been; he was attentive enough in the beginning, and they had been very happy. But what is happiness? A fleeting emotion more appreciated when absent than when present.

Clarice leaned out over the balustrade; her thoughts were melancholy, but time and tears had wiped out their power to make her sad. If anything, she felt a little disgusted with herself, poor blind fool that she had been. All the lies and excuses —whatever he had had to say, she had accepted. Dazzled, that was what she had been.

Of course, the time had come when she could no longer deny the evidence of his faithlessness. She could still remember that day, in a detached way, as though it had happened to someone else. She had thought her heart would break, but it hadn't. And it was only the first of many such days; days of tears, of bitterness. Julian was probably right when he said they had been on the verge of hating each other. The angrier and more upset she had become, the colder and more withdrawn he became. And of course this only increased her hurt.

Clarice laughed a little at the memory. Well, it was something that she could laugh at it. Anne had always maintained that the intensity of her reaction to her husband's falls from grace, the bitter tears she had shed, the scenes she had enacted for him, had gone a long way to make his behavior worse rather than better. Not that Anne condoned his actions, or even suggested that Clarice treat them philosophically; she simply believed that it was foolish beyond permission to cause a man, especially one already inclined to stray, to lose his taste for the companionship of his wife and the comforts of his home. Perhaps Anne had been right; it had certainly gone from bad to worse.

But the intensity of her love for him, the depth of her pain, had made it impossible for her to react any other way. It had come to the point that whenever he was away from her she made herself wretched wondering where he was, whom he was with; and, of course, the damage this did to her peace told on the times when they were together.

And this was what they all wanted her to go back to! Not that it would be the same, of course. Never again would she be that naive: foolish little bride doting so blindly on her husband. She was older, wiser now, and no longer in love with him. But even wives who did not love their husbands, mature and worldly-wise women, could and often did find themselves humiliated and their lives made uncomfortable when married to men of Julian's stamp.

She might be here at Creeley for the sake of the children and to work out some sort of solution with him, but she could not in any way allow him to believe that that solution would ever include her returning to him as his wife. Certainly there could never be a repeat of the scene that took place on this very terrace last night. Even if John Prescott had not come into her life, even if she had not come to care for him and wish to marry him, she would never have gone back to Julian. At the very least, she would have insisted on a legal and permanent separation. One way or another, she would make Julian understand this.

She turned her back on the sunlit scene, and filled with the purpose of her resolve, returned to her room to bathe and dress for breakfast.

Clarice found her way to the breakfast room without encountering anyone except a maid with a bundle of linens under her arm. When Clarice entered the room, it appeared empty, but a sound from behind the open door made known the presence of the countess, gaily arranging primroses in an earthenware bowl. She looked up at the entrance of Clarice and smiled a welcome.

"Good morning, dearest," she said, reaching up from her lesser height to kiss her daughter-in-law's cheek. "I'm afraid we are quite alone this morning. All the men are off to look at a bridge that was quite ruined by all that wretched rain we had last week." She went across to the opposite side of the table from Clarice and seated herself and poured them both a dish of chocolate.

She handed this to Clarice and said cheerfully, "I mentioned to Hal this morning that it's been some time since you've been looking so robust; and the children are grown so jolly! I think Lady Fowle has been good for all of you."

Clarice returned a light reply and helped herself to dry toast and a generous portion of marmalade. She knew that Lady Creeley's words held no snide reference to her neglect of them since Julian had gone away. There was not an ounce of malice in Meg Creeley, and she would have been horrified if she had guessed that her simple words had pricked Clarice's conscience.

When Julian deserted her, the earl had been tact and sympathy itself, and had quite understood why his presence and that of his wife should cause Clarice grief instead of comfort. In the beginning, in her misery, she had simply wanted to blot out anything and everything to do with her husband, and then it had just become habit to rely entirely on her own family, seeing very little of Julian's except when they happened to be in town at the same time that she was there.

Julian was right. This was Perry's home as well as that of Augustus and Julia; she had not been fair to either children or grandparents. And they could have made it so difficult for her, if they had been that sort. Peregrine was joint guardian with her of his nephews and niece and had the same right of decision over their lives that she had; Lord Creeley was principal trustee of Julian's estate; they could very easily have piped the tune to which she danced. But they had trusted her judgment in all things and had never interfered.

Lady Creeley pushed back a lock of straying salt-and-pepper hair and regarded Clarice out of frank blue eyes that had lost none of their once-renowned beauty. She reached impulsively across the table and touched Clarice on the arm. "My dear," she began, "this must be very hard for you to understand, and even harder for you to forgive. But there are things in a man's life that have no place in ours, not because we lack the understanding for them, but because they are outside of our scope and do not govern the actions of women."

Was it out at last? Clarice wondered. Had the siege begun? "It is not a mere matter of understanding or forgiveness, Beaumère," she said carefully.

Lady Creeley removed her hand from Clarice's arm and settled back in her chair. "I know, and I know how very confused you must be. I won't deny what Hal and I hope is the outcome of this, but I want you to know that we do not mean to bring any undue pressure to bear on you. Your problems with Julian are yours and his and must be settled by no one but you. I've seen many examples of what comes of interfering in the lives of one's children, and it is never for the good. But, love"—she leaned forward again—"do not act hastily, be sure of yourself, of your future and of your heart." She rose abruptly. "There! I have said my piece, and I won't plague you anymore. I will go and busy myself in the still-room like a proper housewife, and you may find me there if you need me." She flashed her quick smile, putting Clarice very much in mind of Julian, and was gone, leaving her daughter-in-law prey to mixed emotions.

But not for long. Clarice had just finished the last of her chocolate and was deciding whether to have more or to go at once to the garden where the children were playing, when she heard the muffled sound of male voices.

When Lady Creeley had told her that all the men of the house were out, Clarice had felt cheated of her quarry. She had meant to tackle Julian after breakfast and begin having it out with him at once about their future. Now it seemed she would have the chance after all, and she found she didn't really want it, at least not at this moment. She got up immediately, intending to escape through the door into the garden. She had got about halfway there when the hall door flew open and Peregrine entered, calling her name, so that to ignore him and continue out the door would have been churlish and undignified.

She turned and greeted him and saw her brother, her husband, and her father-in-law come in behind him. They all wished her a good morning and sat down to dishes of chocolate or coffee. Clarice murmured something about leaving them to their business and was about to continue her retreat into the garden when Peregrine jumped up and almost pulled her into the chair beside him. He exclaimed that they would be positively desolate if she deprived their drab table of her brightening beauty, and the others politely agreed, so that she had no choice but to sit down and accept another dish of steaming chocolate.

Lord Creeley inquired after her night.

"I slept rather heavily, I'm afraid," she replied. "I was very tired after our journey, and not at all myself last night." This last was for Julian's benefit, although she did not look at him.

Lord Creeley murmured sympathetically. "Would that we had the recuperative powers of the very young!" he said. "We passed the children playing in the gardens with their governess as we came in; they looked very hale." He paused to sip at the strong coffee he preferred in the morning. "Peter tells me that Fowle has arranged a place in a preparatory school near Devon for young Perry. I wish you had consulted me. I'm sure a place might be had for him at Redfriars, where Julian and Peregrine attended."

Clarice flushed slightly. Her decision to send Perry to that particular school was another example of how she had chosen to disassociate herself from her husband's family. Peregrine, when she had discussed it with him, had mentioned Redfriars, but she had never so much as considered it. She was a little ashamed of herself. "It is very near Fowle's principal seat," she heard herself stammer, "and I . . . I wished Perry to be near me."

Lord Creeley smiled. He was a shrewd man and had noticed the color that had come into her cheeks. "So he might be here. You, as well as the children, are always more than welcome, this is your home. But the boy is quite young yet. Don't you think a tutor would do as well as school for now?"

A retort formed itself on Clarice's lips, and as quickly died. She had been about to exclaim on her own lack of ability to house a tutor, when she realized how greatly the events had altered in the past fortnight. She stole a quick glance at her husband, who was nearly opposite her, but he was regarding some papers he had laid on the table, and apparently chose to take no part in the discussion.

Lord Creeley noted her glance and said, "What do you think would be best for the boy at this stage, Julie, a tutor or school?"

Julian looked up a trifle wide-eyed, as if he had not been attending, but answered, "I think that a year is a long way off, and we have ample time to decide." He looked down and selected a page from the papers he had before him. It was covered with figures and small drawings. "What do you think of that bridge near the home farm? Will it be worth repairing, do you suppose, or should we tear it down and begin again?"

His father frowned, as if annoyed. "I think we will have to go over the matter with Sample."

Right on cue, Mr. Frederick Sample, bailiff of the Creeley estates, accompanied by his lordship's private secretary, came into the room.

In the discussion of estate business that followed, Clarice made good her escape and quickly ran upstairs to her room to fetch her shawl and bonnet. She intended to reach the garden by going through her room and down the stairs of the terrace, and thus avoid a chance encounter with any member of the household on her way there. As she rounded the corner of the labyrinth-like hall into the east wing where her room was situated, she all but ran into the arms of her husband.

She leapt back from him as though he had scorched her. "You!" she cried in dramatic accents, with a hand over her heart, for he had startled her. "Was learning to fly an accomplishment you discovered in America?"

He compressed his lips severely, but his eyes danced. "Not at all," he said amiably. He glanced toward the closed door behind him. "I came up the service stairs in back of the breakfast room, which is almost directly beneath the garden room, while you, on the other hand, chose to get your exercise by crossing the length of the house twice."

"You would think of that," she said darkly.

He looked at her speculatively. "Now, why should that annoy you? I'm sorry if I startled you, but it's quite your own fault for not looking where you were going."

"At least you didn't waste your time improving your manners while you were away," she said coolly. "If you will excuse me, I have things to attend to." She caught at her skirts, intending to sweep majestically past him, but he took a step to his side, into the center of the hall, and successfully impeded her progress.

"Don't you feel that this would be an excellent time for that discussion we have been promising each other?" he asked.

Short of scurrying around him in a most hoydenish manner, Clarice had no choice but to stay where she was. "I have to see to the children," she said rather grandly.

He was not so easily put off. "I saw them when we came in just now; they are well attended."

"I . . . I promised I'd join them as soon as I had my breakfast." Her voice sounded lame in her own ears.

"And so you shall, when we've finished." He paused momentarily to give his next words emphasis. "Unless you *do* wish to avoid talking to me."

"Why would I?"

"*I* don't know. Do you?"

In fact she didn't know, and his striking the nail so squarely on the head ignited the flames of the indignation she was almost determined to feel toward him. She knew herself bested, though. She drew herself up to her full height as he stepped aside, and walked grandly past him into the nearest open door, which happened to be that of a small saloon. She sat down stiffly in a straight-backed chair in full view of the door.

As he followed her and was about to close the door, she said coldly, "I would prefer it left open."

He made her a slight disdainful bow and deliberately opened it to its fullest extent. He sat down near her in a chair more suited to his comfort than properly maintaining a dignified bearing, for which he felt no need. She sat staring straight ahead of her with a decidedly martyred air. It was not lost on him. He smiled.

"Well?" she asked in frozen accents.

"Well what?"

She turned her head slowly to face him and raised her eyebrows a fraction in supercilious amazement. "You have dragged me in here to talk to you," she said. "I presume you have something to say to me."

"I was hoping we might spend a little time becoming better acquainted. So that we could understand each other more fully," he said in his quiet way.

His very manner irritated her. She wished that he was more the hale, hearty, and loud sort of man who always said precisely what he thought and wouldn't have had the least idea how to fence with words. The fact that such men always grated on her nerves in a most disagreeable way, she did not choose to remember.

"Become better acquainted? Understand each other?" She gave a short, stagy laugh. "I can't think of anyone who knows you better or understands you the way that I do, Rown."

"Do you really believe that? I think we have not truly known each other for more than the four years we were physically apart."

"Whose fault was that?"

"Mine mostly."

"Mostly?"

"Entirely. Does that please you?" He smiled slightly. "I am not going to argue with you, Clare, so you needn't waste your time baiting me."

She relaxed a little and lowered her head. "I suppose the truth of the matter is that I still can't think of anything to say. I know that I don't want to be your wife any longer. You have made it clear that you don't wish to divorce me. I think you believe that eventually I will change my mind. I won't." She raised her head. "Is there anything else to be said?"

"A great deal, I think. None of which has anything to do with that. You might begin with your life during the time I was gone," he suggested. "I know nothing about it."

Clarice snorted in an unladylike manner. "You will forgive me, I am sure, if I thought you had little interest in that."

He didn't answer, but sat watching her expectantly. With a sigh she obliged him. She began in reverse chronological order, telling him of her meeting with Mr. Prescott, how they had come to care for each other, how he had helped her and wished to make a home for her and the children on his estates in Hampshire. She studied him carefully for his response to this, but as usual, he did not give away his thoughts. He listened to her with the appearance of perfect ease and calm.

She went on, regaling him briefly with tales of visits to family and friends, and came backward to the time when he had left her. She told him unreservedly of the anger, frustration, mortification, and misery she had felt when she received the note she had supposed was from Therese Rouane informing her that her husband would not be returning to her; of the pain and grief she had all but thought she would die of when she was told, at the Fowles' in Devonshire, where she had gone to escape the wagging tongues of the ton and to nurse her wretchedness, that he had died at sea. She began calmly enough, but at this point she could not hold back her tears. In some way, telling this to him was almost like reliving it. She put back her head and bit at her lower lip. "I think," she said unsteadily, "one of the worst things was remembering what I had said to you the last evening that I saw you. I know I told you that I detested you, that I would give anything to be free of you, but it wasn't true. Not then. I said it to punish you, because I was hurt and I wanted to hurt you. After that, I felt that perhaps if I hadn't said those dreadful things you wouldn't have gone off with that creature, wouldn't have gone to your death. Oh, God, how I loved you!" She finished in a voice totally choked with tears. She gave in to them for a moment, but then forced them back. "Is that what you wanted to know?" she asked as calmly as she could.

"Yes, it was," he said gently. And it was. Exactly. It gave him more hope than he had dared to have since his return. He had very wisely refrained from any attempt to comfort her, knowing full well that any such gesture from him would be instantly suspect. "I'm sorry, Clare. If I'd had any idea it would upset you so, I wouldn't have asked it."

Clarice made a great business out of smoothing out the creases in her damp handkerchief. "I am not upset, not really. It was saying all those things out loud, I suppose; I don't think I ever have before."

He didn't agree with her reasoning, but he didn't dispute it.

"That brings us back to where we are right now, doesn't it?" she said, looking up at him for the first time in many minutes. "*Point non plus*. I really meant it when I said that I can't be your wife again. Even if it weren't for John, I know now what I was too naive to realize eight years ago: I could never be happy married to a man such as you are."

"Was," he corrected. "I, too, realize many things that I didn't when we were first married. Much of my cavalier treatment of you was the result of the habits I had fallen into in connexion with my work for the government and the fast set I was in. I knew I was unhappy in the life I was leading, but it was easier to go on in the way that was expected of me than to change the style of my life, and it wasn't until change was forced upon me that I began to realize that most of my discontent had been my own fault." He paused and then added softly, "I am not the man I was then, Clare. I'd prove it to you if you'd let me."

Clarice smiled sadly. "Does the leopard ever really change his spots? I don't believe it."

"Perhaps the leopard doesn't," he said seriously, "but a man may mature and appreciate the good things that he has, or has lost. I am not trying to excuse myself, you know. I know perfectly what I was then. That doesn't mean I'm incapable of change."

"Does it mean that you have suddenly become the ideal husband who never even looks at another woman?" she asked with a watery laugh.

He answered her with a smile. "I doubt if I'm capable of that much perfection."

"What *are* we going to do, Julie?" she asked despairingly. "Our problems go much deeper than just your past infidelities or my possessiveness. You probably think I can't or won't see your side of it, but I do. You want your wife and your children back so that you may be comfortable again, and you don't want the sort of public scandal that divorce would mean. Neither do I, really. I just don't see what else is to be done, for nothing you can ever say or do will change my mind. Unless you plan to become like one of those tiresome medieval knights and carry me off by main force, there is simply no way that you will ever convince me to come back to you."

"I don't fancy myself as Lochinvar. I expect he would have been a very wearing sort of person to know." More seriously he added, "We could compromise."

"Compromise? How?"

"I don't know; I haven't begun to think of it."

"I think it would be a waste of our time," she said decidedly. "I love John and I am going to be with him, no matter what."

He was beginning to find this constant reiteration of her intention irritating. "I see," he said, his manner cooling abruptly. "You intend to elope with him."

"Elope!" Clarice was horrified. "No, of course not. At least," she added, in case it was a point in her favor, "not unless you force me to it. The obvious answer is divorce."

"It is not. Rid yourself of that notion, Clare." His voice was gentler than his eyes, which looked to her like two black rocks, cold and impenetrable.

Clarice took a deep breath. She wondered how far she dared to defy him. In the end it was very possible that her entire future would depend on what he would or would not do for her. She said in a voice calmer than she felt, "It is very possible, if you will only agree to it."

"I won't, though. And nothing *you* can ever say or do will persuade me to change *my* mind. As you've said, *point non plus.*" His tone was mocking.

In spite of herself, Clarice's temper flared. "I could force you to it," she snapped at him, throwing caution to the wind. "I could leave you and live with him openly. Then you'd have no choice."

"Do you really think so?" His voice hardened. "I think that you would find that even more unpleasant than I would; and it would avail you nothing."

Clarice knew she had gone too far, but she was not in a mood to care. "I think it might be *just* the thing. A proud man like you would never bear *that* disgrace for long."

"Longer than you would, my love." He spoke from a frozen depth. "You'd never set eyes on Julia or the boys again."

"It is you who would not! They would be with me."

"I'd see you in hell first."

He was so icily vehement that Clarice imagined she felt a chill come into the room and she crossed her arms as though to warm herself. Rousing his temper, which she knew from experience could be formidable when full blown, was more likely to hurt her cause than to help it. She took another deep breath to allow her anger to cool, and was at least partially successful.

"Giving our tempers free rein will not serve either of us," she said in a much less emotional voice. "But I cannot believe that you would be so cruel about the children," she could not help herself from adding. "It would be worse for them than for me; they have never really known any other parent."

"Then you should consider them before you act too rashly," was his answer to this. "In this matter, dear wife, you have no ordering."

Fright chilled Clarice to the bone. She was not the careless, offhand mother so many women of her class were, and to be parted forever from her children was a horror that even the prospect of a happy, comfortable life with John Prescott could never compensate for.

She said bitterly, "I might have expected this from you. Why should I go back to you? So that you could invent new ways to hurt me? You may not be able to touch my heart as you once did, but I don't doubt that you would manage somehow to make me wretched. I'd sooner enter a convent than be your wife again." She rose and almost ran from the room. He made no attempt to stop her.

He stood up slowly and thoughtfully and made his way downstairs to the library, his favorite place to sort out thoughts that troubled him. He was troubled not because of anything that Clarice had said to him—that had been no more than he had expected—but because of his reaction to what she said. He had lost his temper when he had had no intention of doing so, in fact, had been determined not to do so. It was a rare experience for him, and one that displeased him not a little.

He poured himself brandy from a decanter that was kept in a hidden niche in one of the bookcases and seated himself in one of the comfortable leather reading chairs that were scattered about the room. He knew, as Clarice did, though for different reasons, that anger would never serve his purpose. If she were to learn to love him again, and he wanted nothing less, she would first have to like him again as well. That for now had to be his primary goal. The rest, he hoped, would fall into place, given time. Though unaware of that man's words, he agreed with John Prescott that the fact that she was legally his wife and had once been in love with him was to his advantage.

The existence of a Mr. Prescott in Clarice's life did not dismay Julian in the least. He knew it was only by the greatest good fortune that he had not returned to discover her married to someone else, perhaps setting up a new nursery. Unpalatable thought! Frankly, he did not regard Prescott as an insurmountable obstacle. This was not vanity, it was simply the belief he had formed based on what he knew. Clarice claimed to be in love with Prescott, yet here she was with him at Creeley, over, he had no doubt, the vociferous objections of her "beloved." No great store, therefore, could be put in Prescott's power to influence her. More importantly, though she said she wanted desperately to be Prescott's wife and never again his, last night on the terrace she had allowed him to make love to her. True, she had fled from him at the first physical advance he had made toward her, but not before he had felt her quick response.

Whatever Clarice might say in anger, he felt he knew her well enough to know that she would not act hastily or rashly, or do anything that would leave her bereft of her children. She needed time, he believed, to get used to the idea that he was back, that he was indeed alive and that they were still married. The longer he could keep her with him, at least outwardly his wife, the better the chances were that they would stay together.

Julian's years as an intelligence agent had impressed upon him the importance of planning ahead, and this is what he did now as he sat absently sipping his brandy. Time was probably on his side, but there was no harm in increasing the odds in his favor, even if it involved risk. Within the hour he knew precisely what he had to do; had, he supposed, known all along.

6

Clarice, after her interview with her husband, foresaw such upsetting scenes for the entire course of her stay at Creeley, and was heartily wishing that she had taken John's and her brother's counsel and remained in London. She felt herself the victim of her husband's caprice and her children the hostages of it, so she squared her shoulders and prepared to do battle with the enemy, but to her surprise, and even suspicion, the enemy had had his teeth drawn. For the next several days Julian was everything that was considerate and charming, displaying no coldness or rancor even when she had deliberately introduced John Prescott's name into their conversation once or twice to gauge his reaction.

At first she greeted this behavior with suspicion, responding in kind only when publicly forced to do so, expecting moment by moment a change in his tone. Still, as the days, gorgeous full-blown days more like summer than early spring, passed and he continued a delightful and considerate companion, never mentioning their problems, never, in even the smallest way, attempting to make love to her, her suspicions, if not allayed, were at least dulled as the rapport between them deepened.

In the mornings she usually rode with him, for pleasure or on estate business; in the afternoons they spent time with their children and took leisurely walks through the formal gardens; in the evenings they played piquet or whist or sang in parts to the accompaniment of Lady Creeley on the pianoforte. They talked and laughed and shared their time in a way that spoke of the easy familiarity that generally exists between a husband and wife.

It was a homey, comfortable existence, and Clarice was willing enough to call a truce and enjoy what, contrary to her expectations, had become a very pleasant time for her and her children.

During this time they received many calls from their neighbors from surrounding estates and from the village of Creeley Combe. It would have been impossible to keep such a nine days' wonder quiet for long in the city: here it was impossible, and everyone came, invited or not, to satisfy his curiosity. Several times a day the family could count on being interrupted by arrivals and subsequent explanations, and this, too, was a pleasant diversion.

The only drawback, as far as Clarice was concerned, was that being with the family, at Julian's side, it was taken for granted that she was overjoyed to be reunited with her husband, and the good wishes expressed at his miraculous return were extended to her as well. She found this occasionally embarrassing, but as she could hardly explain to these people the complexities of their situation, she simply smiled and said all that was proper.

On one occasion a bluff old bachelor colonel whose small property marched with the Rowns' teased her in an overfamiliar way that he used with all pretty young women, and made Clarice even more uncomfortable than usual. It was bad enough that Lady Creeley was present, but then Julian came into the room, and as Clarice caught his eye, she thought that he seemed amused by her discomfiture. This boded ill for their newfound harmony, but after the colonel had been helped, puffing away like that new invention, the steam locomotive, into his ancient carriage, Julian quizzed her so totally without rancor or self-satisfaction that she was forced to see the absurdity of it and instead of quarreling she found herself laughing.

Clarice had not seen a great deal of her brother during this time, that is to say, she had had little opportunity of private conversation with him, and that little had been brief and not at all concerned with her and Julian. She believed that Peter was giving her the latitude to sort out her confusions on her own, and was grateful for his forbearance; she knew well his opinion.

She was a little surprised that he had remained so long at Creeley. She had understood his original intention was merely to escort her and to remain a few days to see how she had got on, before going on to join his wife and children at Lydia's sister's in Shropshire.

She asked him about it one afternoon near the end of her proposed fortnight's stay, and he had replied offhandedly, seeming almost annoyed and asking her if she found his presence irksome.

"Of course not," she replied, "but I don't want you to put off your plans for my sake. You can see for yourself that I am managing very nicely. Not at all in need of a champion," she added with a smile.

"So far," he said succinctly, with a glance at her that held a wealth of meaning.

Clarice laughed. "At least he didn't try to ravish me the moment I walked through the door."

His only response was to return her smile, and they jogged along in silence for a while, part of a riding party consisting of a few friends and neighbors. Clarice was about to ask her brother if he had heard from his wife, when Arthur Hobalt, an overbearing and pompous little man, the eldest son of a neighboring family, trotted up to them, making an inane comment about the weather as he drew rein.

Peter, who made it a point to avoid Hobalt whenever he could manage it, spurred his horse, and his only reply to an entreating glance from his sister was a sympathetic grin as he moved forward to join Miss Hobalt and Peregrine, who were riding just ahead of them.

Hobalt began at once to shower on her his ponderous and unwanted attentions, and Clarice groaned inwardly; once collared, his victims seldom found escape an easy matter. She had just about resigned herself to his company when Julian abruptly rode into the narrow space between their horses.

Clarice was slightly startled, and her bay gelding shied in a halfhearted way that posed no difficulty for her, but Mr. Hobalt's horse's reaction to this was an immediate flattening of his ears and a very wholehearted attempt to kick at the flank of Julian's horse, forcing Hobalt to shorten rein and put his horse back together. He had no choice but to move farther to the side to keep his disturbed mount in check, and he cast a jaundiced glare at Lord Rown for his ill-mannered and reckless horsemanship.

Julian threw Hobalt a quick, unconcerned glance. He had successfully maneuvered Arthur Hobalt precisely where he wanted him. Clarice looked up at her husband in a way that clearly showed that she thought him the answer to her prayers, and he gave her a reassuring smile and addressed himself to Hobalt. "My father tells me that your father is thinking of selling a few acres near the east forest," he said. "I hope you'll let us have first bid."

Hobalt, whose only interest in his father's land was the extent to which it housed his hunters, had no intention of being drawn into agricultural or business discussions, and seeing that his quarry was now firmly protected from his reach, he mumbled something about neighbors and duty, and with a swift bow in their general direction, applied his spurs.

Clarice, as soon as he was out of hearing, laughed. "Do you know, it is quite amazing! You have the same effect on him that he has on me. It takes little more than your presence to tie his tongue and make him wish himself elsewhere as quickly as possible."

"Yes," agreed her husband, "but in his case it's a guilty conscience."

"And in mine? Perhaps a long-suppressed passion?"

"Good God, I hope not!"

"No fear, I wouldn't leave you for *Arthur*," she said, casting him a provocative glance.

"Thank you," he said dryly.

"They look so well together, don't they?" Clarice said, referring to Peregrine and Mary Hobalt, who were riding ahead of them. Julian agreed that they did. "Do you think they will make a match of it at last?" she asked.

"And have Arthur as a brother-in-law?" asked Julian, shocked. "I love my brother and wish him happy, but he has a duty to his family!"

"Seriously, Julie, is it likely?"

He considered for a moment. "Possible, but not, I think, likely."

"Why? She's a lovely girl and not at all tiresome like her brother. I think they would suit very well."

"I think so too."

"Then why not likely?"

"I don't think it is that way between them. On his side at least." He paused and then added, "Perry may sometimes appear to be a rattle, but he always knows his own mind when it matters. I think that if he meant it to be more than friendship he would have done something about it six years ago when he first started to dangle after her. He may have been a little infatuated then, but I believe it passed."

"That is a deplorably male point of view!" she exclaimed. "Did it ever occur to you that perhaps he offered for her and was rejected?"

Julian laughed. "Not for a moment. How little you know Lady Hobalt. If she so much as suspected that she could call Perry 'son,' poor Mary's wishes would have counted for nothing."

"And that," admonished Clarice, "is a perfect example of arrogance. Mary is a very pretty girl, and well dowered, I understand. Why should Lady Hobalt be so very anxious for the connexion with a younger son?"

"Because she is only two generations away from trade," he replied. Seeing the martial light in her eyes, he moved his hand as if to ward off a hit. "No, don't upbraid me. You know quite well how she fawns on my mother. She married Hobalt, which took her family back to the Restoration. Now, if she can catch a Rown, she'll go back to the Conqueror, or at least her grandchildren will. It matters to her, you know."

Clarice sighed. "Yes, it's a little sad, I think."

They rode on for a while in companionable silence. They were almost abreast of a long grassy trail leading into the forest at the edge of Rown land. He asked if she wanted to stretch their horses' legs, and she agreed, so they separated from the rest of the party and were soon galloping beneath the sparse canopy of budding branches. No one from the rest of the party had joined them, so that when they came to the end of the stretch, they were quite alone, not even the sounds of the others' horses reached them. Clarice pulled up breathlessly behind Julian, who turned his horse to face the direction they had come. Clarice turned her mount as well, and by tacit agreement they began to retrace their steps at a more sedate canter.

When they came out of the forest into the clearing again, there was no sign of their party, so they concluded that they had gone on ahead, and turned their horses in the direction they had originally been headed. They jogged along in silence and finally sighted the others on a rise not far ahead. Clarice slowed to a walk, and Julian followed suit.

"I'm glad we have spent these days getting on so well," she

said to him. "I greatly disliked being at loggerheads all the time."

"So did I," he agreed. "We have spent this time together well, I think. Pressing you and pressuring you, as I rather think you expected me to do, wouldn't have served either of us."

She stole a glance at him from beneath her lashes and said tentatively, "It wouldn't have served *you,* Julie. Pressure wouldn't have made me change my mind." He didn't reply, so she went on, "And neither will amiability. What I have rediscovered is that I do like you very much, when you are like this, at least. But it hasn't changed anything. I am afraid we are as much at a stalemate as we were from the beginning." He still said nothing, so her curiosity prompted her to ask if he had thought about their situation at all.

"Of course I have!" he said affably. "Actually, I have thought of little else. I think that now that we are more in charity with one another, we might try discussing it again, more calmly this time, I hope."

"Is there anything new to be discussed?" she asked cautiously.

"Yes, I think there is."

"What?"

"We'll talk later."

"Why not now?"

He looked at her with faint surprise. "Surely lumbering along on horseback is no way to have a serious discussion. See, we are almost up with the others. If we jog a bit, we can catch them up." He suited his actions to his words, and Clarice, finding herself alone, followed him.

It was nearly time for dinner before Clarice finally sought out her husband. Curiosity had made her wish to do so at once, but this had been denied to her. After their ride, the other members of the party had been invited to luncheon by Lady Creeley, and immediately following this, Clarice's attention had been taken up by her children and Miss Poll's fears that Gussie was taking a head cold. By the time Clarice had finished with her and seen to the various possets necessary to relieve her youngest son's symptoms, the day was far advanced.

As soon as she could, she went in search of Julian, but to

her dismay was told that he had left the house some minutes earlier in the company of her brother, so Clarice was left to control her impatience as best she could.

It was coming on seven before she heard them return, and as she was in the middle of dressing for dinner, there was no hope of heading him off as he came in. So she rushed a bewildered Eddly through her toilet, and by half-past the hour she was standing before the door of his dressing room. The door was opened by an impassive Boddle, valet to Lord Creeley, who had been lent to Rown until his return to London could secure the servants he required. Clarice was determined not to be denied or in any way put off, and without preamble she walked past the waiting servant and walked over to her husband at his dressing table. He looked up questioningly at her reflection facing his own in the large mirror above the table and paused momentarily in applying the finishing touches to his neckcloth. When she said nothing, he continued with this delicate operation and then turned to face her. Clarice could think of no way to begin in front of the aged servitor and didn't like to request Julian to dismiss him.

"I'll only be a moment, my dear, and then we may go down together," Julian said helpfully.

She smiled gratefully and sank into a nearby wing chair. "I'll wait for you, if you don't mind," she said for the benefit of Boddle.

"Not at all," Julian replied, and stood up for Boddle to ease him into his perfectly fitted coat. He nodded dismissal to the servant.

When the valet had gone, Clarice watched as her husband adjusted the set of his coat and then slid his ruby signet onto his finger.

"I shall, of course, be honored to take you in to dinner," he said, "but I don't think that is why you've come here, is it?"

"No," she replied, and then plunged ahead. "You said we might have something new to discuss about our . . . our difficulties."

He smiled a little at this euphemistic understatement. "Now?" He paused in the act of inserting his watch in its pocket and flicked it open. "It's rather late. We'll keep everyone waiting for dinner."

"We have some time; dinner's not until eight." Though Clarice had been glad enough to push the subject into abeyance until now, with her fortnight at Creeley nearing an end she wished to have it out and over with at last. She said as much to Julian.

He closed his watch with a sharp click and put it away. "Aren't you afraid we'll get out of hand again and spoil each other's appetites?"

Clarice gave him an elfin smile. "Better that than talking later and upsetting our digestions."

He returned her smile and obliged her by sitting down again on the edge of the broad stool in front of his dressing table. "What I want to talk about is compromise," he said at once.

"Compromise?" Somewhere in the back of her mind Clarice had been hoping that he had mellowed into agreeing with her wishes. It had been a very faint hope, but she still felt a little disappointed. "I thought we were agreed that compromise was a waste of time," she said more sharply than she intended.

"You said that," he reminded her. "I believe that if you will hear me out, and enter into my plan with a proper spirit, it will do very well."

"For whom?" she asked cynically.

"That remains to be seen."

"Well, you must think it will be you," she said reasonably.

"Yes, of course. At least, I hope it will, though I could be wrong," he added magnanimously.

She acknowledged this handsome admission with a slight mocking incline of her head. "At least you're honest about it," she said.

"I'd be a fool not to be. The situation as it stands is this," he went on. "You feel that you cannot be a wife to me again and wish a divorce so that you can marry another man, despite the complications and consequences. I, on the other hand, very much want you with me, and consider the complications and consequences insurmountable. A stalemate, as you've said. I have tried very hard to see your point of view, and I know you have done me the same justice.

"It is now April," he continued briskly. "If you will return to town with me on Monday as my wife for the world to see, and remain with me until the beginning of next year, I will then, if you still wish it, agree to a divorce and even do everything I can to assure you of the dispensation necessary for you to remarry."

She made a motion as if to protest, but he forestalled her. "What I am asking is not unreasonable. I am *asking* you, Clare, but I could force you to it, and far worse, if I chose. We both know that; but I don't choose. Spending the rest of our married life together with you resenting and hating me does not appeal; nor have I the smallest intention of presenting you as a gift to John Prescott, certainly not without trying to win you back to me first. You may think it vanity to hope that I can, but I do hope it. Nine months can be a short time or a long one, depending on how one uses it. The compromise is, I think, a fair one."

Clarice sat, lips pursed, deep in thought. This might not have been what she had hoped for, but wasn't it more than she had dared to expect at this stage? Nine months *could* be very short. Shorter, surely, than simply holding out against her husband and doggedly trying to force him to give in to her; that could take years. But what would John say? Could she make him understand why she would be living with her husband; would he be willing to wait for her under those circumstances?

Of even greater concern was how far she could trust Julian. He might not be making up to her now, but she did not delude herself into thinking that he would not, were she to encourage him in any way. Once they were alone, living together, at least outwardly, as man and wife, would she be able to trust him, or for that matter, herself? Their relationship at the present might be as platonic as it was possible for it to be, but the undercurrent of their attraction for each other was always present; unspoken of, unacted upon, but always there, at least for her.

"It may sound reasonable," she said, "but I don't think it will answer."

"Why not? Are you afraid of how I might behave when we are living alone together?" he asked, coming uncomfortably close to reading her thoughts. He gave her a brief, cynical smile. "If I had intended to force myself upon you, I could certainly have accomplished that by now. It will be on your terms, Clare. I understand perfectly what those are."

"It isn't only that," she said hastily, discomposed. "Please don't think I mean to hold against you forever our unhappy past. That is over and done with, but, Julie, so are we. In these last few days together I have rediscovered the dear friend and cousin of my childhood; that's all. To give you any reason to hope that there is or ever will be more would be very bad of me."

"Let me worry about the damage done to my sensibilities," he said perfunctorily.

"There are other considerations," she persisted. "There is John."

Julian raised his eyes briefly heavenward. The mention of that man's name was beginning to have the power to rub him quite the wrong way. "If he has a grain of common sense"—Julian's tone clearly expressed that he doubted this (he knew better, but he couldn't help himself)—"he will applaud this measure rather than otherwise."

Clarice was astonished. "You can't believe that!"

"I don't see why not. As matters stand, his position is tenuous at best; he is 'betrothed' to a married woman. He has nothing whatever to lose and everything to gain if you prevail."

"He wouldn't at all like my living with you again."

"No, I don't suppose he would," Julian agreed. He rested his elbow on the dressing table and leaned his head on his hand. "I feel sure you will tell him how the land lies, though," he said silkily.

"You may depend upon it! *If* I decide to go along with your compromise, which I am by no means convinced is one." After a moment she added, "How will it look to the world if after nine months of presenting myself to them as your wife we are suddenly divorced?"

"No worse than it would if I were to divorce you tomorrow or five years from now. They'll damn you whatever the time span."

Unhappily, Clarice knew this was true. "What about the children?" she enquired, seeking a new avenue of objection.

"What about them?"

"Would you let me have them?"

"No, of course not. You can't suppose for a moment that I would let my children, my heir, to be raised by another man."

"Then we have nothing further to discuss," she said, and started to rise.

"If you would let me finish?" he said quietly. "We will work out an amicable arrangement through which I will have control of their education and upbringing, but you will be permitted to be with them whenever you wish and their schooling allows. In view of the alternative, which is not to see them at all, I think that is generous. There will be those who will damn me for such leniency."

"Oh, very generous indeed!" Clarice cried with bitter sarcasm.

He stood up and held out his hand to her. "Let's not come to cuffs now, when we've managed so well," he said soothingly. "You don't have to give me an answer tonight, or even tomorrow. Think about it for a while. I think you will see that you can't possibly hope for better."

She permitted him to help her out of the chair and took his arm as he led her down the hall and the stairs to the ground floor and the Great Hall.

"I don't think it will answer, Julian," she said suddenly, breaking the silence that had fallen between them.

"Only think about it," he replied patiently, standing aside to allow her to enter the Great Hall ahead of him.

7

For the next two days Clarice's thoughts refused to focus on anything else. One moment she resolved to reject his compromise as unworkable, and the next she agreed with him that it was the best answer. She longed to confide her predicament to someone, but the Creeleys and Mr. Rown, of course, would urge her to accept Julian's plan, while Peter would undoubtedly urge her against it. No one was likely to give her the impartial advice she felt she needed. In all justice to her husband, he did not bring up the subject again, or in any way try to persuade her, even when they were alone. They went on in the same amiable fashion as before.

On the day after her talk with Julian, little Perry, looking up from a game of soldiers he was having with his brother, innocently asked her if she thought Papa would take them to Astley's Circus to see the famous horses when they were all living together in London again. At first Clarice was angry, believing that Julian had put him up to it, but a moment's reflection made her realize that this was a base thought. It wasn't at all in her husband's character to stoop to such a low ploy. Of course Perry believed that his father would be with them now, as other children's fathers were. She gave him an evasive answer, and felt very bad about it, wishing there was some way that the children could be saved from becoming embroiled in their adult problems, but that would not be possible. Whatever affected her future would of necessity affect theirs, and the realization gave her even more to think about.

She was glad that tonight they would be dining at the Hobalts' and attending a ball there afterward. It would give her a breathing space, a chance to enjoy herself and put aside the turmoil of her thoughts.

Up until now the family as a whole had refused all of the many invitations that had been showered on them by the neighborhood since Julian's return, pleading a very natural desire for time alone with their son after his long absence. At Julian's insistence, though, they had accepted this one. He said that he would have to make a start at appearing in public—if a private ball could even be considered that—and becoming used to the stares and whispers, and it was better to begin here with people he had known all his life than with the gawkers who would strive to put him out of countenance in town.

When all of the Rown family that was in residence at the Lodge ascended the main staircase of Hobalt Hall, where Lady Hobalt was waiting to receive them, she swelled with pride and self-satisfaction at this social coup so visibly that her daughter Mary, who stood at her side, wondered with alarm if Mama's stays were giving way.

Arthur Hobalt stepped out of his place in the receiving line and put Clarice to the blush by bowing over her hand as though she were royalty, and planting on the back of it an energetic kiss. He said in what was meant to be a soul-wrenching manner that he would be quite devastated if she did not promise him at least one of the two waltzes to be danced that night. Clarice's heart sank and she hastily explained that she had already promised them to her husband and brother-in-law, though it was the first either of those gentlemen had heard of it. Mr. Hobalt was visibly and comically crestfallen.

Peregrine and Julian took pity on her and both interrupted his protest to say that they considered her bespoken to them, Peregrine adding with a familiar gleam of mischief in his eyes that Mr. Hobalt would have to convince the band to play another waltz if he wanted her to dance it with him. Clarice turned and threw him a darkling look over her shoulder, to which he responded with a wicked grin. Mr. Hobalt knit his brow and looked thoughtful.

Julian used this opportunity to usher his brother and wife into the large saloon where his parents and Lord Ardane were already waiting with the other guests who had been invited to dinner.

"Perry, if he does . . ." Clarice began ominously as they entered the room, and then caught her husband's eye and had all she could do not to laugh aloud as her sense of the ridiculous was kindled.

"Don't worry, love," he said gallantly, "I'll protect you."

"From Perry, too?" she asked, her eyes dancing with laughter.

Having made his mischief, Peregrine left them to greet friends of his, and almost immediately the Rowns were swamped with greetings from friends and neighbors who, though many of them had seen him at Creeley in the past week, looked at him as if they were only just convinced that he was real. Even in her minor role as his wife, Clarice found the attention uncomfortable, and marvelled at his ability to smile and converse with them as though unaware of their curiosity.

If Julian was able to eat much at dinner, Clarice wondered how he managed it. His dinner partners on either side of him vied for his attention, and others with more curiosity than good breeding spoke to him from across the table, even cater-corner. After dinner the men joined the ladies in the drawing room very quickly so that they could all go to the ballroom before the other guests arrived.

Clarice, as the wife of the man of the hour, was not permitted to sit out even one dance, and this suited her perfectly, as she loved to dance and was very good at it. The time passed quickly and pleasantly. When Peregrine dutifully came up to claim her for the first waltz, she ticked him off soundly for his reprehensible behavior and was only mollified when he assured her that Mary Hobalt had told him that the program was prearranged and could not be changed. Peregrine, like his older brother, was a superb dancer, so as she had no fear for her toes, or that he would lose his timing, Clarice relaxed in his arms and enjoyed his light inconsequential chatter as they glided across the floor.

She had barely set eyes on her husband since they had come into the ballroom, as he had again been surrounded almost at once by well-wishers and the curious. Now and then she caught a glimpse of him on the dance floor, which was no doubt a great respite for him, though the young ladies he partnered seemed to regard him with a species of awe that would have seriously disconcerted a man of less aplomb.

When the first strains of the second waltz were sounded, the last dance before supper, Julian managed to disengage himself from the ever-present circle and went over to where Clarice was standing by his mother.

"Julian," said Clarice when she saw him, "you must be quite worn out with all this attention. We can sit this out if you like. We'll pretend to be in profound conversation, and no one will bother us."

"Not at all! Why should we?" He held out his hand to her. "You promised me quite publicly, you know," he added as she seemed to hesitate.

Clarice took his hand and allowed him to lead her into the middle of the floor. She chided herself. It was silly to be disconcerted at the thought of being in his arms again. It was an innocent dance in the midst of a crowded room. Still, she moved into the circle of his arms stiffly. If Julian noticed, he made no sign and guided her slowly into the group of turning couples on the dance floor. She made an attempt at light conversation, but got so little response that she soon gave it up. He looked into her eyes as they danced, and Clarice felt her color rise, thinking he looked devastatingly handsome tonight and very much aware of the strength of the arm that encircled her waist.

He quickened their pace in time to the music. It was a very fast waltz, and she was beginning to feel breathless, but in an exhilarating way. He tightened his hold on her slightly and brought her closer to him. They whirled across the floor with abandon, or so it seemed to her, their bodies flowing together almost as one to the rhythm of the dance. Her lips parted and her eyes sparkled with excitement as he looked down at her with an enigmatic smile that just might have held a touch of triumph.

Clarice was quite sorry to see the evening come to an end. Not only had her problems not plagued her, she had not so much as thought of them once. As she sat in the carriage on the way back to Creeley, half-listening to the conversation of her husband and her brother about the excellencies of Lord Hobalt's cellars, she was conscious of a disquieting feeling of letdown. It was well after midnight, but early by town standards.

Apparently the others felt the same, for on arriving at Creeley they congregated in the small, cheerful, obviously well-lived-in yellow saloon used for family amusements, to discuss the events of the evening. Clarice would have liked to prolong the evening indefinitely, but within the hour their small party broke up and Clarice reluctantly returned to her apartments.

Once there, she undressed and then dismissed a yawning Eddly. She crawled between the sheets and lay there for what seemed to her like hours, with sleep as far from her as it had ever been. Thoughts of the ball and of her waltz with Julian kept flitting through her head, disturbing her rest. Finally she threw off the covers with disgust and put her feet over the side of the bed. She looked longingly toward the French doors that led to the terrace, but it was impossible to go outside tonight to clear her head. A sharp wind had come up since their return from the Hobalts', and spatters of rain, the first since her arrival at Creeley, clattered against the panes.

Clarice decided she might as well read for a while, but the books she had brought with her were all old favorites, and tonight she felt the need for something new to divert her. With a sigh she slid off the bed and hunted for her slippers, and finding them, she slipped them on and put on the dressing gown which matched her blue silk nightdress, and let herself into the hall.

It was quite dark, for the moon was hidden behind the clouds, but her eyes were adjusted to the gloom and she knew her way about the house. When she reached the downstairs hall, she went to the cupboard where bed candles and a tinderbox were kept. She lit a candle, and guarding the flame against drafts with her cupped hand, went down the corridor and opened the door into the extensive library. The room was cavernous and two stories high; her tiny light did little to dispel the blackness. Despite this and the wildness of the night, Clarice, who was not of a fanciful nature, calmly entered and shut the door behind her. She had spent many hours in this room during her married life with Julian, so she knew it well and unhesitatingly moved toward the section she wanted. She set her candle on the floor and knelt down to examine the titles on a bottom shelf. She found one or two that seemed likely to interest her, then sat back on the floor and prepared to examine them by the dim light.

A slight sound, a movement perhaps, caused her to look up sharply, across the room to the cathedral-sized arched windows that spanned both stories and overlooked the park. She became aware of the figure of a man seated, almost slouched, in one corner of a sofa near the windows. She stood up and raised her candle.

"Julian?" she hazarded. "How long have you been there?" she added, her voice sharpened a little from the fright he had given her.

"Before you," he said quietly.

"Well, you might have given me some sign," she said with asperity, but keeping her voice down as well. "You nearly startled me out of my wits."

"I beg your pardon. I didn't intend to."

She bent down to pick up the books she had been going through and then walked over to him. "What on earth are you doing, sitting here in the dark?"

"I don't wish to go to bed yet; I'm not tired."

Clarice sighed. "I know, neither am I." She sat down in a chair on the other side of a small table from him, placing her books and her candle on it, near a crystal decanter. She looked at him and saw that he held a nearly empty glass in his hand. "Are you foxed?" she enquired suspiciously. She had not paid attention to the amount he had drunk at the Hobalts'.

"No," he replied with a slight smile. "At least, not much."

"Then why are you sitting here drinking by yourself in the dark?" she asked, curious.

"No reason. Just thinking."

The words "About what?" formed on her lips and would have been spoken in an earlier time, but now, somehow, she felt it was too personal. Instead she said, "I thought you had gone up with the others. It really is too bad of you to keep poor Boddle up so late; he's not very young anymore."

"I'm not keeping him up. I told my father to send him to bed when he was through with him. I think I can contrive to undress myself." His words were sarcastic, but not his tone.

"You must be very glad that this night is over," she said conversationally, reluctant to gather up her books and return to her room.

"It wasn't too bad," he replied, and finished off the drink in his glass. He filled it again about halfway.

He may not be drunk, she thought, but he means to be. The wise thing to do, she knew, would be for her to take herself up to bed, leaving him to his solitary musings and his brandy, but she continued, "It's not as if you hadn't been in company all these years. You must have attended many balls in America."

"A few," he agreed.

"Were they the same?" she asked, really wanting to know.

"Yes, they are always the same."

Clarice could not quite gauge his mood. He was behaving amiably enough, but he answered her offhandedly, almost as if he were not really attending. Perhaps he did wish to be alone.

"I suppose I had better go to bed," she said, but not enthusiastically.

"Is that what you want to do?"

"No, but it is very late and becoming quite cool in here with the wind outside." As if to underscore her words, the wind gusted sharply and rattled the leaded panes of the arched windows. Clarice shivered slightly.

He turned his impenetrable dark gaze on her for a moment and then straightened up and rested his right arm over the back of the sofa. "If you mean to bear me company, come here and be warm," he invited her, his voice devoid of inflection.

Clarice's eyes widened at his daring to suggest it.

He gave her his cool, sardonic smile. "I promise not to bite you, Clare."

"That's not what I am afraid of," she said meaningfully.

"You have *nothing* to be afraid of," was his answer. She hesitated, indecision writ plain on her countenance. Still, she made no attempt to leave him.

"Come here, Clare," he repeated very softly.

Hardly knowing why she did so, Clarice got up and sat down beside him. He put his arm around her and drew her nearer. It *was* warmer. "Better?" he asked, and she agreed in a small voice that it was.

If she had expected him to do something dramatic like pounce on her the moment she was beside him, she was disappointed; he understood her too well to do that. He merely reached over to snuff the candle between a thumb and forefinger and then settled back in his corner to sip at his drink. He said nothing, looking out toward the windows, which the wind still rattled from time to time. Clarice shivered again, but not from the cold.

He turned to her and offered her his glass. "Drink it," he said quietly. "It's very warming."

She took it from him and did as she was bid. She did not really like strong spirits, but this was the finest French cognac and went down smoothly, warming her from the inside out. He took the glass from her hands and set it on the table next to the decanter. Then he turned toward her, took her in his arms and kissed her very gently, as though she were made of fragile crystal. As she responded to him, the kiss deepened and she returned his embrace with fervor. Fears that she might be surrendering more than her body to him raced through her mind, but all at once this didn't seem important. Sensations of arousal surrounded her, penetrated her, and she yielded to them almost gratefully, luxuriating at his touch, at the warmth of his mouth on hers. As the blue silk slipped softly from her body, the fine hairs all over her skin stood on end. She lay back against the soft leather of the wide sofa and reached out for him, suddenly impatient for his lovemaking.

8

The morning after the ball found Lord Ardane pacing the length of the garden room between the tall windows and the French doors for perhaps the fifth time; and for the fifth time he nearly collided with a small piecrust table which was directly in his path. He swore at the inoffensive object as he glanced his thigh against it, and absently reached out a hand to steady it.

As soon as the post had arrived, shortly after breakfast, he had sought out his sister, only to have her tell him that as the day had after all turned out fine, she was on her way to join the children for a drive in the pony cart; but she did agree to meet him in her room at an hour when she expected to be back. It was now three-quarters of an hour past the appointed time, and he cursed her specifically and women in general and was just about to leave and go in search of her when the door flew open and Clarice ran in rather breathlessly.

She went over to her brother and kissed his cheek. "Oh, dear, you look quite like a thundercloud!" she exclaimed. "Have I kept you waiting so long?"

He withdrew from her embrace and held her at arm's length. He surveyed her critically; her hair was coming down in two places, there was a black mark on her cheek and grass and damp stains on her skirt where she had been kneeling; her lips were slightly parted, her cheeks and eyes glowed with healthy radiance; she looked about sixteen and, he thought, as beautiful as he had ever seen her. He was in no humor to pay compliments, though, so he merely said, "You look the perfect hoyden! Twelve instead of six and twenty. Where the devil have you been while I've been cooling my heels in all this blasted clutter?"

Clarice gazed around the elegantly appointed room; it was anything but cluttered. She was about to point this out to him when he said abruptly, "You've a smut on your cheek," and offered his handkerchief. She took it and rubbed at the spot he pointed out.

"What on earth can be so urgent to make you so impatient?" she asked as she sat down on one of the straight-backed chairs flanking the tall windows.

He sat down on the other and replied, "If I'm impatient, it's because we haven't much time. You'd best ring for your maid to start packing at once."

She put down the handkerchief and asked if the smudge was gone. Receiving an affirmative reply, she asked, "Why should I start packing? I thought we were leaving on Monday."

"Yes, but I've had a letter from Lydia this morning. She's left Frances and gone on to Jane's and wants us to join her there for a ball Jane's giving tomorrow night, and then we'll all go on to London next Tuesday or Wednesday. It's only some forty miles or so from here, so we ought to be able to do it comfortably if we get a good start in the morning."

"Travelling half the day, getting the children settled in the other half, and then dancing all night?" Clarice laughed. "You must think me very young indeed!"

"We might have left this afternoon if I hadn't spent the whole of the day waiting for you," he said pettishly. "What the devil made you go out in the pony cart?"

"The children wished it."

He rose. "Well, just the same, you'd best get started. The earlier we leave, the sooner we'll get there, and no doubt you'll have time for a little beauty rest before dinner."

Clarice looked up at him. "If you don't mind, Peter, I wish you will give Lyddy and Jane my regrets. I believe I'll stay on until Monday as we'd planned, and go straight on to town."

"I really can't, Clare," he said. "Lyddy's expecting me and isn't best pleased to begin with that we haven't joined her before now."

"Well, you could have," Clarice said reasonably. "I never intended to go anyway unless things were dreadful here. There was nothing to stop you, though. I told you I didn't wish to upset your plans."

Ardane put his hands on his hips. "If that don't beat all! Who said before we even left town that she would be more comfortable knowing there was someone here who would take her side?"

"After you positively insisted on escorting me," Clarice replied, nettled at his tone. "I told you I could manage if I had to, and I have. Very well, thank you!"

"Pretty thanks indeed!" he snorted.

Clarice had the grace to be a little ashamed. His intention, after all, had been to protect his younger sister from being hounded; he had had no more idea than she had that it wouldn't be that way.

"I'm sorry, Peter," she said contritely. "Of course I was very glad that you were here with me. I know that first night especially would have been dreadful to get through without you."

"And after that I might have taken myself off with your blessings?" he retorted, refusing to be mollified.

"No, not at all!" she said hastily. "I'm sure it was your being here, knowing that I could count on you for support, that . . . that you were here if I needed you . . ." She tried again. "I know I wouldn't have been nearly as comfortable without you beside me. I just didn't want to put you out in any way."

He gazed at her coolly for a moment and then said, "You haven't. I wasn't mad to go to Frances' anyway. She *will* let those seven brats of hers run all over the house screaming their heads off. No discipline whatsoever. But," he continued, "the fact is that we will have to go to Jane's. I can tell by the sound of her letter that Lyddy's in a rare taking. She'll hand me my head if I don't show up for that damned ball."

"Then please go, Peter," she pleaded. "The Creeleys are accompanying Julian to town on Monday, and I can go with them. It's only two days; I'll be fine on my own."

"I think it would be best if you left tomorrow with me. If you mean to stand up to Rown, you won't accomplish much by attaching yourself to his family," he pointed out.

"I've quite made up my mind, Peter," Clarice said firmly. "I have already told them I'd be leaving on Monday, and all my plans are arranged."

"Very well, if you are determined," he said, giving in. He walked over to the door leading into the hall, then he turned, his hand on the handle. "I should be back by Thursday or

Friday at the latest. I'll stop by Anne's to see how you got on."

Clarice dearly wanted to say that she would be happy to see him at their sister's, but she knew that she would have to tell him sooner or later of the decision she had come to that morning, and the truth now would be easier than explaining away a lie later.

"I won't be at Anne's," she began cautiously, and quickly and briefly told him of Julian's plan for compromise that she had at last agreed to.

Peter drew in his breath with a low whistle of respect. He walked back over to her and sat down again. "Well, well, well. Very nice. Clever, too. I must admit that I underestimated him. I thought you'd be leading him a pretty dance for a while yet at least."

"What is that supposed to mean?" Clarice asked sharply, not caring for the insinuation in his voice.

"Just that I thought it would take him longer than a fortnight to get you back to his bed and board."

"It is no such thing," Clarice said indignantly, and colored slightly. "He has agreed to go along with my terms, and those are that it be for appearance' sake, in name only."

"In name only," he mocked her. "Do you really believe that?"

"Yes, I do," she said coolly. "Julian does not go back on his word. I had to do it, Peter. It was the only way. I know I meant to stand firm against him, but after ten minutes' conversation with him I realized that that wouldn't serve. He is just as determined as I am. It might have taken years to convince him that I mean what I say; I couldn't expect John to wait forever for me."

Ardane tilted his head to one side and regarded her thoughtfully. "What do you think Prescott will have to say to this arrangement?" he asked.

"He won't like it, I know," Clarice said, "but I will convince him that it *is* in our best interests. He is a conventional man, after all. I'm sure he'll want us to get through this with as little fuss as possible. I am lucky that he cares enough for me not to let the stigma of divorce matter to him."

"You will also be very lucky if he doesn't come to realize that Rown's little plan certainly isn't in *his* best interests," Peter said caustically.

Clarice smiled a little. "I hope I'm clever enough to realize that Julian has hopes that at the end of the time I won't want the divorce any longer, he even admits it, but he is mistaken. I shall want it."

Peter snorted. "If you're clever enough to know that, you also ought to realize that he'll bring out the heavy artillery, trying to get you back to him."

"I know he will," she said mildly.

"And that don't concern you?"

Clarice raised her chin slightly, but didn't meet his eyes. "No," she replied, "not now."

"Why now in particular?" he asked, studying her closely.

To her intense annoyance, she blushed again.

"What is it, Clare?" he asked, puzzled by her reaction. "Has Rown been making love to you?" he guessed, and her face told him, accurately. "Did you find his rather too flamboyant charms easier to resist than you suspected? Is that why you think you can stand up to him?"

Clarice was looking down at her lap, where she was nervously pleating permanent creases into her handkerchief. Peter stood up and went over to her. He took her chin in his hand and raised her face. "Are you sleeping with him, little sister?" he asked bluntly.

Clarice tried to move her head away, but he held her in a grip of iron. "That's it, isn't it?" he said quietly, and dropped his hand.

"No, it isn't," Clarice retorted, looking away from him.

"Dissembling is not your forte, dear sister," he said with a slight sneer.

"I don't see what business it is of yours," she snapped defensively.

"Why, none at all!" he said easily. "Just the purely natural concern any brother would feel as he watched his sister throw herself headlong into unhappiness."

"I have no intention of doing any such thing!"

"I hope you may be right," he said sadly. "I personally doubt it. I remember, if you don't choose to, all the other times you forgave him and took him back."

"It isn't going to be that way this time."

"Isn't it?" he asked sarcastically. "Did Rown promise you that?"

"It doesn't matter what he's promised!" She stood up and

looked out the window, turning her back on her brother. "I am not returning to him as his wife," she added more quietly.

"It seems to me that you already have." She didn't reply, so he went on in a resigned voice. "There was really no reason to make up that nonsense of a compromise. It is your life, Clarice; I haven't the ordering of it. If it is Rown that you want, and think you can manage this time, I wish you all the luck in the world. I never much fancied Prescott as a brother-in-law anyway. Though," he added, "of the two, he'd make you the better husband."

Clarice turned to him and on him. "I didn't make anything up!" she bristled. "It *is* a compromise. Ask Julian, if you like. I trust you will believe him."

"I believe that you believe it," he said gently. "Or that Rown has made you believe it."

Clarice returned to her chair and sat down again. "I know that I denied that I was still attracted to him in . . . in that way, but almost as soon as we arrived here, I realized that you were right. I won't try to deny that we have made love, but I now believe it was the very best thing that could have happened. Before that, I couldn't bring myself to accept Julian's compromise, mostly, I think, because I was afraid that it *would* happen. It was not so much making love with him that I feared as what would happen afterwards. I thought it might rekindle the feelings I once had for him that went far deeper than the mere physical.

"But, Peter, it hasn't," she explained, looking up at him. "If anything, my resolve to be free of him has strengthened. Last night I was confused and frightened. I thought that I was giving up all my hopes for the future I so desperately wanted, throwing myself, as you've said, headlong into unhappiness, but this morning I awakened for the first time since he's come home with my mind clear. It was as though it was a piece of our past that had to be played out. It is truly over between us. I know I can agree to his plan now with no apprehensions at all. At the end of the nine months, he will free me and I will be with the man I truly care for. And," she added a trifle defensively, "it is not as if I have done anything wrong; he is my husband."

"But a husband you no longer wish to have," Peter reminded her. "Well, I must say you sound very confident. After what has occurred between you, do you really think you will be able to keep him at arm's length, living together as you'll be? Do you think he'll let you?"

"Yes," she stated without hesitation. "I spoke with him directly after breakfast this morning, and I was completely honest with him. I told him exactly how I feel, that nothing had changed, that in agreeing to his compromise I hoped to be free of him. He accepted it all quite calmly, even when I made it clear to him that it would be as we had originally agreed, in name only."

"That must have done wonders for his vanity," Peter said with a bark of laughter. "He probably thought that his problems were over."

Clarice shook her head. "No, he understood. It was just an . . . an episode. He was quite amiable and not in the least put out or offended. In any event, it won't do him any harm to know that I now find him totally resistible," she added with a smile.

"The question is, do you? Or do you just want to believe that you do?"

"No, Peter," Clarice replied. "It won't do. I'm not going to let you harangue me into having doubts. Everything is going to go perfectly now. It can't possibly fail."

Lord Ardane said nothing, although far from convinced.

By the time they were ready to leave on Monday, changes had been made in their original plans and the terms of their compromise had been worked out in greater detail. Julian also suggested, and Clarice eventually agreed, that it would be best if the children remained at Creeley while they travelled to London for Julian to show himself to the world by doing the season and to handle the legal matters of his return. The children adored life at Creeley, and Clarice was forced to admit that they would probably be much happier remaining in the country in the care of Miss Poll and their nurse, Mrs. Cratchit, both of whom she trusted implicitly and knew the children loved, than shut up most of the time in their town house.

Lady Creeley, who had made up her mind to go to town herself to help open the house for her son and his wife, also intended to return to Creeley at the end of the week to be with her grandchildren, as did her husband, Hal, as soon as the legal matters were well in hand. Clarice was still feeling a little guilty over her neglect of their grandparental rights, and this went a long way toward convincing her that her babies would manage quite well without her for the two months or so that she and Julian meant to remain in London.

Peregrine, too, declared his intention of joining them in town, though he had his own lodgings in a fashionable house not far from his clubs and would not be staying with them at Creeley House. He had said in his usual provocative manner that he would not for the world miss the stir that his brother's return would cause in fashionable circles and that he fully expected to gather to himself the overflow of lovelies who would no doubt be hanging all over Julian to hear of his interesting adventures. Julian gave him a quelling look at these words, as Clarice was present, but her good humor continued unabated, as did her bright outlook for her future.

As their entourage, consisting of three carriages and several outriders, made ready to leave, Lady Creeley determined that no sad partings should mar their start, and so kept up a brisk cheerfulness that pervaded the whole party. Clarice did hug her boys and her little girl fiercely and shed a few tears, but these were kept to a minimum, and soon they were off, Lord and Lady Creeley riding in the same carriage as Clarice to bear her company, as Julian and Peregrine had elected to ride beside them for at least as long as the weather held.

As the carriages pulled onto the main post road, Julian and his brother jogged along behind them in silence. Julian's horse, a large handsome chestnut nicknamed Silver from a portion of his long pedigree name, was unusually restive, constantly sidling and tossing his head and occasionally kicking out with his hind legs as though he meant to unseat his rider.

Julian, like most men raised in the country with the very finest horseflesh at their disposal, was an excellent horseman, and it took most of his considerable ability to control his difficult mount, which had also made several attempts to bolt. When they were a mile or so from the lodge gates of Creeley, Julian trotted over to the side of the road and abruptly halted, motioning to the puzzled outriders and coachmen to continue on. Peregrine followed him and held Silver's bridle while his brother dismounted. It was as well that he did, for the horse bucked as Julian put his weight in the stirrup and he was forced to leap away from him to keep from being thrown.

Peregrine whistled under his breath. "What the devil's gotten into old Silver today? I've never known him to act like an unbroken colt before."

"I'm damned if I know," replied his brother as he checked the girth and then pulled back the saddle to see if it was rubbing the horse's withers. He ran his hand partway under the side of the saddle, down under the girth, and up to the other side, but everything seemed normal; the pad beneath the saddle was smooth and not bunched up, the girth was exactly the proper tightness, and the horse's stomach was not distended and suggested no disorder. Failing there, Julian went on to satisfy himself that Silver's legs and haunches were sound.

Julian returned to the horse's head to take the reins from Peregrine to remount. As he put his hand on the pommel of the saddle and his foot in the stirrup, Silver shied violently, ramming hard into Peregrine and his horse and nearly pushing them down the bank and into the ditch. Silver raised his head so high that Peregrine's arm ached trying to keep him down. Julian cursed softly and with a swift movement was back in the saddle. At once the horse attempted to bolt again, and actually came up on his hind legs as Julian shortened rein. Peregrine had no doubt about his brother's horsemanship, but even the best of riders could be undone by a truly bad mount. He suggested that they call the others to a halt, stating that if Julian preferred to remain astride, he would be glad to give up his horse and ride in the carriage. Julian was touched by his concern but declined the offer.

"You can't ride that brute for the next fifteen miles," said Peregrine emphatically.

"I don't intend to. I'm not convinced that it is just bad temper; normally there isn't an ounce of vice in this horse. It is possible, Per, that something may well be the matter with him, even if I can't find what it is. We'll stop at the Owl and I'll have one of the grooms look him over; they've good men there." With this he urged the prancing, sidling Silver into a canter to catch the others up.

The Owl was the local watering place for the residents of Creeley Combe and was popular and respectable if unpretentious. It was less than a mile down the road and was sighted by Peregrine with undisguised relief. His nervousness for his brother was transmitting itself to his horse, making his own ride less than comfortable.

They had already warned the others of their intention, and the entire party turned as one into the wide lane that led to the Owl, which was set back a distance from the road. The brothers were the first to enter the courtyard of the inn, a rambling two-story building flanked by stables and numerous outbuildings, and were met by Gretcham, the landlord, on the threshold of his taproom. He had heard the clatter of hooves and wheels and had come out in surprise. Though on the post road, his was a primarily local establishment and did not cater to the quality and the carriage trade. On seeing the brothers, he instantly recognized them and called out a greeting.

He had heard of the miraculous return of Lord Rown, as had everyone in the small closed community of the village, and was about to congratulate him on his return, when before his horrified eyes the dismounting viscount was cast from the side of his suddenly rearing horse and thrown in a heap on the cobbles at his feet.

For a moment neither the landlord nor anyone else reacted. Then, as though a wand had been waved bringing everyone back to life, the courtyard was filled with voices and everyone began to move at once. Peregrine, who had quickly dismounted, was the first at his side, and for one terror-filled moment he gazed down at his brother's still form and feared the worst; but then Julian, only stunned, lifted himself up.

The first thing Julian saw after his brother's anxious face were the wide, frightened eyes of his wife. She was kneeling in the dirt beside him, and her hand reached out to touch him.

"Julian," she gasped, relief flooding over her, "I thought . . ."

"I am not so easily disposed of, as you have cause to know," he said with something that was not quite a smile. "We Rowns are tough stock."

He started to stand up but was prevented by Peregrine and his father and the landlord, who insisted that he make certain that he was not seriously injured and that no bones were broken. When this was done to everyone's satisfaction, he was at last permitted to stand with the helping hand of his brother.

He dusted himself off and made a light, self-mocking comment on his horsemanship.

His mother, horrified that he should make so light of what she considered a serious accident, insisted that they should all enter the inn so that Julian might recover a bit and have something bracing to drink. His protests that the only thing that was shaken was his pride were put aside and he was firmly steered inside to the taproom by the rest of the party.

The landlord, almost as shaken as his noble guest that such a thing should have happened on his doorstep, hovered solicitously about them and barked sharp orders to the tapsman and kitchenmaid, and was clearly disappointed when his lordship insisted that brandy would be sufficient and could not be persuaded to lie down for a time in the best bedchamber. He contented himself at last with giving Julian the brandy with his own hands and saying he would see to it that Jem, the stable boy who was a rare turn with the horses, he was bound to say, looked over every inch of the chestnut to see if he could discover any physical reason for the horse's unaccustomed bad behavior.

Julian felt all the usual male horror at a public fuss, but bore his mother's and Clarice's ministrations with equanimity, fortified by the sympathetic glances of his brother and father.

After dutifully, and not ungratefully, drinking the brandy, he declared himself quite the thing again and suggested that he and his father and brother go out to the stable and have a look at Silver. The ladies naturally protested at this but were overborne, and the men soon found Jem rubbing an evil-smelling ointment carefully into the back of the now docile Silver.

"What's his trouble?" asked the earl, who reached him first.

Jem touched his forelock and said, "All tore up, 'e is, m'lord." He indicated two raw-looking spots high on the back of the otherwise shiny coat of the chestnut. Julian examined the sores carefully and enquired after the nature of the ointment.

"Damn Snidley!" exclaimed Lord Creeley with bitter thoughts for his head groom. "He'd better have one damn good explanation for letting a horse out of the stables in this condition."

Jem flushed and dared to put himself forward. In almost any other circumstance he would have preferred to suffer tortures rather than break in on the conversation of such august personages as those from up at the Lodge, but the stableyard was his domain and he knew himself a master in it.

"Begging your pardon, m'lord," he said, touching his forelock again, "but I don't know that it be the fault of Mr. Snidley." He led them over to the paddock fence, where the saddle rested alongside the light, matted wool pad. "When I took 'im off," he said, pointing to the saddle, "I saw the sores was fresh like." He picked up the saddle pad and turned it over, revealing bloodstains. "Feel this, then," he said, offering it to Lord Creeley.

The earl touched the spot indicated and immediately drew his hand back. He took the pad from the boy and touched the spot more carefully. He looked at the attentive faces of his sons, who were beside him, and handed the pad to Julian. Julian fingered it gingerly and then quickly began to part the fibers.

"Thistles!" he exclaimed in surprise, and examined the pad in more detail. He handed it back to his father, who did the same and then gave it to Peregrine.

The three men exchanged glances. "How the devil would thistles get embedded like that in a saddle pad? You didn't untack your horse on a ride and lay it on the ground, did you, Julie?" asked Peregrine, his face a classic mask of puzzlement.

"No, of course not."

Lord Creeley ran a finger over one of the spots. "And it would be wonderful indeed, would it not, if they just happened to become embedded like that in a row, and so deeply."

Peregrine regarded him fixedly. "Are you suggesting that they were deliberately put there?"

"Of course he isn't," said Julian, casting a warning glance toward the attentive Jem. "He is merely saying that it is remarkable that it should have happened like that."

Peregrine and the earl caught his meaning and murmured assent, and at that moment they were joined by Gretcham. Lord Creeley showed him the offending pad and undertook the explanations. They made arrangements with him to stable the chestnut and have him sent on later in the day to the Lodge, as it was agreed that his sores would make him unridable for some time.

They rejoined the ladies in the taproom, who exclaimed with amazement that such an accident could have happened. The men by tacit agreement gave them no opportunity to delve more deeply into the matter, but insisted that they must begin their journey again immediately if they were to reach the inn where they were to spend the night before dark. This was agreed to, and Lord Creeley went in search of Gretcham to pay for the brandy and the stabling of Silver, while Perry escorted his mother, and Julian his wife, back to the carriage. Julian and Clarice had just crossed the threshold into the courtyard when Clarice exclaimed that she had forgotten her reticule and dashed back into the inn, followed by her husband. She located it under a table where it had fallen, and taking her husband's arm, began once again to leave the taproom. They had almost reached the door again when they all but collided with a man who was hurrying in from a side door. He took a step back, mumbled an apology, and then stood stock-still, his jaw slack and his eyes wide open in amazement.

Though the light in the room was too dim to easily discern the finer points of the man's features, there seemed to Julian something vaguely familiar about him, but surely nothing to account for such startled recognition on the stranger's part. Julian turned to his wife, and it was his turn to be surprised, for she, too, seemed to be suffering from the same malady, her face a study in blatant astonishment. Julian turned back to the man, who had apparently come out of his trance and was again disjointedly apologizing and then all but dashed out of the room and up the stairs. Clarice had recovered as well and murmured something just barely coherent about the others waiting for them. Julian regarded her blandly and led her out into the brightness of the day.

As their carriage turned into the post road, Clarice rested her head against the squabs, recovering from the shock of running into John Prescott at an inn not two miles from Creeley Lodge; she thought she had never been more surprised by anything in her life. She had had no idea that he was there, and the magnitude of the discovery momentarily pushed from her mind her concern over Julian's accident.

Julian sat beside her now in the carriage, and she stole a sidelong glance at him. He was conversing earnestly with his mother and father, for the purpose, she suspected, of allowing her to recover herself. Impossible to hope that he had not noticed her reaction to seeing John, or worse yet, John's reaction to seeing her; as though he'd been struck by lightning! Julian clearly didn't intend to question her about it, at least for now, no doubt for his own reasons, and she was too grateful for this to look into what they might be. The only hope she could cling to was that the ill-lit taproom would make it impossible for Julian to recognize John again when they met in town, as they were bound to do. She might have to explain to John about her decision to live with her husband again, but John Prescott, she inwardly fumed, would most certainly have a thing or two to explain to her. What if Julian did recognize him again? What might he not think about John's presence so close to Creeley? It could overset everything.

It was full dark by the time they reached the George and Crown, the hostelry where they were to spend the night. When they had been shown to their rooms and had refreshed themselves and relaxed after the tedious journey, the members of the travelling party met in a large private parlor for dinner. After much quizzing by Clarice and his mother, Julian was forced to admit that he was feeling a bit sore from his fall, but on the whole, the incident was treated so lightly that it was quickly passed over and all but forgotten.

The ladies did not withdraw after the meal, as was the usual custom, and it was nearly ten before they retired to their bedchambers, leaving the men to their private enjoyment of a final glass of wine.

When they had gone, Perry said, "What I don't understand is why anyone would want to pull such a prank."

"If it was a prank," said Julian.

Both Peregrine and Lord Creeley stared at him.

"Do you mean you expect it was more?" asked the earl.

Julian considered this for a moment. "As it turned out, it was nothing more than an annoying mishap. It could have been more, perhaps intended as more."

Lord Creeley drew his brows together. "Who the devil would hurt you at Creeley?"

"Who indeed?"

Peregrine looked thoughtful during this interchange and now said tentatively, "It was your saddle and pad, but anyone might have used it in a pinch. Perhaps it wasn't directed at you."

"Perhaps," agreed his brother.

Perry, who gathered from the terseness of his brother's tone that he would prefer to drop the subject, nevertheless persisted. "Is there any possibility that it could be laid to Mr. Smith's account?"

"Mr. Smith?" asked the earl, puzzled.

Julian cast his brother a warning glance, and heartily wished that he had said nothing about his suspicions. He turned to his father with a slight smile. "You must remember," he drawled. "Perry means the relic from my days as an intelligence agent."

"Good Lord!" exclaimed the earl. "Surely that is all done with now."

"I'd hoped so," responded his son with a sigh. "I've given the government enough of my life, and they agree; my services are no longer required. Mr. Smith, whether he appreciates the fact or not, is free to go on his way, and that suits me; I just want to be left in peace to get my life back in order."

"If Mr. Smith will let you," said Peregrine caustically.

"Pray don't be so melodramatic, Perry," admonished the earl, becoming alarmed.

"Just the same, I have been off my guard, and that may have been foolish," said Julian. "I shall take better care in the future."

"I find it most interesting that such an incident should have happened at Creeley," said Peregrine thoughtfully. "It is difficult to believe that he would have the power to harm you there, but what else is there to think?" He shot a defiant glare at his brother, who sat looking down at the table, carelessly running a finger around the rim of his glass. "Of course, it was not necessarily someone in the house," he added, "or more accurately, the stables, but certainly someone who had access to them."

Julian stretched out his legs and slouched in his chair in a lazy, unconcerned motion. "You mustn't mind Perry, Father. You know his imagination runs to the fanciful," he said, looking not at his father, but directly and coolly at Peregrine.

Lord Creeley looked thoughtful. "I think perhaps I had

better go back to Creeley. I think it would be worth having a word with Snidley and the boy who saddled the chestnut."

Julian slowly drew himself upright again. "That is exactly what I don't want you to do. This was intended to be seen as an unfortunate accident, and we'll treat it as such."

"No!" said Peregrine defiantly. "Someone tried to hurt you, perhaps even kill you. I for one have no intention of letting whoever is responsible get away with it."

Julian reached across the table and touched his brother's arm. "Nor do I, dear brother," he said earnestly. "If it was the work of Mr. Smith, you may depend upon it, he has covered his tracks; he has managed, has he not, to avoid discovery for equal and worse crimes. We will do no good by stirring up gossip in the neighborhood, and it may be no bad thing if he thinks that I am still off my guard. It may even keep him off his."

"Well, I think ignoring this would be the worst possible thing," insisted Peregrine.

"You are mistaken. Trust me to know my own business," Julian said levelly.

Lord Creeley listened to their conversation carefully. "Is there something you're not telling us, Julian?" he asked suddenly. "Do you know more about Mr. Smith than you admit?"

Julian sat back. "Perry is convinced of it. But don't suppose," he said, turning again to address his brother, "that you are going to frighten or bully me into making any hasty accusations." He then abruptly turned the subject, and his father let the matter drop, realizing that his elder son did not wish to discuss it any further.

The decanter was passed around again, and after a short while they rose to go to bed, as they planned to resume their journey at an early hour of the morning. As they reached the door, Julian stopped them. "By the way," he enquired casually, "did either of you notice a man who came into the taproom by the side door just before Clarice and I came out of the Owl this morning?"

Both men disclaimed any knowledge of him, but Peregrine asked why suspiciously.

"I thought there was something familiar about him," replied Julian evasively.

Peregrine opened his eyes wide and was about to speak

when he received a playful cuff on the shoulder from his brother.

"Take your imagination to bed, you young fool," laughed Julian.

Smiling in response, Peregrine passed through the door and followed his father up the stairs.

9

The following morning the unpredictable April weather turned sour again and it began to rain, and it was with profound relief for all that Creeley House was reached late in the afternoon on Wednesday. A bare half-hour after the carriages had stopped before the door, Lady Augusta Hook, Julian's younger sister, swept into the saloon where the ladies and Peregrine were enjoying a bracing cup of tea.

This lovely and vivacious young matron of about the same age as Clarice had been unable to post to Creeley when she had first been informed of her brother's return because she had been recovering from the confinement of her fourth child, but it had been settled by correspondence that Julian would make his first public bow to the ton at a small but select card party and musicale at her home.

On entering the room, she dutifully kissed her mother, brother, and sister-in-law and then exclaimed impatiently, "Where is he?" She hastily removed her gloves, making a small tear in the finger of one of them in the process, and cast herself onto a sofa.

"Poor George," she said with mock sorrow. "He had to all but tie me down to keep me from coming the moment I heard that the carriages had arrived." She dimpled. "I have my spies, you know."

"Very likely," returned Peregrine dryly. "Did they also tell you that Julian left with Papa to see Mr. Bolt about twenty minutes ago?"

"Oh, no!" she wailed. "I made sure that you would all be quite prostrate from your journey and quite easy to track down." She recalled the rest of her brother's statement and added, "To Mr. Bolt? The solicitor? Whatever for?"

"I don't suppose it would occur to a widgeon like you that

Julie's return from the dead would occasion not a few legal problems," Peregrine said sardonically.

Lady Gus refused to take umbrage. "No, it didn't," she said simply. "I suppose he's got to prove that he's himself for the succession, and I suppose there's his will as well." A sudden thought struck her. "Does that mean I'll have to give back that beautiful ring he bequeathed me? Oh, and I've had it sized down for me, too!"

"Of course not," soothed her mother. "He knew how much you liked it and always meant for you to have it."

"Yes, but it's not the same thing." She turned slightly on the sofa and caught sight of Clarice again; she had quite forgotten about her. She sprang up and went over to hug her. "How thrilled you must be, love!" Lady Gus knew as well as the others that Mr. Prescott had of late grown particular in his attentions toward Clarice, and had speculated to her husband that she considered Clarice's remarriage a distinct possibility. But now she had no doubt whatsoever that Clarice would welcome Julian back with open arms; nothing else had even occurred to her.

Clarice returned her embrace but was spared the necessity of answering her sister-in-law as that loquacious lady gathered her breath and went on, "And surprised too, I'll wager. He probably burst in on you or some such thing and nearly frightened you to death. Has he seen Julia and the boys yet? But of course he has! I was forgetting that you were all at Creeley. In fact, I suspect the whole world was at Creeley except me. Not just confined, love, but another girl! Can you imagine my humiliation!"

"Beaumère was kind enough to show me your letter," leapt in Clarice, glad for a change of subject. "I think Corrine is a delightful name."

"Yes," agreed Lady Gus, "but how much better Corey, or rather George, which we should call our son, if we had one." She pulled a face, which did nothing to mar her essential prettiness. "Four girls! And where we are to get decent dowries for them all, heaven knows. I shall have to start searching in the nurseries of my acquaintances for rich husbands for them at once. I made quite sure that dear George would put me aside like poor Queen Katherine."

Clarice, who had an interest in history, was able to sort out her obscure allusion without much difficulty. "But that was a kingdom at stake, and only one daughter," she laughed. "I think George will manage to forgive you if only you will give up your passion for yellow gowns."

Lady Creeley shook her head sadly. "Gussie is beautiful, she is intelligent, but no one has ever been able to persuade her that yellow makes her look brown. And dowdy," she added as an afterthought.

Lady Gus tossed her reddish-gold curls, the only fair-haired member of the family, and said, outraged, "Dowdy! Brown, I will give you, and I don't really see what's wrong with that. With everyone striving for the whitest possible complexion, it makes me an original. Never dowdy!"

"Copper-headed," put in Peregrine. "Makes you look like a kitchen candle."

Lady Gus's indignant gasp was cut off abruptly. The door opened to admit Lord Creeley and his elder son, and at once she was on her feet and rushing headlong into the arms of her brother. Almost as soon as she was embraced by him she pulled back to look at him again. She reached out and began to trace his features lovingly with her fingers. "Oh, Julie, it really is you," she said, her voice catching.

He smiled down at her. "Did you think an impostor had come to claim my place?"

"And fool Mamma? Never!" Her voice was fully tremulous and she burst into tears on his shoulder and hugged him as close as she could.

Everyone in that somewhat phlegmatic family was affected by this display of sisterly emotion, and even Peregrine's irreverence was for once silenced.

Julian took her over to a love seat by the windows and made an effort to laugh her out of her tears. At this the others seemed driven by a need to discuss trivialities, and did so at once, Clarice especially. The effect of Lady Gus's emotion on her was one of acute discomfort. For a reason she could not identify, she felt embarrassed and a little ashamed that Julian should have found such a joyously tearful welcome from his sister when he had found such a different one from his wife. True, she too had cried, but it had been from surprise and shock, not joy.

Shortly afterward Clarice went to the Fowles' to arrange to have the rest of her things gotten together and taken to Creeley House, and the children's sent on to the Lodge. Anne listened quietly enough to Clarice's explanations for staying with her husband, but did not even bother to conceal the fact that she clearly thought it the beginning of Clarice's return to him for good. Her joy and approval were so obvious that Clarice left with feelings of severe apprehension that it was precisely what John Prescott would think as well.

The following night, as Eddly helped her into a gown of green shot silk, Clarice looked forward to her evening at the Hooks' with some misgiving. The memory of the way they had been lionized at the Hobalts' was still fresh in her mind, and she knew that it would be far worse in town.

There was one thing, though, that could make Clarice view even this unpleasant probability with composure, and that was that there was no chance of Mr. Prescott being present at Lady Gus's party. She knew it was likely that he had returned to town, but Lady Gus probably would not have even thought to include him on her guest list of Julian's family and near friends, and if it had occurred to her, she wouldn't have invited him anyway. If Prescott had followed her back to town, as was likely, he had thus far made no attempt to seek her out, and as she rather dreaded the interview she knew she had to have with him, she was glad of the reprieve, however temporary.

At this point her reflections were interrupted by a discreet knock at her door. Eddly, who had been chattering trivial nonsense all the while, broke off and went to answer it.

"Begging her ladyship's pardon," began a voice, for Eddly had opened the door little more than a crack and Clarice could not see who stood there. "Lord Rown presents his compliments and wishes to inform her ladyship that he has just returned from a meeting with Mr. Bolt and will be a few minutes late."

As she listened, recognition slowly dawned. Clarice ran over impulsively, heedless of her dishabille, and wrenched the door out of Eddly's hand. "I don't believe it!" she exclaimed. "It *is* you, Rodgers!"

The dapper little man, elegantly attired as befitted a valet in a noble household, made her a low bow. "It is a great honor, my lady, to be serving in this household again."

"But I thought you had gone to Sir Edmund Berburry. I didn't think Lord Rown had any hope of getting you back."

"Lord Rown took the liberty of writing to me to see if my sentiments might allow of my leaving Sir Edmund, my lady."

Clarice smiled. "I take it they were."

"A very superior gentleman, Sir Edmund; most refined and elegantly turned out." He paused for effect. "But not entirely what one would like, my lady."

Clarice bit back another smile. She was always entertained by Rodgers, with his airs and affectations, which she knew were largely tongue-in-cheek. "No?" she enquired innocently. "I have always thought that he cut a superb figure, and his reputation is spotless as far as I am aware."

"Just so, my lady," he agreed primly. "But there are ways and ways of cutting a good figure."

"Oh! Padding, I collect. I never guessed! They must be very good," she laughed, amused at this interesting discovery about an acquaintance of hers.

Rodgers' eyes opened wide in alarm. "My lady, I never—"

"Quite so," said Clarice soothingly. "His secret is safe with me. But you may depend upon it, I shall look more closely at him next time we meet."

Rodgers bowed again, his eyes twinkling, and was off.

Clarice shut the door and turned to scold Eddly for not telling her that Rodgers had returned to their employ. Eddly begged her pardon but said that she had assumed that Lady Rown had known. Aware that the servants were ignorant of the businesslike nature of her arrangement with her husband, Clarice quickly turned the subject and went back to her dressing.

They arrived at the London house of the Hooks well in advance of any other guests.

"I knew that the last thing you would want would be a collective gasp and then a dead silence when you entered the room," Lady Gus said to her brother in her forthright way. "Now that you are here with us when they come in, in ones and twos, it will go easier, I think. Of course I have done exactly as you and Mamma wished and told anyone who would listen about your 'miraculous' return, but hearing and seeing aren't the same thing, are they? It has been the *on dit* of the season so far, I promise you; no one talks of anything else. I cannot leave the house, since the story has gone around, without being positively accosted everywhere I go. Everyone, and I do mean everyone, wants to hear about it. Even Countess

Lieven, who seldom has more than a stiff smile for me, has absolutely insisted that I bring you to Almack's as soon as possible; and Silence, who can be quite sweet when she chooses, gave my ear blisters wanting every bit of information I could give her. I daresay I may have made some things up along the way, just to be obliging."

Julian accepted a glass of wine from his brother-in-law and softly murmured his thanks. "I hope you remember what those things were," he told his sister, "or one of us is bound to end up in the suds."

"Well, I don't, you know, but it doesn't really matter. All the details, no matter where they come from, are bound to be exaggerated and garbled as the gossip goes the rounds, so no one will be likely to remember just what they really heard or from whom."

In a short while the peal of the bell was heard and the family made ready to receive their guests. They were in what was known as the Grand Saloon, which had been opened up with two others on either side of it to allow for the free movement of the gathering. In the one on the farthest left, tables had been set up for play, and in the one on the far right, a small group of musicians had been hired to provide dancing and entertainment for those who wished it. The main, central saloon was clustered around with chairs and sofas arranged to give every opportunity for elegant conversation or, as was more likely, comfortable gossip. Across the wide hall in the formal dining room, a buffet supper was even now being laid out, to which the guests would repair around midnight.

In a few moments, after the noises of arrival had floated into the saloon, the butler announced in stentorian tones the arrival of Sir John and Lady Hamlish and Mr. and Mrs. Reginald Rown. As the former were cousins and the latter the aunt and uncle of Julian, Clarice allowed herself a sigh of relief. If mostly family arrived first, it would doubtless go easier.

As soon as those announced entered, after the briefest of greetings to their host and hostess and the rest of the family that civility allowed, they immediately converged upon Julian. Lady Hamlish was the first to reach him. She came toward him, hand outstretched for him to take.

"It really is you!" she exclaimed. "I must admit that I came here not entirely convinced."

Before he could reply, his hand was being warmly shaken by Sir John, and immediately behind him, also anxious for the honor, were his uncle and aunt. Lady Hamlish passed on to Clarice; she commented on Clarice's good fortune much as Lady Gus had, and Clarice smiled and replied vaguely and, she hoped, suitably, and wondered to herself how soon the rooms would fill up and she would be permitted to efface herself from the circle of admirers and well-wishers surrounding her husband.

Her wishes were soon granted. In less than an hour the rooms were all but packed, and Clarice managed to slip away to a quiet corner to sit beside her sister Anne and her sister-in-law Lydia, who had returned to London that morning with Peter and their children. Julian was not so fortunate. Whenever Clarice managed to spot him in the crowd, he was surrounded by a group; it was not until supper that she found herself by his side again, and even Lady Creeley remarked in the carriage on the way home that for all she had seen of her elder son this evening, he might still have been in America.

The surprise of the evening had been the arrival of Lord and Lady Jersey. They were particular friends of Lady Bergemet, Lord Creeley's youngest sister, and came in the wake of her and her lord. Clarice had no wish to meet them and be subjected to Lady Jersey's brand of elegant cross-examination if she could help it, and escaped into the farthest saloon, where several groups of people were standing about, talking or listening to the music being played. She was about to make her way to the side of two elderly cousins of Julian's, when she felt a touch at her elbow. Turning without apprehension, for not even Silence could have talked her way in that far yet, she met the laughing eyes of Peregrine.

He led her farther into the room to two chairs that were, incredibly, unoccupied. "Can you believe that she has managed it?" He grinned. "We might have guessed, though; Aunt Sarah and Sally Jersey have been bosom cronies since their first season together."

"Yes," agreed Clarice, "and leave it to Silence to make certain she was the first outsider to set eyes on the returning prodigal."

"Oh, she's done more than that," he said ominously. "You won't escape her so easily tomorrow night."

"Why?" asked Clarice, surprised. "What is tomorrow night?"

Peregrine smiled slowly and wickedly. "Her ladyship has invited you and Rown to a ball she's giving tomorrow for some Portuguese something or other, who will now be quite eclipsed. Another coup for her, you see; two lions, and both in her den."

Clarice groaned.

"Don't worry, love," he said soothingly. "It will be a sad crush, and you'll be able to lose yourself in the crowd. Have you seen Prescott since you've returned?" he added suddenly, throwing Clarice off balance and causing her to wonder for one panicky moment if he had perhaps seen and recognized John Prescott in the courtyard of the Owl.

"No," she said cautiously. "I understand he is not in town."

"You had better hope he stays that way," said Peregrine. "If there is any chance that Silence can draw his cover and have him at her thing tomorrow night, she'll do it. Entertainment, don't you know."

Before Clarice could answer this or even digest it, her sanctuary came to an end as Aunt Sarah, closely followed by Lady Jersey, effectively routed Peregrine and put Clarice to the inquisition she had been dreading.

By the next night Clarice decided that her dread of society and its vulgar pryings had been far greater than the actual fact warranted. Having cleared what she considered the highest hurdle, nearly thirty minutes conversation with Sally Jersey the previous night, she felt equal to anything that that lady's ball might cast in her way.

She regarded herself in her mirror with satisfaction. Her rich brown hair was dressed to perfection, braided with a blue ribbon and studded at coy intervals with tiny sapphires, and became her to perfection, as did her gown. Its rich blue satin folds shimmered to equal the sapphire teardrops in her ears, the only adornment besides the chips in her hair that she wore. Set off as they were by her dark brown eyes and fair complexion, they were all that she needed; the effect was at once exciting and dramatic and gave her the confidence of knowing that she looked her best.

It was as well that she did, for the ball was indeed a sad crush, made all the more so by the hastily spread word that the Rowns would be present. It seemed to Clarice, as she accepted the hand of yet another bejeweled matron, that the whole world had come. Someone touched her from behind, and she heard her husband's voice say softly in her ear, "Come with me and pretend that we are totally lost in conversation. It might keep a few of them at bay for a bit."

She nodded and permitted him to excuse her to the matron who had been gushing at her. It was difficult going, as they were stopped several times on the way by friends and acquaintances, but at last they found an empty seat near the musicians.

"If I have to answer one more discreet question that hopes to lead me into indiscretion, what little good temper I have left will vanish entirely," he said wearily.

Clarice smiled. "It serves you right. If you will leave dramatically and then return with even greater drama, you must suffer the consequences."

"I know," he agreed ruefully. "I wonder if I can bribe an impecunious distant cousin to kick up a lark that will set all their tongues wagging in a different direction?"

"It would have to be quite a lark," laughed Clarice, "like running off with one of the royals; nothing less will do for a while. And this is only the beginning," she added. "By tomorrow I have no doubt that we will be swimming in invitations."

"Very likely. We will accept them all."

"All?" she cried plaintively.

"All," he repeated. "The sooner they get tired of looking at my face, the sooner we shall have peace."

"At that pace, will we be alive to enjoy it when it comes?"

"Kill or cure," he said, smiling.

Their privacy had been respected until this point, but now they were interrupted by their hostess, who came up to them with a smile. "Here is someone who is all agog to meet you, Rown," she said sweetly, and then stepped aside to reveal Mr. Prescott advancing on them; Clarice's worst fears and Mr. Rown's prediction had been realized.

It was widely said that while Sally Jersey loved to create a sensation, there was no harm in her, but Clarice revised this opinion of her at that moment. The scrapings of the musicians and the murmurs of conversation about them went on, but it would have been foolish not to suppose that anyone within earshot would be straining to hear what was said among them.

Clarice turned to look at her husband, but he was simply looking calm inquiry at Mr. Prescott, who was now sketching a bow before them. Julian was, in fact, carefully scrutinizing Prescott in the subtle way that only a man trained to do so can. He was not fool enough to write Prescott off as negligible, but neither did he consider the obviously nervous and uncomfortable man who stood before him the threat he had been fully prepared to face.

The thing that interested Julian most, however, was that Mr. Prescott proved to be the man who had run into them at the Owl and had elicited such a surprising reaction from Clarice. As well it might, thought Julian grimly. He rose, and meeting Prescott's gaze with polite aristocratic indifference, held out his hand, offering only two fingers; not for nothing was he the son of an earl.

"I am pleased to make your acquaintance, Mr. Prescott," he said in his soft voice. "But I believe we have met before."

"I daresay," replied Prescott, a faint reddish tinge creeping into his cheek. "Several years ago, no doubt."

Julian appeared to muse for a moment. "No," he said slowly. "It was more recent than that. I don't believe we were introduced at the time."

Mr. Prescott's color deepened at this, to the delight of the onlookers, and Clarice quickly intervened. "Mr. Prescott has been in Hampshire recently, visiting his mother," she invented, "so you must be mistaken."

Mr. Prescott, taking her lead, hastily assented, and then annoyed her by filling in a wealth of unnecessary, contradicting detail that wouldn't have fooled one far less astute than her husband. Julian smiled and commented when necessary, and in general gave Mr. Prescott all the rope he needed to hang himself. Clarice announced almost in despair that the cotillion they were playing was quite a favorite of hers, and this, accompanied by a judicious and, she hoped, unobservable kick, prompted Mr. Prescott to ask if he could have the pleasure of leading her into it.

He flushed again and stammered, "With Lord Rown's p-permission, of course."

This was freely given, along with a quick smile of unholy mirth for his wife, and the star-crossed lovers took the floor. For a while they danced in silence because neither could think of a thing to say that could be freely overheard among the other dancers.

Clarice felt something between disgust and despair over the way Prescott had handled himself, or rather had not handled himself, with her husband. She realized now just how much she had wanted John to shine before Julian, to show him the manner of man she considered worthy of her regard. But John had stammered and gabbled, appearing inarticulate and provincial beside Julian's polished address and cool sophistication, and the honors had certainly gone to her husband in that encounter.

Prescott interrupted her thoughts with an attempt at light conversation. He, too, was aware that he had not appeared to advantage, though how that had come about, he was not at all sure. He had intended to be calm and masterful, making it clear to Rown that he was a man to be reckoned with, but Rown's cool, dark gaze and soft, pleasant-sounding voice had somehow made him not only seem but also feel loud and bumptious. He had hoped to find in Clarice's response to him reassurance that it had not gone so very badly. She replied appropriately and pleasantly, for the sake of those about them, but his tattered self-esteem did not receive the assuagement that it needed.

If she had been aware of his need, Clarice might have pandered to it, for she had no wish to make him feel any worse than she knew he already must, but the frustration of not being able to speak her mind, hampered on all sides by the eyes of the ton, made her insensitive.

Mr. Prescott unwisely suggested, as the dance came to an end, that they try to slip quietly away and talk.

"Are you mad?" Clarice hissed at him. "It would be all over town in ten minutes. We're the center of attention tonight; you must know that. Whatever possessed you to come?" she asked with a brilliant smile for the benefit of the onlookers.

"I was invited," he replied, surprised and not understanding her meaning.

"Will you please try for a little countenance?" she said, exasperated, but still with an outward smile. "Everyone is looking at us. No, don't look about, just smile at me as though we are discussing inanities." She took a breath and went on before he could interrupt, "I meant why would you accept when you must have known Julian and I would be here. They're all hoping we'll say or do something to give them more grist for their gossip mill. Vipers!" she added meaningfully under her breath as she nodded pleasantly to an acquaintance who was trying to wave them down. She steered him purposefully toward the anteroom where champagne punch had been set out for the refreshment of the dancers. She had no intention of letting him take her back to Julian and risk exposing himself further.

"I'm not afraid of Rown," he said staunchly.

"I never said you were," she replied, "but it was foolish of you to force a public meeting before we had a chance to speak privately."

"Well, I did try this morning," he said defensively. "Your sister's damned starched-up butler told me you were not available. Whether that was supposed to mean that you were out or just not receiving, I'm damned if I could tell."

Clarice glanced at him quickly, but did not reply, as they were entering the anteroom and were hailed by a mutual friend. So, he had not heard that she was living at Creeley House; Clarice didn't know whether to be sorry or glad, and decided it was just as well. She would try if she could to keep up the pretense another day and arrange to meet him on the following day at Anne's. She informed him of the hour she wanted him to be at the Fowles', and suggested that it would be best if he left her, so that they wouldn't be seen too much together. He began to protest, but was forestalled by the arrival of Lady Augusta, whom Clarice greeted with barely disguised relief.

To Clarice's surprise, the rest of the evening went smoothly, even gaily. She did not see John Prescott again, and assumed that he had left, which relieved her. She had had a half-thought that he might do something tiresomely Byronic, like spend the evening glaring at her with smoldering eyes as she stood by her husband's side. Clarice had to laugh at herself for this flight of imagination; surely there was nothing less likely for the prosaic Mr. Prescott to do. It was much more in Julian's line to be so dashingly romantic, but then again, neither would he have ever done anything to so publicly display his emotions. Behavior only for books, she reflected as she got into bed at an advanced hour of the morning; and she heartily wished the whole of the events of this last month were between covers and not really happening to her.

Clarice went to Anne's the next day much earlier than the time she had appointed for Mr. Prescott to come there. When the time of his arrival approached, Clarice was still sitting in the green saloon arguing with her sister, as she had been for most of the morning.

"But, Anne, this is ridiculous," she said for at least the tenth time. "Come, what harm can there be? Can you honestly believe that this is to be a stolen lovers' rendezvous of the kind one finds in a novel? I must talk to him, explain to him all that has happened since I left for Creeley."

"If that is so, I don't see why I can't be here. It was one thing for you to be alone with him before Julian came back, but now . . ." Anne let her voice trail off expressively.

"Oh, Anne. What do the proprieties matter? No one will know but us."

"The servants will know, and you know how they gossip."

"All right, you stay here with us for a few moments and then make an excuse to leave. Stay in the very next room if you like; jump in on us at will, only please give me just one half-hour alone with him." She paused, seeing the set expression on her sister's face. "He was very nearly my husband, your brother-in-law; don't you think he deserves a private explanation? I can't be sure how he is going to take it, you know; it may be most difficult and embarrassing for him if you are with us. Please, Anne!"

Anne pursed her lips, looked down at the floor and back at her sister. She didn't want to give in, but felt the force of her sister's argument. "I suppose it might cause him some embarrassment," she admitted.

"Oh, yes, indeed, I am sure it would," said Clarice quickly.

After a few moments' hesitation, Anne said grudgingly, "Very well. But only a half-hour, mind, and I shall be directly in the next room."

Clarice gratefully accepted these restrictions and got up to hug her sister. Anne returned her embrace, but could not forbear adding, "It is just this once, Clare. If you must plot to leave Julian for this man, I cannot stop you, but I *will* not aid you."

Clarice bit back a retort that it was Julian who had left her four years ago, and said instead, "It is just this once, Anne, and I thank you very much."

Almost immediately afterward the bell was heard, and in a matter of minutes Mr. Prescott was shown into the presence of the ladies. He was a trifle taken aback to find Anne with Clarice, but was relieved when after a few moments of civilities she made an excuse and left.

Before he could say anything, Clarice sat him down and plunged into the story of the arrangement she had made with Julian and the results she hoped to achieve from it. She had lain awake for most of what had been left of the previous night rehearsing what she meant to tell him, and she wanted to get it over with as quickly as possible while she still had a hold on her trumped-up courage.

He had exclaimed from time to time, but she had not allowed him to interrupt her, and now that the first shock of her disclosures had worn away, he faced her grimly.

"I suppose I knew all along how it would be. I never should have let you go to Creeley," he said, forgetting that he had not possessed the power to stop her. "Should I make you a pretty speech about the honor you have done me, and how I regret that the life we planned together cannot be?"

"John . . ."

"I saw it for myself last night, didn't I? Though I hadn't the sense to recognize it." He stood up, too agitated to sit. "Made a damn cake of myself; must have been the only fool in the room not to know you were his wife again."

"I was that the moment we knew he had come back," she interjected, a shade tartly.

"Yes, and he used it to his advantage, just as I told you he would."

"John," she began, getting up and taking hold of his arm. "John, please sit down and listen to me. I *am* his wife, there is nothing I can do about that; but I haven't taken him back, and I don't intend to. It is for appearance' sake until January, and then he will divorce me and we *will* be together. We should be thankful that everything is working out so well for us."

"Well for us!"

"It is," she affirmed. "We would never have won through stubbornness; it might have taken years before he gave in, if at all, and he could have made it very unpleasant for us. This way, in nine short months it will all be over."

"I think it's over now."

"You know what I mean. How can you claim to care for me and not trust me?"

He looked a little ashamed. "Of course I trust you. It's Rown I don't trust. I know his type; an out-and-outer. Saw it the moment I clapped eyes on him. He'll pull out all the stops now that he has you where he wants you, and that sort usually get their way."

"Not this time," she said gently yet firmly. "You must have faith, John; we will come through this and be together."

"Let's make certain that will happen," he said, suddenly seizing her in his arms and kissing her in a way that was more earnest than skillful.

Clarice made a smothered protest and pulled a little away from him.

He tightened his hold on her and said urgently, "Don't you see, Clare, if we are lovers he will hold no temptations for you. I understood and respected your wishes before, though it was hard, and I still do; but now it is in our best interests."

He tried to kiss her again, but this time she pulled away from him completely. "No," she said sharply; so sharply that he looked at her with surprise. "No," she said more gently, but moved a greater distance from him. "Anne is just in the next room and could come in on us at any moment."

He took her hand in his. "We could be together if we wish it. We could arrange it," he said huskily.

"That is the very last thing we could do," she said. "It is only because we agreed to meet here at Anne's, which is above reproach, that I dared to see you alone today. It wouldn't do at all for Rown to know that we were alone together today or anytime before next year."

He stared at her in amazement. "I can't believe you are telling me that you must take care that Rown doesn't suspect that you are being unfaithful to him—to him who all but made a career out of being unfaithful to you!"

"The situation is different. It is I who want something from him, and at all costs he must not be given any reason to be offended with me or . . . or wish for revenge."

"Offended with you?" He gave a short laugh. "What do you think he will do during the months of your 'arrangement'? Suddenly take up celibacy? I think you know him better than that!"

Clarice flushed a little. "That is of no consequence," she said shortly. "The important thing is that *I* maintain an uncompromised position. And you very nearly undid that on Monday, didn't you?" she added, suddenly remembering Prescott's appearance at the Owl, which had been pushed from her mind by the first part of their discussion. "What on earth were you doing in Creeley Combe? I nearly had the vapors when I realized it was you!"

"To what purpose is that now?" he hedged. He had cherished a hope that she had forgotten all about that incident.

"To every purpose. I had hoped that Rown wouldn't recognize you again when you met in town, but I should have known better; it was obvious that he did."

"Perhaps he didn't."

"Of course he did, John; that was why he baited you," she told him caustically. "I hadn't the least idea that you were there, but he doesn't know that, and trying to explain it to him would only make it look worse. Suppose he thinks that we were meeting secretly? He might suppose that we are lovers and be furious that I'd stoop to such a thing, especially at his father's house."

"Dammit, Clare. He has no right to be furious over anything!"

"Right or not, your presence there could have compromised me at a time when I cannot risk offending my husband; when *we* cannot risk it. Suppose that he said that he considered my behavior had nullified our agreement? Then where would we be? Exactly where we started, and with precious little hope. And don't think his treatment of you at the Jerseys' ball wasn't deliberate," she added, waving aside his spluttering protests. "Oh, I know he said very little, really, and that it was all polite and proper, but he managed to tie you into knots just the same. He's a master at that sort of thing, John, and he'll show you to disadvantage every time he gets the opportunity, if you let him. You must be very circumspect, and avoid him as much as possible."

Prescott gasped in angry amazement, but Clarice ignored him. "Well," she continued coldly, "do you mean to explain to me what you were doing in Creeley Combe?"

"Dammit!" exploded Prescott wrathfully. "I was trying to look after you, small thanks though I get for it!"

"Look after me?" she asked, astonished. "At an inn at least four miles from the house, and without even letting me know that you were there?"

"I . . . I thought it would be better if you had someone in the neighborhood who could take care of you if you needed it," he stammered lamely, his anger cooling rapidly in the face of her cool incredulity.

"But I didn't even know you were there! Did you imagine that someone at Creeley was going to publicly beat me into submission so that you could hear of it and come rushing to my rescue?" she asked with bitter sarcasm.

"N-no, of course not. I just wanted to know that you were well. I . . . I thought . . ." He faltered and was saved having to further explain himself by Anne, who, their half-hour being up, came in at that moment. Clarice allowed the matter to drop, and after a few minutes' desultory conversation, he took his leave of Clarice and her sister.

10

The next few weeks were as hectic as Clarice had feared they would be. As Julian had insisted, she accepted all invitations, even if it meant only putting in a nominal appearance at some of the events.

During their first full week in town, many hostesses who planned daytime entertainments were disappointed to find Clarice arriving on the arm of Mr. Peregrine Rown instead of the much-sought-after viscount. Julian and his father were spending most of their daylight hours closeted in Lord Creeley's study with Mr. Bolt and a perfect profusion of efficient-looking men who trooped back and forth across the vaulted front hall of Creeley House.

One afternoon, on the day before Lord Creeley was scheduled to return to Creeley Lodge to join his wife and grandchildren, Clarice was called into the study and requested by Mr. Bolt to read and sign a document which turned out to be a testimony that she, Clarice, knew the man who had returned to be Julian Francis Henry Halcott de Varley Rown, known by courtesy as Viscount Rown, her lawful husband and the rightful heir to the earldom of Creeley, put forth in such convoluted legal language that Clarice could barely grasp the meaning of it. She signed readily, but that night at one of the four ton parties they were scheduled to attend, Clarice quizzed Julian, suggesting that she might have put an end to all her troubles by simply looking Mr. Bolt straight in the eye and denouncing her husband as an impostor. Julian laughed and replied in kind, and it wasn't until much later in the evening that Clarice realized what a comfortable stage their relationship had achieved: to think they could be laughing and joking over a subject that had such a short time ago unleashed his temper and reduced her to angry tears.

This harmony between them continued unabated. Clarice was greatly enjoying being mistress of her own establishment again, after so many years as a perennial guest in the homes of others, and this buoyed her spirits tremendously. Julian, too, was in unflagging good humor; not even the tireless social round caused either of them to be short-tempered or at outs with each other.

Clarice began to discover that the occasions she enjoyed most were those they shared together; these were the times she laughed the most and everything amused her. Julian was attentive, but not aggressively so, and he made it clear, in a flattering way, she had to admit, that he preferred her company to any of the dashing young women who cast out obvious lures to him. If he was trying to convince her that he had changed, he was going about it in the right way; but the only thing that Clarice was convinced of was that he wanted her to think that he had changed. She had been hurt too much, too often, to have any real trust in him yet, and anyway, she told herself, her future did not lie with him. It did, however, bring the inevitable and doleful thought of how different things might have been if only everything had been this way eight years ago when they had first married; and it was the remembrance of their early, less happy times together that kept Clarice from being completely seduced by his charm.

Though she no longer found herself attracted to him with the intensity she had felt at Creeley, she did not fool herself that it had altogether disappeared, and she was constantly aware of how fatally easy it would be to succumb not only to his lovemaking, should he renew it, but to loving him again as well. Though she had resolved to be free of him, she felt safer with her guard up. But there were moments, after a particularly convivial evening, a delightful ride in the park, or a quiet hour of reading to each other, when she had doubts about the course she had adopted and wondered if the easy way out of her difficulties could be so bad after all. But then she would bring to mind again just what her life had been like before as his wife, and this fortunately did the trick and brought her back to her senses.

Clarice saw Mr. Prescott frequently during this time, but always in company. He continued to try to persuade her to meet him privately, and was inclined to be pettish when she refused, but she was adamant, using the argument that the present sacrifice was worth the good they would achieve in the months ahead. Nor would she permit him to call on her even in the most formal way at Creeley House. Though he protested that even Rown could not object to such an acceptable social convention, she claimed that she would be too acutely uncomfortable knowing that Rown might come in on them at any moment, however innocent his calls might be. But Prescott was clearly disgruntled and did not bother to hide his feelings.

His inevitable encounters with her husband were a trial to her as well. Julian was far too clever to disparage Prescott in front of her or to speak poorly of him in any way that might come back to her, but his subtle manipulation of every situation that brought them all together invariably caused John Prescott to come off badly by the comparison. She told herself that Julian was at home in the fashionable world of the ton, while John, living retired as he had, had never properly learned to function there; but she, too, was a creature of that world, and she found she could not help being annoyed by Prescott's lack of social grace. All in all, there were times when she found it almost a relief to discover him absent from a social gathering she and Julian attended together.

Much as Julian had predicted, as time went on and the world ceased to regard his presence as a novelty, they were no longer mobbed wherever they went, and some three weeks after their arrival in town, an obliging countess eloped with her daughter's dancing master and the ensuing scandal pushed them firmly into the background. Julian was very glad of this. He was bored telling his story (or rather its watered-down version) again and again, and an imp of mischief, not unlike the one that afflicted his brother, occasionally crept upon him and caused him to embellish the story with startling improbabilities conjured for his own amusement, which endangered its being believed as a whole.

He found it was now a very real pleasure to be able to enter one of his clubs for conversation or a quiet game of cards with a few old friends, without being collared by half the men in the room before he even got his foot in the door.

He was at White's, sitting not far from the fire on an unseasonably chilly day during the second week of May, enjoying his newfound solitude, when it was brought to an end by the arrival of his brother.

"I can't believe I've found you alone," Peregrine said as he eased himself into a wing chair. "I've tried calling at Father's a couple of times lately, but you're never at home."

"I told you of my plan to make the world sick of my face," replied his brother with a smile. "It has worked, as you see, with a little help from Lady Stoneby and her proficient dancing partner."

The brothers discussed this tantalizing bit of gossip for a while and then progressed to other matters of mutual interest.

After a while, when there was a lull in their conversation, Peregrine said, "There is something that I'd like to ask you about, but I'm not sure I should; you'll probably tell me it isn't any of my business."

Julian awarded him a lazy smile. "I can't recall that that has ever hampered you before."

Peregrine acknowledged the hit. "Should I take that for encouragement?" he laughed. "I know a little of your affairs," he went on more seriously. "At least as much as the rest of the family knows, and a little that Clarice has told me. I can't help but wonder how matters progress between you and Clare; whether we're all to be tossed into a scandal broth in the near future, or whether you've decided between you to live happily ever after." Enquiries into his private life, Peregrine knew, usually caused a shuttering effect on his brother, but this time Julian only shrugged slightly.

"Matters are well enough, I think," he replied. "It wouldn't pay to be overconfident, though; she's not precisely throwing herself at my head. But I believe she has come to like me again, and that's a beginning."

They were interrupted by a greeting from behind them, and both men turned to discover Lord Ardane. He came over to them and sat down in a chair beside Peregrine.

"Hope I'm not interrupting anything," he said in the tone of one who has no doubt of his welcome. He was mistaken. Peregrine, at least, was wishing him at the devil; but before he could say so, Julian said, "Not at all, dear coz. Please join us. I was just telling Perry that my hopes with Clarice are not yet dashed."

"I should think not! Not after what passed between you at Creeley," said Peter dryly.

Julian showed mild surprise. "She told you that, did she?" he asked quietly.

Peregrine looked from one man to the other, an interested spectator. Obviously Ardane possessed a knowledge that he, Peregrine, did not, and it was equally obvious that Julian was not at all pleased that he did.

"In all fairness, no," replied Peter. "I thought it out for myself and bullied her into admitting it." He rubbed his chin thoughtfully. "I must say you seem to have routed Prescott pretty successfully. I saw the neat way you handled him the other night at the Bosleys'. Getting him to make a cake of himself, are you? He hasn't been on the town much and hasn't any polish, so it should serve. As far as I know, they never meet except in company, and he goes about with a Friday face. Causing some comment, that; but at his expense. If you like, you can rid yourself of him for good."

"Can I?" asked Julian with polite interest.

"Simplest thing in the world. Just point out to him that the very handsome jointure that Clarice enjoyed as a 'widow' is bound to cease now. He's a bit of a slow top, in my opinion, and I daresay he hasn't thought of it. Bound to throw him for a loop; I mean, it isn't likely that you'll give her an allowance if she leaves you and marries him."

Julian regarded his cousin thoughtfully and then said, "There would be her marriage portion; it is customary, I believe, to return it when a marriage is dissolved."

Peter shook his head. "Not in this case. If you recall, it is in the marriage settlements that it be tied up in the children. It remains hers in a way, but only through her children. She can't touch it."

"It would be mean of me to hold her to that, don't you think? I shall be quite able to provide for our children."

"Generous, ain't you?" snorted Peter. "More fool you if you do."

"You don't rate your sister's charms very high, do you?" Julian asked.

"They have nothing to do with it. I daresay you know that the night before you returned, Lyddy and I were at Anne's to celebrate her betrothal to Prescott. The beggar has property in Hampshire and he's forever prosing on about making it a model farm like Coke or some such thing. Do you know that he took me aside that very night and damn near bored my ears off about the place. Actually said that now he'd have the blunt to really do something with it." Peter shook his head in disgust. "That very night. Loverlike, ain't it?"

Julian said nothing, simply digesting this piece of information, and a moment or so later Peter leaned into the circle their chairs formed and said conspiratorially, "Speak of the devil himself! There's Prescott standing next to Halsley, not three feet from your elbow, Julie."

"Then it is to be hoped your voice didn't carry, Peter," remarked his cousin. "Your comments have not been complimentary."

Peter shrugged. "Much I care. I don't love him, and that's no secret."

"This is a turnabout for you, isn't it?" asked Julian. "I rather thought I could not count you as my friend in this matter."

Peter smiled slowly. "What I am is Clare's friend. If she's fool enough to want you, so be it."

"And does she?" wondered Julian. "Is this yet another confidence she's entrusted you with, or merely conjecture?"

Peter's grin broadened. "That remains to be seen, don't it?"

Peregrine raised his hand to catch the attention of a passing servant, and as he did so, Mr. Prescott chanced to turn his head in Peregrine's direction and their eyes met. Prescott took in the small family party and began to turn away, but the devilry ever at work in Peregrine's soul caused him to set the cat among the pigeons. Having caught the servant's eye, he turned his attention to the hapless Mr. Prescott and hailed him in a voice heard by half the room.

Dearly as Prescott, and, for that matter, the two men flanking Mr. Rown, would have wished it, there was no chance of pretending not to have heard. Reluctantly he turned back to face the little group and was peremptorily summoned over to them. He obeyed the summons, but declined Peregrine's offer of a chair.

"You are most kind," said Prescott stiffly, managing with difficulty not to look upon Lord Rown, "but I have an appointment in the City and I'm afraid I am already late."

As he obviously had been chatting at his ease only a moment before, this was not a very convincing excuse, and Peregrine had no intention of letting it stand.

"Nonsense," he drawled. "Never worry about those fellows,

does them good to wait. I know you've met my brother," he added with a quick teasing glance thrown to Julian.

Prescott bowed slightly in Julian's general direction. "I've had that pleasure several times," he said in a stilted voice.

"Yes, you might say we've run into one another," agreed Julian provocatively, not above the family weakness.

Prescott was conscious of a powerful desire to plant a facer on Lord Rown, who continued to regard him with a cool, faintly sardonic gaze. He took a step aside to permit the servant to set down a small table containing a decanter of wine and glasses, the motion serving effectively to hide his confusion; and before he could speak again to extricate himself from this unpleasant situation, Peregrine rather loudly requested another glass for their guest. With the feeling of one in the throes of a nightmare, Mr. Prescott presently found himself sitting by the very side of his rival, unwanted glass in hand.

Julian turned to him and gave him his most ingratiating smile. "I understand you farm, Prescott?" he said pleasantly.

Under the full force of that smile, which had caused both men and women made of harder stuff than Mr. Prescott to melt, he forgot the cold civility with which he had meant to treat Lord Rown and said clumsily, "I have a place in Hampshire. Nothing much, not large . . . not very interesting, I'm afraid."

Julian laughed softly. "By which I take it you mean *I* would not find it interesting. You mistake your man, Mr. Prescott." He paused to let this sink in with whatever interpretation the listener chose. "I, too, am a farmer," he then added, robbing his previous words of offence. "Perhaps you have visited Creeley? If you have, I trust our bailiff showed you about; I am quite proud of the improvements we have made in the home farm."

Mr. Prescott had not the least idea how to answer to this, so once again he covered his confusion by resorting to action. He placed his glass on the table and in the process accidentally knocked over the glass that Peter had just placed there. It worked far better than he dared to hope, for at once Peregrine was up dabbing at the mess with his handkerchief and Julian was forced to reach for his own glass, which was now in danger of being toppled by Peregrine's ministrations. Mr.

Prescott begged pardon and took the opportunity of dabbing at the spill to rise.

"Most clumsy of me. I do hope you'll forgive me; I really must leave now," he said jerkily, and without waiting for a reply, made good his escape.

"Ass!" exclaimed Peter after he had gone.

"A trifle graceless," agreed Julian. "So much the better for me. He does not improve on acquaintance, and I find that quite encouraging."

The cousins remained for a while longer drinking and talking, until Julian rose and took his leave of the others. Outside, he declined the porter's offer to call him a hack and began to walk toward Creeley House. There was still ample time for him to dress for dinner, but he had no wish to fall into the trap that easy companionship offered of imbibing too freely. Though by the standards of his contemporaries he was not a heavy drinker, he had a hard head and was almost never genuinely drunk; but he preferred to be more cautious than usual now, when matters were going so well with his relationship with his wife. He had himself and his emotions well in check and meant to make no misstep.

Clarice screwed on the figured gold cap of the small crystal bottle and set it back in its slot in the open dressing case. She rose from her position on the floor, tossed the treated cloth over the back of a chair, set her hands at the small of her back, and took a few stretching steps. She was beginning to regret refusing Eddly's aid in going through and cleaning the small bottles and jars in her dressing case. She had decided on impulse to take on the neglected task, and it was proving to be a larger chore than she had bargained for. She had gone through only half the contents, and the job seemed endless.

Her sitting room was at the back of the house, away from the noise of the street, so she was surprised at the arrival of Moreton, the Creeleys' town butler, who came with the information that she had a visitor.

"A gentleman?" she enquired. "Didn't he give you a card?"

"No, my lady," replied the servitor. "But he did give his name as Mr. Prescott, in case you should enquire."

"Mr. Prescott?" cried Clarice, her voice rising a little in surprise. Recovering herself before the butler's polite stare, she said, "Yes, of course, I had quite forgotten. Please show him up, Moreton."

As soon as he left, Clarice hastened to shove the dressing case into a corner, half behind a chair, and then, tearing off her apron, ran to the mirror to see what a little patting would do for her disordered locks. She had just accomplished this, though not entirely to her satisfaction, when Mr. Prescott was announced and came into the room. Moreton made to pull the door shut after him, but Clarice intervened and told him to leave it ajar, and to bring them some refreshment. When he was gone, Clarice turned to face Prescott.

"Why are you here?" she asked angrily. "You know perfectly well that I told you I do not wish you to come. Suppose Rown came in and found you here?"

"He won't. I left him at White's with Ardane and Mr. Rown a few minutes ago," Prescott replied.

"Left him? Do you mean you were with him?" she asked, surprised.

Mr. Prescott nodded grimly and proceeded to tell her of his uncomfortable encounter. "I can't help but feel that he deliberately baits me every chance he gets," he finished, speaking of his brief conversation with Julian. "This is intolerable, Clare. He is the one who has wronged us both, yet whenever I am in his company, I feel that I am the one in the wrong."

"Well, then, it is a good thing you are so seldom in his company," said Clarice reasonably, but seeing the dark look that this produced, she went over to him and placed her hands in his. "Don't despair, dearest," she said gently. "Every day that passes is one day closer to the time that he will divorce me."

"If that day ever comes," said Prescott pettishly.

"It will," said Clarice calmly, but she was aware of the rising exasperation that his constant reiteration of his wrongs at the hands of her husband caused her to feel.

"I shall believe it the day that it happens, and not a moment before," said Prescott, snorting. "Look at you here, in his house—"

"His father's house," she interrupted quietly.

"Whatever!" he snapped, annoyed. "The fact remains that you are here with him. I am not permitted to see you or even speak to you except in a room full of people. It is intolerable!"

Seeing that he was genuinely upset, Clarice applied herself for the next hour to soothing him and reassuring him that all would be well, but always at the back of her mind was the nagging thought that Julian might at any moment return home. The sooner she could get him into a happier state of mind and out of the house, the better.

Lord Rown handed his hat, gloves, and walking stick to Moreton and enquired casually if his wife was at home.

"Yes, my lord," replied the butler in his usual expressionless voice. "She is in her sitting room with a visitor, a Mr. Prescott. Shall I inform her ladyship that you wish to see her?"

Lord Rown gave him a long, unrevealing look and told him it wouldn't be necessary. He went up to his dressing room, a spacious and comfortable apartment that also served as his sitting room. He walked directly to a small cabinet and removed a decanter of brandy; the hand with which he poured was not entirely steady.

Clarice followed Mr. Prescott from her sitting room to the front hall. She stood making polite conversation with him while Moreton retrieved his belongings. Her reason for this singular attention was simple: she wanted to be on hand should Julian choose that particular moment to return home. Experience had taught her to place no great trust in Prescott's ability to dissemble.

At last the door was shut firmly on Mr. Prescott and she could not forbear a small sigh of relief. As she started up the stairs, she hesitated. "Moreton," she said, turning, "please inform me when Lord Rown returns home."

"He has returned, my lady."

"Oh," said Clarice, then added casually, "Did he ask for me, Moreton?"

"Yes, my lady," replied the butler impassively. "I informed him that you were with a visitor."

Clarice thanked him and then continued up the stairs. So he knew. Moreton hadn't mentioned whether or not he had told Julian the name of her visitor, and she didn't dare ask, but it was a fairly safe assumption. The question was, how had he taken that piece of information? She would find out soon enough at dinner, but she dreaded the wait. By the time the servants left them to private conversation, the food would have long turned to ashes in her mouth and the tension would have put her nerves on edge to the point where her tongue might be unguarded. The simple thing to do would be to face him at once.

Timidly she knocked on the door of his dressing room. She knew that she would most likely find him there at this hour, and if Rodgers was with him, she would have to contrive to get rid of him. On being requested to enter, she opened the door and discovered her husband sitting in a chair by the window; his expression was not encouraging. She closed the door and advanced into the room.

"You are returned early," she began conversationally.

"A surprise to you, no doubt," he said evenly. "I take it Prescott has gone."

"I had no notion he was coming. If I had, I would have forbidden it."

"Yet you received him," he said sharply. For some time now he had been feeling decidedly unwell, a sensation that could not be blamed entirely on his anger or the incautious amount of brandy that he had drunk in the last hour. The pain, which seemed to be growing slowly but steadily in the depth of his body, was honing his already quickened temper to a fine edge.

"I . . . I didn't think. I was afraid that there might be unpleasantness in front of the servants if I refused." She paused and then went on in a firmer voice, "I think, if you are fair, Julian, that you will admit that I have kept to my side of the agreement most assiduously. The world knows nothing of our difficulties—in their eyes we are a contented couple."

"Yes, and the moment my back is turned, you entertain your lover in your room," he said nastily. "It was never part of our agreement that you were forbidden to meet Prescott; my objection is that you have seen him here. I will not have that man running tame in my house. If you refuse to obey me in this, I shall see to it that you have no choice."

Clarice's contrite concern for having offended him dissipated on the moment. "Running tame!" she exclaimed indignantly. "I will not stoop to answer that vile implication."

Nevertheless, she went on, "We were in my sitting room. Talking."

Julian said nothing. Under his cold, steady appraisal, Clarice, to her total fury, blushed. She had permitted John to kiss her before he left, because it had been necessary to his composure and thus, in her mind, to getting him safely away from the house, but she would never have dreamed of allowing it to become more. Now, as her eyes met her husband's, she felt soiled, as though she had done something unforgivable.

In her anger, she fairly spat out her words at him. "You have a vulgar, filthy mind. Just because you reduce everything to the most base physical terms, you have no reason to suppose that I or John would stoop so low as to cuckold you here. No doubt your narrow outlook has us making passionate love on the sofa, or perhaps even in my bedchamber." She stood a few feet from him, her bosom heaving with indignation, her eyes alight with anger. She drew herself up to her full height and said, "It gives me consummate pleasure to inform you that John and I sat talking in full view of the open door. If you don't choose to believe *me,* you may ask any of several servants who passed."

He applauded her. "Excellent, Clarice, quite excellent. You ought to be on the boards." He paused, not to gather his thoughts, but because a sudden knife thrust of pain momentarily made speech impossible. "All the more excellent because you know that I never would," he added as soon as he could.

"Well, you might," she snapped. "And you might question Anne's servants as well, if you please. I cannot think what I have ever done to make you think that I would be fool enough to repeat with John the mistake I made with you."

He raised his brows. "Indeed? What I do question is why you think it necessary to tell me that now."

Clarice herself had no answer to this, so by way of reply she turned sharply on her heel and strode purposefully toward the door. She had almost reached it when the sudden sharp intake of his breath caused her to turn. What she saw made her rush instantly to his side. He was doubled over in obvious pain, his head almost resting on the arm of the chair.

"Julie, what is it?" she asked breathlessly, her anger forgotten in fright.

"I don't know." His voice was little more than a gasp. "Get Rodgers. Quickly."

Obediently she ran to the bell pull, tugged at it furiously, and rushed back to his side. He sat back, very straight, his eyes closed, his breath quick and labored. She put her hand to his head and found it cold and damp. Terror creeping up on her, she ran again to the bell and pulled it. In her anxiety she began to pace about the room, but never taking her eyes off her husband. He hadn't moved a muscle, as if he were afraid to do so, and he was so pale that his skin seemed almost transparent. She returned to his side and possessed herself of one of his hands. It, too, felt cold and clammy, and her fear grew by leaps and bounds.

"Rodgers will be here in a moment," she told him soothingly, and in her heart prayed that she was right.

11

Clarice frantically paced the length of her sitting room. The doctor had been with Julian for more than an hour now, and the suspense was making her half hysterical. Never in all their lives together, even when they had been children, could she remember him being truly sick; never, for that matter, could she ever remember anyone being quite that sick. Even if he had been flushed and feverish, she would have been far more at ease, but he had been so cold, so white. What was keeping the doctor! She heard footsteps in the hall outside her door, and expecting it to be the doctor at last, ran into the arms of her brother, who was just coming in.

"What the devil is amiss?" he queried. "The house seems in an uproar. What's this Moreton tells me of Julie being taken ill?"

"Oh, Peter," she sobbed, relaxing into his embrace. She vented her overwrought nerves in tears on his shoulder. "Oh, Peter," she said again when she could, "I am so glad you are come. I sent word to Gussie's, but they had left for Carlton House and I didn't want to bother them there until I knew what the doctor had to say, and Perry is out too! I have been frantic."

"I had no idea!" said Peter, astonished. "I only came by to have a word with Julian before dinner. But come, tell me what has happened."

Briefly she told him, and when she had finished, and before Peter could comment, the doctor, Sir Walter Beamish, came into the room. Clarice immediately went to him and begged him to tell her his diagnosis.

The doctor smiled slightly. "Nothing to be concerned about, my lady," he said vigorously. "Obviously something Lord Rown ate disagreed with him most violently."

"Surely not," said Clarice, sceptical. "He was so unbelievably ill; it couldn't be just that."

"Nevertheless, it was," replied the doctor stiffly. "I have left some powders and strict instructions with his valet that he is to rest tomorrow and be given nothing but a liquid diet. After that and a day or two spent quietly, he will be as well as ever."

"But he was in such pain!" said Clarice, not yet convinced that her fears were groundless. Sir Walter gave her a quelling look, and she added hastily, "But of course you know best. If you will tell me, Sir Walter, what he is to have, I will see to it in the kitchens." She went to her writing desk and fetched a pen and paper and carefully wrote down everything the doctor told her. When Moreton had shown the doctor out, Clarice sank gratefully into a corner of the sofa.

"Thank heaven it was nothing more!" she cried with relief. "I don't suppose I ought to disturb Gussie now, do you? I don't think Julie would like it if I did."

"Probably not," agreed her brother, sitting himself across from her. "Tell me, why did you question Beamish's opinion?" he asked thoughtfully.

Clarice shrugged. "I don't know. Very likely I was frightened into believing it worse than it was. Do you remember the time at Lodin when Little Perry and Gussie got into the wild strawberries? Do you remember how sick it made them?"

Peter's eyes rounded slightly. "Remember? I am not likely to forget. I never saw anything quite like it before."

"Well, Julian was worse. He could hardly breathe for the pain. Have you ever heard of anything disagreeing with a person to that extent?"

"Was he better after he was sick?" asked Peter.

"Oh, yes, at least the pain seemed to leave him. Only, then he fainted." She shivered a little at the memory. "I thought—"

"Yes," broke in Peter, "I can guess what your abundant imagination came up with. Now you see, don't you, how silly you were to be so worried."

"I am not silly," she said petulantly. "It might have been very serious. If you are here to lecture me, I wish you will go."

Peter smiled lazily. "Not to lecture you, little sister, to

comfort you, by being brisk if necessary to keep your imagination from running away with you. You say that you have never seen him so sick. Well, if it comes to that, you haven't seen him at all for the past four years. Who knows what outlandish things he fed upon in the colonies. Very likely it was due to the change in his diet."

Clarice looked at him doubtfully, but agreed. Peter rose. "Do you think it would be all right if I left you now? Will you be all right alone? We are having the Colbys to dinner, and I must dress."

Clarice assured him that she would manage quite well. As she walked him to the door, a thought struck her. "What was it you wished to see Julian about?" she asked.

Ardane looked at her blankly for a moment and then said, "Oh, nothing that won't keep." He kissed her lightly on the cheek and left.

Julian shifted restlessly under the sheets. The crippling pain and overwhelming nausea had left him, but he felt drained and exhausted as a result of them. His restlessness was caused by the fact that though his body had given in to weariness, his mind would not follow suit. He had accepted blandly and without comment the doctor's verdict, but he didn't agree. The attack had been too sudden and too violent to be mere food poisoning; in fact, he thought he knew quite well what had caused it. One of the "outlandish things" he had eaten in America had been food which had been accidentally contaminated by rat poison. The attack then had been similar, though far less severe, which led him to believe that the poison this time had been purer or a stronger dose. Enough to kill? he wondered. It was possible that his body had rejected a larger dose before any permanent damage had been done. He wished he could have consulted with the doctor, but that, of course, was impossible.

Rodgers came into the room carrying an empty and sparkling clean decanter on a tray. He wore his most disapproving look, which caused Julian to smile a little.

"You can stop pouting, Simon; I am doing this for the best."

"Not for your own best, my lord. I should be talking to Sir Henry this moment."

"Simon," chided Julian gently.

"I know what you think, my lord," said Rodgers with a rueful grin, "but he would want to know. You were trained, same as me. You know that."

"Yes, I do," agreed Julian, "and if I were sure of my facts, I might even let you go, but it wouldn't answer. Suspicion is not proof."

"It's the suspicion that often leads to the proof," replied Rodgers with mild reproof.

"We had this argument four years ago, Simon," said Julian quietly, "and I still don't agree with you; especially now. I had nothing on him then and have even less now. He has had four unmolested years to cover and recover his tracks."

"I always thought there might have been something if we'd had the opportunity to go on with it," persisted Rodgers. "After all, my lord, we were dished rather early in the game, before we could really get into it."

Julian sighed bitterly. "I botched that properly, didn't I?"

Rodgers shook his head sadly. "It wasn't your fault, my lord. Those things happen in our way of business, so to speak."

"So they do," said Julian tonelessly, and then added, "I still can't thank you enough for the help you gave to me back then, nor for the messages that you got to me in America. They meant a great deal to me."

"As to that, my lord, it was just my job," replied Rodgers a trifle briskly to cover his embarrassment.

"But you do it so very well, Simon," said Julian with the smile that had originally won the little man's heart nearly ten years earlier.

An ostensibly retired batman gone into service, though in reality employed by the government in intelligence, Rodgers had been assigned to recruit a member of the aristocracy with French connexions in the Old Regime. It had taken him some time to find exactly the right man, but once he had, he had never for a moment regretted it. A warm relationship that went beyond that of master and servant had developed between them, and now that neither was technically involved in intelligence any longer, it still suited both to throw their lot together once again.

"So do you, my lord," replied Rodgers as he busied himself with refilling and returning the decanter to the cabinet. "The information you gathered in America was most valuable to our men there. I know Sir Henry has commended you."

"To be honest, Simon, I never liked my job less. The Americans were people fighting for their homeland; I felt like a man betraying a friend while under his roof. Montreal was much better. At least there it was those dear, detestable frogs that I was stabbing in the back again."

Rodgers shook his head and clucked slightly. Ambiguous morality was a very real part of being in intelligence, as all of the men involved in it knew; though few ever spoke of it. It was not, for most of them, conducive to peace of mind. He returned to the bed and fussed with the pillows and covers to make his lordship more comfortable, and begged him to remain in bed and to call him for anything he might need.

"There is one thing that you can do for me, Simon, if you will," said Julian. "I want you to search the house thoroughly. Very thoroughly. I don't care how long it takes, and nothing is to be sacrosanct, do you understand?"

Rodgers opened his eyes a little in surprise. "Do you think it likely that we'll find anything here, my lord?"

"Perhaps not," Julian replied, "but I would like to limit the possibilities. It was either in something I had here or in the wine I had at White's; I took nothing else today. If possible, I would prefer to know which." Seeing the spark in his servitor's eyes, he added, "Yes, I know you would handle it another way, and I also know that the possibility of the poison still lying about is small, assuming that the person who is decidedly not fond of me has any sense; but please do as I ask. Check belowstairs as well. See if any rat poison looks as if it has been used lately."

Rodgers nodded. "It also might be wise to make a few enquiries about who called at the house today. You had some of that brandy last night, my lord, if that is where it came from."

"Yes, but take care you are very discreet."

Rodgers looked mildly offended. He took up the tray on which he had brought in the decanter, and was about to leave when he recalled something he had meant to say. "Begging your pardon, my lord, I was forgetting. Mr. Peregrine is with her ladyship, and both would like to see you for a few minutes, provided you are up to it." His voice clearly stated that he did not believe that he was up to it.

Julian was about to agree with him, but then changed his mind. "I am quite well now, Simon, only very tired. I'll see them for a few moments."

Putting on his most expressionless face, which voiced his greatest disapproval, Rodgers bowed himself out of the room.

"Trying to stick your spoon in the wall again, Jul? You *must* be part cat!" said Peregrine cheerfully as he entered the room.

"My life does seem to be fraught with unusual perils, doesn't it?" agreed Julian, who was sitting up, comfortably propped against his pillows. He looked at his wife, who was standing a little to one side of his brother. There were small lines of tension about her mouth and eyes that he found most interesting. He stretched out his hand to her, and she moved beside him and took it. "I treated you to quite a spectacle this afternoon," he said quietly. "I am sorry if I frightened you."

"You certainly did," said Clarice with a shaky laugh. "I was nearly frightened out of my wits. I was afraid . . ." She stopped, discovering it difficult to go on without a break in her voice.

"That I had stuck my spoon in the wall?" quizzed Julian in perfect mimicry of his brother's tone.

Clarice smiled and nodded, and Peregrine protested that his voice wasn't *that* high, and for several minutes they made light conversation until Clarice insisted that they both leave to let Julian rest.

Not long after they had gone, Julian gave up the unequal battle with his weariness and fell into a light doze. There was a slight click as the door opened and Rodgers came into the room.

Julian was instantly awake. "Damn you, Simon," he said sleepily. "If you want me to rest, go away. Whatever it is, it'll wait until morning."

Instead of coming back with the expected retort, Simon Rodgers stood at his master's bedside, quiet, set, and grim.

At once Julian was alert, his exhaustion momentarily forgotten. Silently he took the small glass bottle with a plain silver top which Rodgers held out to him. He unscrewed the top and examined the grayish powder it contained. He took a little on the tip of his finger and placed it on his tongue.

"Where did you find this?" he asked crisply.

"In Lady Rown's dressing case," replied Rodgers without inflection.

Julian returned the top to the jar and turned it over thoughtfully. "This isn't the sort she keeps in her dressing case," he said.

"No, my lord. Those belonging to the case are crystal with gold tops. This was in a side compartment with several others of the same sort."

"You found it in the storeroom?"

"No, in her ladyship's sitting room." He gave a small deprecating cough. "I thought as you said to search everywhere it would be a good time to go in there while her ladyship was with you. I found the dressing case open and pushed behind a chair. It looked as if someone had been rifling through it."

Julian said nothing but continued to regard the bottle.

"Shall I inform her ladyship that you wish to speak to her?" asked Rodgers in the same toneless manner.

"No, not tonight." Julian put the little bottle in the drawer of his bed table and lay back on his pillow, giving himself up to much-needed sleep.

Although it was late, Clarice had not yet changed for bed. She had finally been persuaded by Eddly to take a tray in her room to make up for the dinner she had never had, but she was still so overwrought from the events of the night that most of it had gone back to the kitchen untasted. Since Peregrine had gone, she had busied herself with various little nonsense tasks to make the time pass and had finally curled herself up in a comfortable chair with a book. It lay open in her lap, unread.

Thought after thought raced through her head so rapidly that she could hardly keep track of them, but they all returned to the same end. Everyone, it seemed—Peter, Anne, and even John Prescott—had known her better than she knew herself. There was no point in denying it any longer, she had not the temperament to go on lying to herself when reality stared her straight in the face. In that moment when she had seen her husband so white, so desperately ill, she had known that she loved him. The realization had hit her like a blow and had filled her with unadulterated terror; to have lost him again would have been past bearing.

Was it possible that in spite of everything she had never

stopped loving him? Was she the fool her brother so obviously thought her, letting herself in for the unhappiness he predicted? To all appearances Julian had changed, but in fact had he? Once he was sure of her again, would he return to his old ways? Would she, too, fall into the old weeping, shrewish patterns?

She shifted in the chair, and the book fell to the floor unheeded. She was very confused as to what she should do next. If she loved Julian, she could hardly allow John Prescott to hope any longer, but if she gave him his congé now to spare him any further pain, Julian would be sure to realize it, and she wasn't at all sure she wanted him to know her feelings yet; the knowledge was still so new to her that she did not entirely trust her heart. And when she thought of giving herself totally to him again, she felt so vulnerable that it frightened her. On the other hand, she longed to pour out her love to him, to laugh with him, to plan their future, to be in his arms, to make love.

With a sigh, she got up and rang for her dresser. She knew that if she didn't make a push to go to bed she would sit up all night with her thoughts, and they were frankly making her head ache.

She rose with the dawn on the following morning and in spite of the late hour at which she finally fell asleep, she found that she was surprisingly refreshed. She decided against sending for Eddly at so early an hour and quickly washed and dressed herself in a light morning dress of spotted muslin. She left her room and went down the back stairs to the kitchens.

It was nearly eight when she tapped lightly on the door of her husband's bedchamber. It was answered at once by Rodgers.

"Good morning, Simon." She smiled. "Is he awake yet?"

"Yes, my lady," replied the valet, but he did not move aside for her to enter.

"I've made him some barley water and gruel for his breakfast," she said, indicating the tray she carried.

Rodgers gave a slight cough. "I am afraid, my lady, that the doctor left the strictest orders—"

"I know, Rodgers, he left them with me as well. I promise you I have followed them to the letter."

"I beg your ladyship's pardon, but I think his lordship's meals had better be left to me for the next few days."

Clarice felt her temper rising. "Rodgers, you will please stand aside," she said, very much the Viscountess Rown. "I wish to see my husband."

For a moment Rodgers didn't move; then he dropped his eyes and made room for her to pass. She cast him an imperious look and went into the room.

Clarice pushed several things aside and put the tray down on the bed table. "Good morning, Julian," she said cheerfully. "I've brought you your breakfast, as you see, and there is no point in complaining that you'd rather have ham, because you won't get it."

"I don't think, my lord—" stated Rodgers, who had followed her to his bedside.

Clarice rounded on him, a martial light in her eyes. "You don't think what, Rodgers?" She turned to her husband, who had thus far sat silent, but watchful. "What on earth is the matter with Rodgers? Anyone would think that I was trying to poison you!"

The two men exchanged glances, and this was not lost on Clarice. Before she could speak, Julian said quietly, "That will be all, Simon. I'll ring if I need you."

The valet looked mulish, but bowed and left the room.

Clarice pulled a chair over to the bedside and sat down and began to stir the gruel. "What is it, Julie? Am I supposed to have fed you bad food?" She laughed.

"Would you open that drawer for me, Clare?" he said, indicating the one in the bed table. "At the back of it you will find a small glass bottle."

Clarice did as she was bid and handed the bottle to him. He watched her intently as she gave it to him. "Is this the medicine that Beamish left for you?" she asked conversationally.

"No," he replied. "Does this bottle belong to you?"

She took it from him in surprise and turned it over in her hand. "It might. I think I have some like it, but it's common enough. Why, what is it?"

"Arsenic, I believe."

"Arsenic!" she repeated after him. "What would I be doing with arsenic?"

His eyes never left her face. "I believe some women use it to improve their complexions."

Clarice laughed. "I thank you, my lord, that is most flattering. I don't need any such thing, and I think it would be a rather dangerous thing to use in any event."

"Most dangerous," he agreed. "Taken in too large a dose, it has rather alarming effects on the body; severe pain, nausea, vomiting . . ." He let his voice trail away.

She stopped stirring the gruel, her brow knitted. "I don't understand what . . ." She broke off as his words combined with his steady, grim regard enlightened her. Her lips parted in surprise. "You can't be serious!" she said with a tremulous laugh. "Really, Julian," she said as she turned back to the gruel, "this is a very tasteless joke. First of all, what you had was food poisoning, not *that* sort, and second, it is really very bad of you, even joking, to imply that I would ever do anything to harm you."

"It isn't a joke, Clare. Rodgers found this bottle in your dressing case."

The seriousness in his tone made her stare at him. What she saw convinced her that this was no jest. "Good Lord! You mean it! Julian!" she exclaimed, aghast. He met her stare unblinkingly and said nothing. "What was Simon Rodgers doing in my dressing case?" she added indignantly.

"He was under my orders to search everything in the house," replied her husband. "Everything, Clare, not just your things. I would have given anything if he had found it elsewhere."

Clarice let the spoon fall on the tray with a clatter. The sheer absurdity of the charge he seemed to be making against her momentarily forestalled any anger. "Julie, you have been very ill and you are letting your imagination run away with you," she said gently and very carefully. "If you say that Rodgers found that in my dressing case, I suppose I must believe you, but I certainly didn't know of its existence or at least its contents, and even if I did, why would I ever wish to poison you?"

"It would be a solution to your difficulties, wouldn't it?" he said evenly.

Clarice would have laughed had the situation not been so deadly serious. Had she behaved so badly toward him since his return that he could suspect she would stop at nothing to rid herself of him? His expression told her that he could and did suspect it. Slowly anger began to kindle. So this was what he thought of her!

"A solution! Oh, yes, a splendid solution," she cried wrathfully. "I would be free of you, and John and I could be wed from my prison cell."

"Not necessarily. Even Sir Walter suspected nothing."

"But you did. Without a moment's hesitation you immediately assume that your wife is trying to poison you and set your valet to search my things," she raged, whipping herself into a fine fury. "Do you send for the constable now, or am I simply to be incarcerated with a keeper at some remote property of your father's for the sake of the family name?"

"I suspected poison because it is not the first time that it has happened to me," he said calmly in marked contrast to her heat. "It happened before, in America, an accident. I did not for a moment suspect you."

"Until Rodgers found that in my dressing case." She sneered. "And this, of course, could not have been an accident."

"No," he said in his quiet manner, "it could not be."

Turning again to the table, she picked up the glass of barley water and deliberately drank some; she did the same with the gruel. "There," she cried defiantly. "Does that convince you? Or do you accuse me of wishing my own destruction as well?"

"I only want you to tell me that my suspicions are groundless."

"And then you will suddenly believe me?" she jeered. As she placed the spoon back on the tray, her anger suddenly left her. She looked at him sadly. "What *I* want, Julian, is for you to believe in me without my having to say so." Afraid that remaining any longer would bring her to tears she did not wish him to see, she turned her back on him and left the room.

After remaining some time in deep thought, Julian rang for his servant. When Rodgers came into the room, Julian tore back the bedcovers and got out of bed.

"Get my bath and put out my clothes, Simon, I've lain about long enough," he said briskly. Rodgers protested vigorously but was overruled, and finally was persuaded to help his master dress.

An hour later the valet gave a final twitch to the tail of his lordship's exquisitely cut coat and then stood back to survey his handiwork.

"Will I do, Simon?" asked Julian with a severity that belied the smile in his eyes.

"Yes, my lord," said Rodgers at his most serious. "If I might suggest—"

"I know. A quiet day of rest. You have nothing to be concerned about, that is all I plan. I still feel a trifle weak." He paused and added, "I said weak, Simon, not sick."

Lord Rown had said nothing to Rodgers concerning his interview with his wife, and Rodgers would have preferred not to question him, if possible. If it was something to do with her ladyship, then beyond the affection in which he held his master, it was no concern of his. If it did not . . . Well, that was another matter entirely and it was imperative that he discover this immediately.

Rodgers gave one of his little coughs. "Begging your pardon, my lord, I couldn't help but wonder if you had any further information pertaining to the bottle I found last night?"

"My wife is not trying to murder me," replied Julian.

"Of course not, my lord," said Rodgers hastily.

"You fraud," laughed Julian. "You trust no one, not even me completely. But you are forgiven; I, too, had my doubts until this morning, may I be forgiven for them. Did you get that other information?"

"Yes, my lord," said Rodgers, and he then went on in a businesslike tone to enumerate the callers who had come to Creeley House on the previous day. As these were mostly family and in no way remarkable, he finished rather quickly and ended up his account by saying, "There is one interesting thing, my lord. Miss Eddly mentioned, without my asking, that her ladyship had spent the afternoon going through her dressing case discarding things she no longer had use for." Lord Rown appeared preoccupied with attaching his fob to his watch and didn't reply, so Rodgers continued, "There were no service calls out of the ordinary, and as far as I can tell, no one had access to anything you ate or drank in this house except Lady Rown and the staff."

"I think we have been following a red herring, Simon,"

said Julian, glancing up at him. "I begin to suspect a plant." He paused, and when he went on, his voice had hardened. "If what I suspect is true, and I am afraid and very sorry to say that I think it is, it is time we took steps to make certain and deal with it once and for all."

After her unhappy interview with her husband, Clarice ran down the hall to her own room, slammed the door with all the force she could muster, and gave in to a fit of tears. While happily preparing his breakfast that morning, she had almost made up her mind to unburden her heart to him. What manner of fool would she have been if she had? He didn't truly love her; he couldn't and think such a thing of her. It was his pride that made him determined to hold on to her, and he would never know how close he had come to success.

"Idiot!" she raged aloud to herself. "He has managed to hurt you in a way that even you never suspected. This is what you would have to look forward to if you stay with him." She began to cry again.

However, when she next saw him, later that same day, he apologized so sincerely and was at such pains to convince her that his suspicions had been a sick fancy and an overreaction due to his years in intelligence that she gradually unbent toward him.

Their companionable relationship continued much as before, but she was no longer truly happy in it. Always in her mind was the knowledge that she was again in love with him, and the quandary of what she was to do with that knowledge.

Tears seemed to come easily to her in the days that followed, and the cause of those most recently shed had been an innocent request by her husband that she accompany him on an inspection of their house on Curzon Street, which had been vacated on the previous day by the tenants to whom Lord Creeley had let it.

She had given him an offhand excuse, and when he had left by himself, she again indulged her lacerated emotions. She had felt that it would be impossible for her to go with him now to that house in which their lives had once been so bound together. How different it would have been if she had been able to confess her love for him on the morning after his illness. They would then have gone there today as lovers, joyfully planning their future together.

She wept for several minutes, dampening the brocaded counterpane on her bed, and then got up and went to her dressing table to dab rice powder under her eyes. The red, swollen countenance that faced her in the mirror instantly disgusted her, and she sat down on the stool in front of the table and buried her face in her hands. Was she going to spend the rest of her life crying, afraid to love the man she couldn't help loving? If her wayward heart refused to be controlled, then it was time she stopped feeling sorry for herself, faced up to the situation, and took it in hand. She could not permit herself to decline into the pitiable watering pot she had been during the early years of their marriage.

She raised her head and forced herself to look at the woebegone appearance she presented. She loved Julian, and that was that. Tonight he would know it, too; beyond any doubt, let the future hold what it may.

"Yes, I think it will be the rose gown after all," she told a flustered Eddly, who helped her out of a gown of green silk about an hour later. It was the twelfth dress Clarice had tried on, the rose gown twice. She and Julian were to attend a ball that night at the Seftons' that promised to be the event of the season, and Clarice intended that the evening would be perfect in every way, down to the last detail of her dress.

"It will have to be pressed, of course," she continued as she again slipped on the rose silk, "and I would like you to lower the neckline a bit." Clarice indicated how she would like this done, and Eddly opened her eyes a trifle wider.

Lady Rown was a woman who could well carry off such a dress, but it had always been her habit to dress modestly, and Eddly, not conversant with her mistress' motives, and very much aware of how things were, or rather weren't between Lord and Lady Rown, never suspected that all this trouble might be for his lordship's benefit.

Eddly didn't much care for Mr. Prescott, but he had made her lady happy those last months before his lordship returned, and if he never had a kind word or a smile for a simple dresser, what did that say to the sort of husband Mr. Prescott would make her ladyship? Those beautiful men like Lord Rown, with smiles that made one's knees watery, certainly didn't make for comfortable husbands; at least her lady had shed an ocean of tears over him. Well, she thought, and clucked to herself, this wasn't going to help matters any. Trouble ahead, if she was any judge. She shoved a pin into place, and Clarice gave a little cry as it stuck her. Eddly was instantly contrite, horrified that her wandering thoughts had led her to be careless, but Clarice brushed away her apologies with a smile, and asked her to help her out of the gown.

Clarice began to rummage through a drawer in her dressing table, and after a few minutes said, "Do you know what became of that rose-colored ribbon that I had for my pink muslin?"

"Yes, my lady," replied Eddly. "It faded sadly in the wash and you bade me give it to one of the maids at Lady Fowle's."

Clarice made a vexed sound. "I'd forgotten; I wanted to wear it in my hair tonight."

"You wore the diamond clusters with that gown last time, my lady," Eddly reminded her. "It looked uncommonly well, if I may say so."

"Perhaps, but I want to dress very simply tonight, no jewels except earrings." Clarice considered for a moment. "If I am to wear that gown tonight, you won't have time to go out and purchase the ribbon for me."

"I could send one of the maids, my lady. If I snipped a bit from the hem, she would bring back the right color."

"No, I'll go myself. I think I want it a shade deeper than the dress."

As Clarice was drawing on her gloves in the hall, Anne called, and Clarice prevailed upon her to join her on her shopping expedition. The ladies got down from their carriage at the head of a street filled with the shop fronts of milliners, modistes, and drapers, and at one of the last Clarice quickly made her purchase, and then she and Anne walked leisurely along the street, stopping frequently to comment and admire the wares displayed.

"Oh, look, Clare!" cried Anne, pointing to a dainty chip straw bonnet adorned with pale blue spring flowers. "That would be perfect with your new blue muslin."

Clarice peered more closely into the window. The bright May sun was high in the sky, and its brightness made the display window a perfect mirror of the opposite side of the street, making it impossible for Clarice to see clearly inside the store without shading her eyes. She agreed with Anne that the bonnet was lovely, but decided that the flowers were a quite different shade of blue from her dress. She stepped back a bit, about to suggest that they go on, when she saw something in the reflection of the other side of the street that surprised her and made her hesitate. Julian was standing across the street in front of a fashionable modiste's talking to a man she didn't recognize and a woman who was hidden from her view by the strange man. But surely Julian had told her that he meant to make a thorough inspection of the house and would not be through until late in the afternoon. She turned from the window to really look at them and discovered that she was not mistaken.

She was about to point them out to Anne and suggest that they cross the street to join them, when the unfamiliar man bowed and walked away. As he left, the woman was brought into Clarice's view, and as she recognized her, Clarice caught her breath. Before her startled eyes, Julian took the woman's arm and led her into the doorway of the shop they had been standing in front of. Clarice turned again to the window, her heart beating a little fast. She was determined not to jump to conclusions.

The entranceway which Julian and the woman had entered was recessed at an angle, making it virtually invisible from the street. By a quirk of fate that morning, the reflection of the rays and the angle of the window at which Clarice now stared gave her a clear picture of it. Julian, in the act of reaching for the door handle, stopped, and lifting the woman's chin in his other hand, kissed her lightly but lingeringly.

Clarice became dimly aware that her sister was speaking to her.

"What is it, Clare? Are you ill?" Anne was saying anxiously. Having received no answer to several comments and at least one direct question, Anne had turned to find her younger sister staring vacantly at the shop window, her face totally drained of blood. Anne quickly put her arms about her, fearing she was about to faint.

Clarice blinked into Anne's concerned gaze. "Oh, Anne," she murmured brokenly. "I must go home."

"Of course you must," said Anne solicitously, still keeping a protective arm about her sister.

Clarice had very little recollection of returning to the carriage or of the ride home. When they arrived there, Anne took her immediately to her room, and Clarice was soon lying on her bed, a cold compress on her forehead, and Anne sitting beside her holding a vinaigrette. She had told Anne nothing but that she had the headache, and Anne had thus far not asked her any questions.

"Thank you, Eddly," Anne was saying. "I'll stay with Lady Rown now." Thus dismissed, Eddly reluctantly left the sisters alone.

Anne put a cool hand to her sister's cheek. "You're not flushed anymore. What is it, Clare? I don't for a moment believe that you suddenly got the headache."

There was no need to dissemble with Anne, and perhaps talking would ease the dreadful ache that came from nowhere and everywhere inside of her. "It was Julian," said Clarice in a voice barely above a whisper.

"Julian!" exclaimed Anne, puzzled. "You saw Julian?"

Clarice nodded with dumb misery.

"What is there in that . . . ?" Anne broke off as she realized what it must have been. "Oh, dear," she said tonelessly. "A woman, I suppose."

Clarice nodded again. "It was Lady Susan." Her voice broke on the name.

Anne knit her brows. "Lady Susan?"

"Hope," replied Clarice in the same numb voice. "She is the wife of Ambrose Hope, you must remember her."

"Oh," said Anne, "I see." She did see. Lady Susan Hope had reigned in Lord Rown's affections shortly before Therese Rouane had come into his life. Anne felt a flash of anger for her brother-in-law. How stupid of him to be seen with a former inamorata. The most innocent circumstance involving him with such a woman would lead Clarice to place the wrong construction on his behavior, as it was obvious that she had, for Anne had no doubt that Julian was innocent. She firmly believed that he was sincere in his feelings for his wife and in his determination to be a good husband to her this time.

"Well, what did you see?" she asked Clarice. "Rown walking down the street with her? There's nothing in that to be so upset over. You would hardly expect him to cut all his female acquaintances."

"He kissed her, Anne."

"What! In the street? I don't believe it!"

Clarice took the damp rag from her forehead and sat up. She sighed deeply. "No, not in the street. They were in the doorway of Mme. Franchot's shop. I saw it reflected in the glass of the milliner's shop."

Anne understood this, for she too had noticed the odd mirrorlike effect in the window. "Nonsense," she said briskly. "What you saw was a fuzzy reversed picture from all the way across the street. Very likely it wasn't him at all. Didn't you tell me he was spending the afternoon at your house in Curzon Street?"

Clarice shook her head sadly. "It was him, Anne. I saw him clearly before that, and not in the window." Her voice was more like her own now. The pretended headache had given her time to gather her thoughts and put what she had seen in its proper perspective. "It is just as it always was, is it not? The flawless excuse to cover his actions. I wonder why he bothers; he seems to care so little that I eventually discover the truth." She drew her knees up and rested her head on them. "What am I going to do now, Anne?"

"I think you should give him a chance to explain."

"Explain!" said Clarice with a hollow laugh. "You mean lie. How many chances have I given him, Anne? How many? And he has betrayed me again. I cannot believe that I have let myself love him again and let myself in for this pain."

"Love him?" asked Anne, surprised, for it was the first she had heard of it.

"Yes, love him. Consummate fool that I am," Clarice said bitterly. "I realized it the other day when he was so sick, but in perfect truth, I suppose I've always known it." She choked on a little sob. "I didn't want to believe it, Anne; I didn't want to be hurt again."

Anne folded Clarice in her arms and said nothing while the sobs racked Clarice's body.

After Anne left her, Clarice used her fake headache to spend what was left of the afternoon undisturbed in her room. In the end her thoughts led her to a decision that was quite different from the one she had come to earlier in the day.

12

Clarice gave another little tug to the bodice of the rose silk gown and announced herself pleased. Privately, Eddly thought it indecent; there was more of the demimonde high flyer about Lady Rown tonight than the demure young matron. With every movement, the soft folds of rose silk, assisted by dampened petticoats, clung suggestively to every voluptuous curve of Clarice's body. The previously rejected diamonds glittered in her dark curls, and a single diamond pendant suspended on a white gold chain unnecessarily accentuated the deep cleavage between her full breasts.

If Clarice had any doubts about the effect she intended to create, they were dispelled the moment she saw the expression in her husband's eyes when he saw her. It was precisely what she had hoped to see and had the effect of raising her color and thus heightening her bold beauty. She flirted outrageously with him on the way to the Seftons', but managed to keep him at arm's length, where she wished him to be for the moment.

Once there, Clarice discovered that Julian was not the only man to appreciate her openly displayed charms. They earned for her not only the admiration of the men but also several sour looks from the women present. Clarice, drinking it all in like a reviving cordial, felt it suited exactly her dangerous mood of suppressed excitement.

In their fashionable circle it was considered very *déclassé* for a husband and wife to spend the evening in one another's pockets at a social event, whatever their private inclinations might be, and it was not until the last waltz before supper that Julian led his wife onto the floor. The signals he had been receiving from his wife's behavior toward him had been unmistakable, and though he had no idea what had caused this sudden turnabout in her, he wanted what she was offering too much to question it; at least until he had secured it.

"I was beginning to wonder whether I would be able to dance with the most beautiful woman in the room tonight," he said softly as they twirled about the candlelit room.

"And were you?" asked Clarice archly.

"Finally," he laughed.

Their bodies moved in perfect unison as they glided along the floor. Clarice gave him a seductive smile and asked teasingly, "Don't you find it dreadfully hot in here?"

"Unbearably," he agreed.

They made their way to the side of the room, where draperies stirred in the gentle breeze from the open windows behind them. Pushing back one of the brocaded panels, he led her out onto a small balcony, one of several that ran the length of the ballroom. Outside, she turned to him, and there was no need for words to be spoken; almost at once they embraced. Clarice let him kiss and caress her without restraint until she felt the familiar rush of pleasure and anticipation surge through her, and more importantly, knew that he must be feeling it too. No need this time to distrust herself; she had her emotions well in hand.

When she judged from the intensity of his lovemaking that her purpose had been achieved, she gently pushed him away. "We can scarcely make love here," she said softly. He agreed but nevertheless drew her closer and kissed her again. She did not move away this time.

When his lips left hers and began to move hungrily down her slender white throat, she murmured quietly but distinctly in his ear, "For me there must be the comforts of a bed, unlike poor Lady Susan." He made no reply, and she went on, "How insatiable you are, Julian! A mistress in the afternoon and a wife at night. Where did you manage it this afternoon? In a carriage? At an obliging friend's? Or was poor Mr. Hope from home?"

He had been paying little attention to her speech, but he caught the word "mistress" and the reference to Mr. Hope. He raised his head to look at her but did not release her.

"What is it, Clare?" he asked quietly, not yet concerned.

"It is simply that I was vastly entertained this afternoon by a delightful scene enacted in the doorway of Mme. Franchot's. But you would not know of it. You were so busy inspecting the Curzon Street house." Her tone was no more than conversational.

He did not answer her at once, so she said bitingly, "Are you trying to think of a convincing lie? I think I liked you better in the old days. Then when you were caught out you had the grace to admit it at once."

"You have put the wrong construction on what I take it you thought you saw," he said carefully.

"Oh, dear, have I?" Her voice dripped sweet sarcasm. "How foolish of me! No doubt you arrived at the house to discover Lady Susan moping under the holland covers. Then you took her to Mme. Franchot's so that she might have something better than a white sheet to wear, and kissed her because she hadn't been with a man for an hour and needed reviving."

"That is unworthy of you," he said, his voice hardening.

She laughed bitterly and pushed herself away from him. "What is unworthy of me," she spat at him, "is that I was fool enough to begin to wonder if you had changed. What has obviously changed is that you have learned discretion, with the notable exception of your lapse today. And even that was just bad luck that I should be there and the reflection in the glass play you false."

He didn't have the least idea what she meant by that last statement, so he ignored it; he was becoming angry in his turn. "I can see that you have made up your mind that I have taken a mistress, so explanation is useless," he said in a tone bitter enough to match hers. "But why this charming little farce tonight, Clare?" he challenged her.

For an answer, Clarice moved even closer to him and pressed her body seductively against him. "Can't you guess?" she asked huskily.

"Unfortunately, I can." His eyes were no longer soft with love, but as hard and brittle as his voice. "Take care you don't go too far."

Clarice felt a shiver of apprehension at his tone, and though she didn't completely admit it to herself, excitement. She started to move away from him, but found herself held fast. He kissed her in a hard, brutal way that she had never experienced before. Genuinely frightened, she struggled and nearly fell when he released her abruptly. She gave him a look of pure venom, and made her escape into the ballroom.

He stood looking at the swaying drapery she had disappeared behind, cursing softly to himself and at himself.

The second part of the plan she had concocted that afternoon in her bedchamber proved to be far more difficult to carry out than the first. It was one thing to bait a man with whom she had been on varying terms of intimacy since childhood; it was entirely another to invite herself to spend the night with a man she had known well for less than a year. She had decided, bitterly, that men regarded women only in base physical terms and intended to bind herself to John Prescott in just that manner.

It was the work of a moment to gather her disheveled thoughts back into order and to find Prescott in the crowded ballroom, but once at his side she was at a total loss how to go on. Prescott, once he began to realize what it was that she wished, was at first surprised and then delighted. Far from regarding her as a wanton, as she had feared he might, he thought her blushing hints became her modesty and would have whisked her away at once to his lodgings, but Clarice insisted on observing the outward proprieties. She left him to seek out her sister Anne.

Anne's behavior toward her that afternoon had led Clarice to think that she might find aid in that quarter. Instead of coming to Julian's defense, as Clarice had feared she might, Anne had been all that was warm and comforting. Well, if she believed her sister to have been wronged, now was the time for Anne to help her put matters to right. But Clarice had misjudged her.

"I could never do such a thing," cried Anne plaintively when Clarice had succeeded in taking her to a small anteroom and explained to her what it was she wished her to do.

"Well, you must," said Clarice patiently. "There is no one else here I dare ask."

"You can't ask me either. Clare, how could you think I would be a party to such a thing!" Anne moaned. "How can you even *do* such a thing!"

"I'm not sure. You had better ask Rown; he manages it well enough."

"It is not the same thing," replied her sister, almost stamping her foot.

"Oh, yes, I know. The husband may please himself with impunity; a wife's place is to sit at home mending by the fire, waiting patiently to greet her man when he returns from his 'adventures.' "

Anne was shocked by the bitterness in her sister's tone. Searching wildly for something to turn her sister's mind from this disastrous course, she said, "You told me this afternoon that you were still in love with Julian. What do you think will become of your marriage if you do this thing?"

"My marriage!" Clarice mocked. "I haven't got one. The sooner it is over, the better. If you won't help me, then I shall manage without you. I shall leave quite openly with John. I am to be ruined in the end, so this is just as well; it will but hasten it."

Anne reached out a restraining arm to prevent Clarice from leaving the room. "No! You mustn't do that!" she cried, alarmed. "Please, Clarice, you are upset and overwrought. Go home and rest. Take some laudanum." The mulish look on her sister's face told her her entreaties were useless, and all at once Anne capitulated. "Very well, I will help you," she said slowly, looking into her sister's eyes and hoping Clarice would forgive her for what she meant to do.

The large upright clock in the hall of Creeley House was striking the hour of four as Clarice quietly let herself into the house. The wall sconce usually kept lit, that any member of the household returning late might light a bed candle, had guttered, leaving the house in total darkness. Clarice groped her way up the stairs and tiptoed down the hall past her husband's rooms, but no light shone from under either of the doors. Very likely he was still out. If he was in a rage, and Clarice thought it probable that he was, he would be in no hurry to return home; and whatever time he did return, it was hardly likely that he would seek out his wife.

With a shudder, Clarice recalled the painful evening she had just spent. From a morning during which she had conceived such hope for her future, the day had provided one disaster after another, and all she wanted now was her bed; and perhaps the laudanum drops that Anne had suggested. Quietly she turned the handle of her bedchamber door and let herself in. She went to the mantel for the tinderbox, and finding it, lit several candles on a bureau.

As she lifted the diamond pendant from about her neck, she decided to manage the little buttons on her gown herself rather than ring for Eddly at that late hour. She heard a sound behind her and turned abruptly to discover her husband standing beside her. "Julian!" she gasped, then added shakily, "I wish you would give up this penchant you have for sitting in the dark."

"I was waiting to say good night to my wife," he said quietly; there was a slight emphasis on the last word. "I have been waiting uncommonly long. What kept you, Clare? Friends met along the way? A carriage accident? Or perhaps Prescott was greedy and loath to let you go?" He mocked her manner of earlier in the evening.

Clarice caught her breath. "How did you . . . ?" She stopped, realizing that she was betraying herself.

"How did I know?" he asked in a silky voice that frightened her. "Your conscientious sister Anne was obliging enough to tell me. I believe she had the notion that I would rush after you and quixotically save you from yourself. She was mistaken. I don't fancy myself in the role of the pitiable cuckold dragging his wife out of another man's bed, and I am just civilized enough to be repelled at the thought of what I would have done had I found you there."

His back was to the candlelight, and Clarice could not quite make out his expression, but something in his stance made her take a step backward. She stumbled over the stool of her dressing table and would have fallen had he not caught her by the arm.

Fear made her retreat into anger. "What an amusing reversal," she said brightly. "You playing the wronged mate, and I the penitent one. Only I am not feeling very penitent."

His grip on her tightened. "You were at some pains the other day to imply that you had not slept with Prescott. Why?"

She shrugged as well as she could with his hand restraining her. "It was true. Then," she added provocatively.

He pushed her away from him so roughly that this time she did fall over the stool, and the table as well, knocking over several things on top of it. As she grabbed at its edge to save herself from falling to the floor, she hit her elbow, and for a moment was helpless as waves of pain washed over her. Across the room she heard the music of crystal on crystal. "You're drunk!" she cried accusingly.

He laughed bitterly. "Not nearly as drunk as I wish to be.

It takes a great deal, it seems, to wash down the knowledge that your wife is a whore."

"Oh, very good, Julian!" she said in a congratulatory tone. "If I am a whore, what does that make you? You needn't waste your breath telling me that it is different; Anne did it for you. If I didn't sleep with John before, it had nothing to do with you; I didn't want our first child together to be born barely seven months into our marriage, as Perry was in ours. But now I don't give a damn anymore; there are no lengths to which I would not go to be rid of you," she taunted.

With icy venom he called her by the vilest epithet that can be used to describe a woman. His anger was white-hot, nurtured by his long vigil and his father's excellent brandy, and the iron control in which he held himself was within a hair-breadth of slipping away from him.

Clarice was instantly furious. "You dare say that to me? What have I done that you and countless men like you have not done to their wives time out of mind? You take your pleasure when and where you please, without even the pretense of love, let alone the feeling of it. So you have spent one wretched night imagining me with John Prescott." She paused to make a derisive sound. "Do you expect *me* to be impressed? Shall I tell you the stages through which your imagination took you? I can recite them by heart, so many times have *I* lived through nights like this. When you walked out on me four years ago, did you suppose that I would spend the rest of my life remaining faithful to your memory?"

"That has no bearing on this night," he said, his voice cold steel. "You speak of no pretense of love? Were you Prescott's whore for love, I would try to accept that as best I might. What you have done this night was for revenge; to pay me out, in the manner of a slut."

The disgust in his voice at last was too much for her, and crossing to where he stood, she attempted to strike him. He caught her wrist and held it in a grip so tight that the pain caused her knees to buckle slightly. He took a step nearer to her, and the fury and barely suppressed violence that she saw in his face made her involuntarily shrink from him. Then jerkily, as though he had suddenly checked himself, he dropped her arm. He turned on his heel and slammed himself out of the room, and a few moments later, out of the house.

Mechanically Clarice walked over to her dressing table, righted the stool she had knocked over, and sat down on it all in a heap. Placing her fingers over her eyes, she waited for the tears that did not come. Perhaps I am beyond them, she thought miserably, or have none left.

Why hadn't she told him the truth? She had let him leave in such a state, thinking such a thing of her! Very likely she had driven him into his mistress' arms.

Wretchedly Clarice gave up the attempt to cry and began to unfasten her gown. To be fair, she couldn't blame Anne for what had happened. Julian probably would have arrived at the same conclusion himself when he discovered both her and John missing from the Seftons'; he would never have believed the story she and Anne had concocted to account for her departure, not in light of what she had said to him on the balcony. And Anne had not made her taunt him with lies calculated to cut him as deeply as possible. She had been a fool to let her pride and temper run away with her. What good had it done her? All she had now was a husband who despised her and thought her a whore, and a lover who was both angry and humiliated.

All had gone well when she had left the Seftons' with John Prescott until he had begun to display his ardor during the carriage drive to his lodgings. Clarice had put him off playfully, as best she could, telling herself that once there her mood would settle and she would be able to respond to him, but it had never happened. She really had tried. If intent was as good as the act, then she was unquestionably guilty of adultery, but when brought to the point, she simply had not been able to go through with it. Prescott had not bothered to conceal his anger and frustration, and Clarice could hardly blame him. It would take considerably more persuasive power than she had to soothe his lacerated vanity this time, she thought, recalling the things he had said to her. But after all, it made no difference; any hopes they had had for a future together had dissolved the moment she had stepped into Peter's bookroom and had seen her husband; and she was feeling far too defeated now to have any regrets for what her life with Prescott might have been.

Or her life with Julian, for that matter. She had, with signal efficiency, destroyed that as well. Her revenge had been complete indeed! Account credited in full. Did he hurt now as she had on that night of her first disillusionment so many years ago? The satisfaction she had imagined she would feel was nowhere to be found, only a dull unhappiness that seemed to oppress her from every side.

13

Clarice awoke heavy-eyed the next morning and wretchedly unhappy. Facing Julian across a breakfast table was out of the question, and she requested a light breakfast to be brought to her room. She knew she ought to do something to mend the shambles that her life had become, but her spirits were so depressed that no solution satisfied her, and trying to focus on one made her head ache.

She was eating her breakfast, tasting none of it, and going through the mail that had been brought up with her tray, when she came upon a letter that bore no direction. She turned it over and saw that it had been sealed without a design. Curious, Clarice broke the seal and unfolded it; a smaller folded piece of paper fell out onto her lap. She put aside the larger paper, which oddly seemed to be printed rather than written, and retrieved the enclosure. She unfolded this and at once recognized her husband's hand.

3 Dec.

I can't make it on Tuesday, you'll have to cross without me. I have nothing for you this time in any event. There is trouble here, and security has been tightened. No need for concern; it's nothing to do with us. You'll know what to do when you get there, and what to say.

R.

Clarice knit her brow in puzzlement and read it over again. It made no sense to her, and she picked up the larger paper she had thrown on the table, hoping for enlightenment. It read in a neat printing without any character:

The enclosed note and several others like it are worth a fortune. They will cost you a total of a thousand pounds apiece; six thousand in all. This is a present to you. If you don't want your husband to hang for a double dealer and a traitor, you will pay that amount when you receive instructions in a day or two. On receipt of the money, the remaining letters will be sent to you in the following post. You will say nothing to your husband or all is forfeit. He is a dangerous man, and if he knew you know of these, I would not be the only one in peril. Lest you have any doubt, you should know that this missive is the mildest of the seven. The others name names and are totally damning. I have them from a frog who had been one of Bonaparte's top agents and whom I found dying at Waterloo. He made me a present of them, along with the details and your husband's identity, in payment for a last few moments of comfort. I trust you will see that his reckoning is paid in full.

There was no signature. Clarice reread it and the smaller note as well and then sat staring at them. She was all but positive that the small note was her husband's writing, and the signature initial, so familiar to her, helped to convince her; but she could not accept that Julian was what the printed letter purported him to be. It was absurd; it was a hoax, it had to be. What, after all, did his note say? Surely nothing that couldn't have a dozen different meanings, all of them perfectly innocent.

She stood up and began to pace nervously about the room. Should she ignore the warning and take it to Julian? After last night, she wasn't anxious to seek him out for any cause, yet she felt that at this point in her life another burden would be more than she could cope with. She needed advice, and she needed it badly. Besides Julian himself, she knew that the only other person she could go to would be her brother. Could she trust Peter with so delicate a secret? Partly because she so desperately wanted to, she decided that she could.

Clarice could not believe her good fortune at finding Peter at home and alone. She had envisioned a fretful hour or so with Lydia while she thought of an excuse to see her brother alone, and as it was, he was about to leave when she arrived, but she persuaded him to put off his plans for her. When they were alone in his study, she mutely handed him both letters and watched him carefully for his reaction.

Brows together, he read both carefully and then read them again, as she had done. When he finished, he turned to her and said in an annoyed voice, "What is this nonsense? Where did you get these?"

She explained.

"Did you ask the footman who brought up your tray how it came to you? There is no direction."

She admitted that she had not. "I didn't think, I was so surprised. It must have come by messenger, I suppose."

"Probably," he agreed. "Perhaps it's just as well that you didn't; until we can decide what this is about, it would be as well not to call attention to it by speaking to the servants. Have you shown this to Julian?"

Clarice looked disconcerted. "No, I haven't seen him this morning. I didn't know what to do; the letter says I must not tell him."

"What this letter is, my dear girl, is moonshine. Do you really believe that Julian would play a double game? Or that he would be fool enough to put evidence of it in writing if he had?"

"I don't want to believe it," she said unhappily.

Peter scanned the note again. "Perhaps it is a forgery. If it is, it's remarkably good. Well, it might be something else, then. What does the note say, after all? Nothing. I daresay there is more than one construction that could be put upon it," he said bracingly, echoing her own thoughts.

"What should I do, Peter? Should I ignore it? Should I take it to Julian?" she asked. "If I follow the instructions, I very much doubt that I will be able to draw such a sum from our account without Julian's being told about it. He'd want to know what it was for."

Ardane considered this. "Do nothing now. Wait and see what the next message brings. Perhaps it is all a hoax and you'll never hear another word about it," he advised, but Clarice thought she heard a shade of doubt in his voice.

"You're beginning to wonder if it mightn't be true, aren't you?" she asked suspiciously.

He began to protest that he did not, but under the scrutiny of her earnest gaze, he faltered. "There is a point or two that troubles me," he admitted. "Probably nonsense." He waved his hand as though to dismiss his thoughts, but Clarice insisted that he tell her. "Well, there's the character of the man himself," Peter said reluctantly. "You know what he's like. Half the time one never knows what's really going on inside his head. He's always been like that, too; even when we were boys. I should think he fell into espionage quite naturally."

"That hardly condemns him as a traitor," said his sister.

"No, I'm not saying that it does. I only mean that given his nature one has to admit that it is not beyond the realm of possibility. There is no one who takes greater pleasure in keeping his counsel than Julian. I think it just possible that when it wasn't women he was intriguing with, it was governments, and all for the pure sport of it."

"How can you say so, Peter," Clarice cried, aghast. "That is the most horrible thing I have ever heard said about anyone. That he would betray his country for sport!"

"I know it is horrible," he said soothingly, "but is it so unthinkable? He made vows to you, did he not? He claimed to love you, and surely he owed you all his loyalty, but did that ever prevent him from committing infidelity after infidelity? Was there anything to redeem his behavior? Was there even one with whom he fell in love and thus couldn't help himself? Of course not! It was sport, pure and simple; and is it after all so very different? Isn't treachery treachery, whatever the source?"

"Certainly that argument is specious! I can't believe it of him," said Clarice staunchly. "I would sooner believe it if he believed Napoleon a savior, as Perry did in his salad days, but he didn't; Julian was amused by Perry's idealistic talk. He has never been political."

"The very fact that he allied himself with the government and agreed to be employed by them shows that he must have had some political inclinations, don't you think? It just proves what I've said about none of us ever knowing what he really feels." Peter paused to look at her critically for a moment and then said, "I can see that I'm upsetting you. Perhaps it would be best if we didn't discuss this any further."

"No, Peter," said Clarice, meeting his gaze steadily. "I want to know what you think, even if I can't agree with you. You said there were one or two points, Peter. What else is there?"

He looked very much as though he regretted having ever mentioned his doubts, but he said, "Well, there is Julian's Mr. Smith. I have been wondering for some time about the validity of his claim to existence. So clever, so mysterious is Mr. Smith, and oh so elusive. I remember the close watchful way that Julian looked at me when he first told me of him, almost as though he were challenging me to believe him."

"But why on earth would Julian make him up?" asked Clarice, surprised.

Ardane shrugged. "To amuse himself, perhaps. That whole damn family has odd ideas about what's entertaining, and just because Julian doesn't carry it to the obvious, as Perry does, doesn't mean that he hasn't the same strange sense of humor. It surfaces from time to time, you know."

"I know, but I can't imagine Julian indulging himself in such a serious matter. Now, *that* would not be like him."

"Perhaps," said Peter grudgingly. "It was only an idea I've played with for want of a better reason, but now that I've seen those letters you've received, another possibility occurs to me." Clarice said nothing, so he went on. "Let us suppose for the sake of argument that his story in its essentials is completely true. He made a mistake, betrayed himself to Mme. Rouane, whom he knew as an enemy agent, and was reassigned to see if he couldn't give away the confidences of our American cousins. I think that is all perfectly true. I also think that Julian is clever enough to know that the best lie is one that is based on the truth."

"What, then, is the lie?" Clarice interrupted.

Peter leaned toward her and said confidentially, "What if his mistake led Therese to discover that he was not just playing a double game, but a *double* double game, carrying treachery to its ultimate? He has painted her as an amoral creature without any true loyalties. If she was that sort, he would have made himself the perfect victim for blackmail. How could he hope to save himself if both sides believed him false? In either case, her continued existence would have been most dangerous to him."

"You think *he* murdered her?" asked Clarice, horrified.

"No, not necessarily," Ardane said testily, obviously impatient of the interruption. "He might have somehow convinced the French that she was better off out of the way. But with that behind him he was free to go to our government and give them the story of Mr. Smith. La Rouane was no longer there to contradict him, and he would be able to give his imagination full rein to convince them of whatever he deemed necessary."

Clarice thought this argument farfetched and did not hesitate to say so. "You don't know that any such things ever occurred any more than I do," she said scornfully.

"No, I don't," said Peter severely. "But if there is any truth to those letters you received this morning, something very much like it may have happened. And if it were the truth, it would go far to explain Mr. Smith's curious behavior of late."

"What curious behavior, pray?" Clarice enquired with a hint of a smile. She was beginning to find her brother's fantastic story and even his gravity a little amusing; it was so like a plot in a wretched melodrama.

"The two attempts on Julian's life."

"What are you talking about?" asked Clarice, surprised.

Peter looked at her with astonishment. "You should know; you were with him both times. The first was when he was thrown from his horse at Creeley Combe, and it is only a sennight yesterday that he was poisoned."

"Don't be absurd, Peter," Clarice said sharply, but at the same time she remembered the little scene she and her husband had played out in his bedchamber the morning after his illness. "They were both accidents," she said firmly, as much to convince herself as her brother. "You were the one, after all, who laughed at me for questioning Sir Walter's diagnosis."

"Yes," said Peter, still very grave. "But that was before I had a conversation with Peregrine the other day. He told me that Julian firmly believes that he was poisoned and that Mr. Smith is the culprit. Did you know that there were thistles in his saddle pad and that they were the cause of his horse's erratic behavior?"

"Yes. Julian said that it was an unfortunate accident. Why would Julian say these things to Perry and lie to me about them?"

Ignoring this, Ardane went on eagerly, warming to his theme. "Mr. Smith is so clever and efficient that not only Julian but the entire network of British intelligence is incapable of unearthing him, but when he seeks to rid himself of a sole man whom he views as a threat, he badly bungles it both times. Is that logical? I suppose Julian might have been killed when he was thrown, but surely it was more likely that he would break his leg than his damned neck; and then he is poisoned, but with so little that it only makes him sick, or perhaps the wrong poison was used. In either case, it makes Mr. Smith look like an expert fool. Is that consistent?" He paused briefly for dramatic effect. "I think Julian may have staged both attempts himself to solidify the credibility of Mr. Smith's existence, and to protect himself should any hint of his treachery ever come to light. If that is true, it frightens me a little to think to what lengths he may carry it."

Clarice stood up and began drawing on her gloves. "This is utter nonsense, Peter, brought on by those wretched letters that even you said in the beginning were moonshine. I wish I had thrown them into the fire at once. I am ashamed that I have been a party to such ideas by even listening to them. Julian may have deceived me in our marriage, but that is an entirely different matter and I cannot, will not, credit him with such abominable behavior." She took the letters which Peter had placed on a table and stuffed them into her reticule. "I made a grave mistake in bringing these letters to you. I suppose I wanted you to reassure me that they could not be true, and instead you have formed ideas which would be laughable were the matter not so deadly serious."

She was so obviously upset that Peter at once apologized. "Forgive me, Clare," he said earnestly. "There is no cause to be upset. It was all just theories, and only valid if there were any truth in those letters, which I am sure there is not." But he made a bad job of this dissembling, and Clarice knew that he believed, at least in some degree, the dreadful things he had said of her husband. She allowed him to think her mollified to get away from his house and the possibility of any further discussion on the subject.

When she returned home she was more confused and in need of advice than she had been before. Although she had defended her husband, Peter's wild imaginings had planted a doubt in her mind that refused to be entirely unseated. Despite a lifelong acquaintance and the intimacies of married life, how well could she honestly say that she knew her husband? In all that time she had never for a moment been aware that he was involved in anything like espionage; what else might she not have known about him?

It was a disheartening thought. Still, she could not reconcile the base character that Peter had described with that of the man that she loved. Julian at his best was gentle, kind, considerate, warm and loving, and generous to a fault. Even at his worst, and heaven knew she had seen enough of his darker side, he had never been the evil, bloodless creature that she had no doubt a traitor would have to be. She could never have fallen in love with a man like that.

Clarice wished with all her heart that there was someone else to whom she could turn, but even if there had been, her experience with her brother had taught her the folly of doing so. What she should have done, she realized, was put her personal feelings behind her and gone at once to Julian.

Having decided this, she still sat irresolute on the edge of her bed, staring at the two letters spread out beside her. If someone were deliberately trying to ruin Julian, it was foolish for her to try to deal with it alone. He had to know about it and take steps to protect himself. If only this hadn't happened now, after the dreadful things they had said to each other the night before, after the dreadful thing she had let him believe. Yet she had to face him, and she knew it. Refolding the letters, she got up and placed them in a concealed pocket in the folds of her morning dress.

She had no idea whether he was in the house or not, and checking the clock on the mantel, she decided it was still early enough for him to be in, perhaps changing to go out. She went immediately to his dressing room and entered it without knocking, afraid that if she did so, he might refuse to see her. Only Rodgers was there, however. He looked up from his work with polite enquiry.

"Is his lordship in his bedchamber, Rodgers?" she asked a little diffidently.

"No, my lady, he is in the study," replied the servitor.

"Oh," said Clarice lamely. She became aware that before she had interrupted him, Rodgers had been putting shirts into a travelling case.

"Are you packing, Rodgers?" she asked stupidly, not knowing what else to say.

"Yes, my lady. His lordship is leaving for Creeley immediately after luncheon." Then, taking pity on her, he added, "I believe he had a message from Lord Creeley."

Clarice sincerely doubted this, but she took her cue and

said brightly, "Has he? Then I had better see him at once. Thank you, Rodgers."

She hastened down the broad stairs to the ground floor, through the entrance hall to the back of the house, where the study was situated. Her heart was beating fast, but it was not from the exercise. Had she given him such a disgust of her last night that he could not wait to be away from her?

Once again she simply opened the door without knocking. He was sitting at his father's desk, straightening some papers and placing them in a leather pouch. He looked up when she entered, but went back to his work without speaking.

She walked up to the front of the desk and said without preamble, "I have something very important to tell you, Julian."

He was unimpressed. Without looking at her, he said coldly, "Not too important, I hope, because it will have to wait. I am leaving for Creeley within the hour, and I haven't time."

"Rodgers said you were leaving after luncheon."

"Did he tell you, then? Well, I've changed my plans. I'm leaving at once."

"He also said that there was a note from your father. Was there?"

"No."

"I see," she said despondently.

"I trust you do. However, it may be just as well that you are here. There is something that I have to say to you." He looked up at her for the first time, and what she saw in his face made her feel cold inside.

"No, please, Julian, this is too important to wait," she said urgently, and pulled out the two letters. She held them out to him, and he took them without speaking. She watched him intently as he read them both through, but he did not betray what he was thinking.

"Where did you get these?" he said at last, his voice as rigid as the gaze he turned on her.

"I found them on my breakfast tray this morning with the mail. There was no direction, and I suppose they were brought by messenger." She paused, waiting for his reply, but it didn't come. He had thrown the larger printed letter down on the desk and was carefully studying the smaller one.

"Someone is deliberately trying to ruin you, Julie," she said, unable to contain herself any longer.

He ignored this and asked, "Did you question the servants about it?"

"No. I was too surprised . . . and frightened, I suppose. Peter said it was for the best that I did not," she added without thinking. She had not meant to tell him that she had gone to Peter with them first. "He said it wouldn't do to call attention to them."

"You've discussed this with Peter?" he asked, looking up at her quickly. "I wasn't aware that he had called this morning."

Clarice reddened slightly. "He didn't. I went to see him after it came. I . . . I didn't think," she added lamely, by way of explanation. Before he would speak again, she remembered what her brother had told her and asked, "Is it true that someone *has* tried to harm you twice? Was it really poison that night?"

"Yes," he said shortly, and then asked, "Did Peter tell you that?"

"Yes. He said that Perry told him."

"Did he?" said Julian in an odd tone. "Did he advise you to bring these to me?"

"No. On the contrary, he felt that I should do nothing, but wait to see what the second message brings. Perhaps they should be taken to . . . to whoever was your superior in the government."

Julian managed to look at her and through her at the same time. "I think not," he said levelly, and got up and walked over to the low fire that had been lit to ward off the early chill of the morning. Clarice watched in horror as he stooped down and put both letters into the grate. She rushed over to him and made a grab for the letters, which were already being consumed, but he held her back.

"Are you mad, Julian?" she asked, incredulous. "We must save them. They could lead us to whoever sent them and is trying to ruin you."

"I know well enough where they came from," he replied. "I suppose I must thank you for bringing them to me, however belatedly. You may trust me to handle this in my own way."

"But surely there was no need to burn them?" she said, unconvinced.

"It is better; certainly safer," he said as he stirred the ashes in the grate, thus obliterating all traces of the paper that had burned.

Clarice rose from her crouched position, horror slowly dawning on her face. Was he admitting that it was true? Was it necessary to burn not only these letters but also the other six that were said to exist? Was it possible? She came out of her momentary reverie and realized that he was staring at her. Slowly he too stood up.

Her thoughts were mirrored clearly in her face for him to read: doubt, shock, horror, revulsion. "It doesn't signify, what you think," he said harshly. "I've done what's best for everyone. No doubt your opinion of me will be easier for you to bear when I tell you I have seen Bolt this morning. He is preparing an action against you, and I will begin it when I return from Creeley."

"An action?" asked Clarice dumbly.

"Criminal Conversation," he said brusquely, and walked back to the desk. Clarice stared stupidly after him.

He looked at her blank face. "Crim. Con., my love," he said, coldly sardonic. "It is necessary in order to obtain a bill of divorce. I am sorry for it, for both our sakes, but there is little to choose from. However, it will doubtless be a comfort to you to know that it at least is not unjust."

"You're divorcing me!" she exclaimed in horrified surprise.

It was his turn to be surprised. "Yes. Isn't that what everything has been about since I returned? You wanted to be rid of me to marry Prescott, and now you will be. I release you completely from our arrangement, you have what you wanted more than seven months earlier than you'd dared to hope for it."

She stared at him, mute in her misery, and he continued in a sneering voice, "What is it, Clare? I rather expected outright relief, if not effusive gratitude."

The floor heaved beneath her feet, and for a moment she feared she really would faint, but she deliberately shut out this new horror and forced her mind to the matter at hand.

"Julian, is that letter true?" she asked in a small voice. "Are you . . . ?" She faltered, unable to think of the right word. Traitor?

"Playing both ends against the middle?" he queried sarcastically. "No, Clarice, I am not."

"Then why did you burn those papers?"

"It was necessary."

Clarice asked what she considered an important question. "Are you going to tell . . . anyone?"

He gave her a cynical smile. "Are you afraid to ask whom I would tell? No, I am not going to tell anyone. Anyone. I would prefer it if you did the same." His tone implied that he placed no reliance on her silence. He bent over the desk, picked up the leather pouch he had placed his papers in, and left without saying another word, leaving Clarice standing numbly in the middle of the room.

14

The next several days were a nightmare for Clarice. Desperately in need of a confidante, she told her sister Anne everything that she dared about those two wretched days, leaving out only the receipt of the letters and their aftermath. Wrapped up in her own unhappiness, Clarice completely failed to foresee her sister's inevitable reaction. Anne was almost beside herself with regret for the part she had played by telling Julian of his wife's intentions, and blamed herself totally for the dissolution of their marriage. Instead of being the one consoled, Clarice discovered that she spent most of her time trying to reassure her sister and thus felt more alone and in the traces of her problems than ever.

After a day or two she gave up all pretense of keeping up appearances. She cancelled all but the most pressing of her engagements because she found being in company intolerable. The small talk and social conversation which she had always enjoyed and shone at she now found insipid, and the constant necessity of pretending that there was nothing whatever the matter in her life made her weary and dispirited.

There was also the necessity of avoiding Mr. Prescott. She knew that she owed it to him to tell him to his face that it was over forever between them, whatever became of her marriage to Julian, but with the weight of her troubles upon her, she could not bring herself to the sticking point of seeking him out. As the days passed and he made no effort to see her either, Clarice decided that his feelings must coincide with hers, and though she knew that if Julian persisted in his plan to divorce her and name John Prescott as co-respondent, she would have to speak with him eventually, she was glad enough to put it off until it was absolutely necessary.

The person who was not as easy to avoid or put off was her brother. Nearly every day he called to discover if she had heard any more from the would-be blackmailer, and his curiosity over Julian's sudden departure was unbounded. At first he had suspected that it was because Clarice had shown Julian the letters, but stung by Julian's obvious lack of faith in her discretion, she deliberately lied to Peter and told him that she had not. When he asked to see them again, she told him that she had burned them herself, and to her relief, after only the mildest protest he accepted it, obviously believing that it was a thing a frightened woman who saw her husband threatened would do.

Clarice did not inform him of the rift in her marriage, and as far as she knew, he was ignorant of the events that had led up to it. She had sworn Anne to secrecy and trusted her implicitly, so at least she was spared the necessity of discussing that with him. Nevertheless, putting on for him the mask she wore for acquaintances and strangers was wearing, and she was glad that his visits were short and that he accepted her reasons for not going out without question.

Clarice vacillated constantly between the belief that Julian had betrayed his guilt by his actions in the study, and the conviction that he was completely innocent. Even these desperate thoughts took second place, though, to her concern for the future, if any, of her marriage.

In spite of his presumed infidelity, in spite of the bitter things he had said to her, in spite of the possibility that he might have been a traitor, Clarice could not help loving him. She didn't even try. She determined that the moment he came back from Creeley she would make him listen to her and convince him that she had not played him false. He was hurt, as she had been, but she didn't believe that his love for her could be destroyed any more easily than hers for him could be. She was fully aware that in doing this she might be returning to the humiliating unhappiness that had once been her lot, but she also knew that she would never forgive herself if she didn't at least try one more time to make her marriage a success. So fierce was her resolve that he would listen to her and give up his plan to divorce her that she was able to bear her lonely days with something like calm.

Still, there were those inevitable times when a listless depression came over her and everything seemed impossibly black to her again. It was on just such a day, a week after Julian's departure, that she sat in a huge leather chair in the very room where she had had her last interview with her husband.

She started a little guiltily when the door opened and Moreton came into the room. She hastily picked up her unopened book and made a pretense of being engrossed in it. Even on her worst days, she was not yet ready to give up hope in front of the servants.

"Yes, Moreton, what is it?" she asked when the butler stopped by her chair.

"It is Lord Ardane, my lady. I told him that your instructions were that you wished to see no one, but he insists." Here he gave a discreet cough. "He says it is of the utmost urgency, my lady."

Clarice had to check herself to keep from making a vexed exclamation. She did not at all want to see her brother, but she knew quite well that Peter was not above making a small scene if he wanted to get his way. "Oh, very well," she said with an assumption of carelessness. "Have him come here."

Peter came into the room so shortly after Moreton had quitted it that Clarice suspected he had been halfway down the hall when the servant had told him she would see him.

"Really, Peter!" she said, exasperated. "I told Moreton that I wasn't at home to anyone because I have the headache and wish to be alone."

"Do you?" asked her brother. "Well, I am sorry for it, for what I have to tell you is not likely to make you feel any better. I'm sorry, Clare, it seems that we have more unpleasantness to discuss."

"Having put me in a state of nervous suspense, you had best tell me your news at once," Clarice said caustically. "At least it can't be that my husband is back from the dead this time."

"Oh, can't it?" said Peter gloomily. "I can tell you that he is back from Creeley, if he ever went there at all."

"What do you mean?" asked Clarice sharply. "Of course he went to Creeley. I saw him leave, and if he were back I would certainly know it. I haven't left the house all day."

Peter shook his head. "He's at your old house."

"On Curzon Street?"

A servant came in at that point with brandy that Peter had requested from Moreton, and conversation was necessarily suspended. When the servant left, Clarice said impatiently,

"The house on Curzon Street is closed up. It is totally under holland covers. Why would he go there?"

"That's exactly what I came here to ask you," said her brother. "Have you decided to separate after all?"

"I don't know," answered Clarice in a numb voice. At her brother's exclamation she knew she would have to confide in him.

"Is he, damn him!" said Ardane with much surprise when Clarice had told him of Julian's plan to divorce her. "Well, it's what you've always wanted. You may have trouble fixing your interest again with Prescott, though, after the damn fool way you've behaved; especially if the rumors I've heard are true."

"What rumors?" asked Clarice unhappily but without real interest.

"I've heard that Prescott's staying with friends in Devonshire and is courting an heiress in the neighborhood. I don't know if it's true or not, but I haven't seen him about town lately," he replied.

"It doesn't matter about him," she told her brother with perfect truth. With a touch of surprise she realized that not even her pride felt wounded. If she felt anything at all, it was annoyance that she had wasted so much time avoiding him to no purpose. John Prescott had certainly wasted no time, and as far as Clarice was concerned, the Devonshire heiress was welcome to him.

"Doesn't matter!" Peter sighed with disgust. He drank his brandy and poured himself another. "If that isn't just like a woman. Carrying on that she wants things one way, and then, when she gets it, hey presto! she's changed her mind. I'm mortified to think I've such a bird-wit for a sister."

Clarice had no intention of being drawn into an argument of personalities. "You haven't told me how you know that Julian is in town. Have you spoken to him?" she asked, calling him to mind of the purpose of his visit.

"No, I saw him through the window of the morning room," he answered. "I suppose I'd better begin at the beginning. Yesterday I happened to be passing the house when I saw a man who I thought looked like Simon Rodgers going around the back of it. I knew he had gone to Creeley with Julian, so just out of curiosity I, too, went around the back of the house and knocked at the service door. There was no answer, so I went around the front again, but the knocker was still off.

"It puzzled me, of course, but I didn't make a lot of it. Julie might have sent him to town on an errand and he might not have heard me knock, but I kept thinking of it, and today I decided to go back and have another look. I knocked as before, but still got no answer. I looked in the windows on the ground floor, and in the morning room I saw that several pieces had been uncovered, and while I was actually standing there, Julian himself walked into the room. I was so surprised that I didn't even think to rap at the window, and in a moment he was gone. Well, I finally found my wits, and after that, nothing would hold me. I all but brought the house down at every door and window I could reach.

"Let me tell you, my girl," he continued, "there is no way in the world that anyone in that house wouldn't have heard me. They didn't choose to hear me. There had to be something damned havey-cavey going on, so I came straight over here to see if you knew about it."

Though Clarice was able to assure her brother that she knew nothing at all about Julian's presence in London, she was nearly certain that she knew the reason for it. She believed that Julian, returned from Creeley, where he had no doubt gone to warn his parents of the coming scandal and disgrace which the Crim. Con. action and subsequent divorce would bring, had wanted privacy to conduct the matter with Mr. Bolt, and had not wanted the embarrassment of her presence. No doubt in a day or two she would receive a formal notice from the solicitor informing her of the action being taken against her, and advising her to quit Creeley House. Julian did not even intend to see her again. Sadly she told her brother her theory.

"So, that's that," he said baldly.

"No, Peter, it can't be," she said in a voice that was almost a sob. "I've got to stop it from happening."

Peter shrugged. "If what you think is true, I don't see what you're going to be able to do about it until it's too late. Once the thing becomes public, my guess is that there'll be no stopping it."

"I know," she replied in near despair. "But I'd hoped . . . Peter, could you talk to him for me? Now, before it goes any further. Tell him that I still love him and want to be his wife again. Ask him to see me, even if only for a few moments."

"You're addled, dear sister," he said bluntly. "I have just finished telling you that I couldn't beat my way into that house."

Clarice bit at her lower lip in thought. "You could wait outside until he or Rodgers come out. If you actually confronted him, he couldn't very well pretend not to be there."

"Ho!" grunted her brother. "I've nothing better to do with my time than lurk about that house for God knows how long waiting for my chance."

She considered this. "No, I suppose that won't do. But there must be some way." She looked at him reproachfully, as though she expected an answer from him.

Peter shook his head slowly. "No you don't, old girl. The only thing that is going to open the door to that house is a key. If you're thinking of anything mad like breaking in . . ." Her face had brightened, and he stopped, fearing the worst.

"Of course! Why didn't I think of it before!" she cried.

"No, Clare. I absolutely will not—"

"Oh, don't be stupid!" she interrupted. "I don't mean for you to break into the house. I doubt you could contrive it," she added a little nastily. "I have a key. Don't you remember? You were there when Julian gave it to me so that I could go over to the house to see about the draperies and hangings."

"By Jove, yes, I do remember." His face fell suddenly. "I don't know that it's much better than housebreaking, though. I mean, I let myself in with the key and then roam about the place until I find someone. Deuced awkward when I do."

"Oh, what is that to anything?" Clarice said impatiently. "If you will not go, I shall have to, and I'd rather not; not until you've spoken with him. It would be so much easier if you would do it, Peter."

"Well, I suppose it would be, at that," he admitted. He thought for a moment. "I can't say I like it, Clare, but I'll do it."

Clarice hugged him and then left to get the key from her sitting room. When she returned, he pocketed it with the admonition that she not get her hopes up too high.

"First off, he might not be there now, and second, it's possible that he won't listen to me."

Clarice nodded unhappily. "I'd thought of that; but surely he will. He wanted so much for us to be together again."

Ardane knew how much she wanted him to encourage her, but he simply said, "I hope you may be right."

Clarice knew that she could not reasonably expect her brother to return to her within the hour, so she determined to keep herself busy and thus keep her anticipation and fears at bay. When the time for dinner came and went, and she still had not heard from him, she sent a message to his house and was informed that Lord and Lady Ardane were both out for the evening and were not expected to return until late. Clarice waited up until an advanced hour of the morning, hoping that Peter would come to her before he went home, but eventually weariness claimed her and she fell into a restless sleep.

After breakfast there was still no word from her brother, and Clarice's impatience pricked at her mercilessly. She called for her town carriage and returned to her room to change for the streets, determined to find her brother and discover his news. Anything—the information that he had not gone there yet, that he had not found Julian there, or even that Julian had refused to listen to him—was preferable to this interminable waiting. She was even willing to sit with her sister-in-law if necessary and listen to her envious complaints and inconsequential chatter if at the end of it Peter had anything to say to her.

Dressed in a very becoming dark gray-and-green-plaid carriage dress, she was just setting the smart hat that matched it at a jaunty angle on her dark curls when a footman arrived to tell her that Lord Ardane was awaiting her in the library. Clarice whisked past the surprised footman and risked her neck running down the stairs two at a time.

As soon as she entered the room, she began to reproach Peter for keeping her in such a fret, but the grim expression on his face soon halted this flow, which had stemmed from her anxiety, and replaced it with silence.

"What is it?" she brought out at last. "He wouldn't listen to you. That's it, isn't it?"

"Not exactly. You'd better sit down, Clare." He suited his actions to his words and gently pushed her into a chair. "I haven't come any sooner because there was nothing to tell until now. I went to the house yesterday after I left here, but no one was there. I waited for a time and then gave it up. I meant to go back after dinner, but in the end I couldn't manage it. I wish to hell that I had!" he added vehemently, making Clarice's heart beat faster.

He took a folded piece of cream-colored paper out of his pocket and continued, "I went there as soon as I could after breakfast this morning, about an hour ago in fact. I'd hoped that by being early I couldn't fail to see him. I found this instead." He turned the paper over in his hand and unfolded it. "It's addressed to you, but I took the liberty of reading it, I hope you don't mind. It wasn't sealed, and I thought perhaps it might lead me to discover his intentions. It certainly did that," he added with heavy irony. "I'm sorry, Clare." He took a step nearer to her and handed her the paper. Clarice took it from him with fingers that trembled and began to read.

My dearest wife,

Though I use the term loosely, for there is little that is dear between us now, and you are my wife in only the legal sense of the word. Your actions of the other night have brought home to me, far more clearly than any words could have done, that since I have returned we have been acting out an elaborate farce. I apologize. My first mistake in this, my role, if you will, was being fool enough to suppose that I could have things as they had been four years ago. My second mistake, and perhaps even more unforgivable, was imagining that I could change myself into the sort of husband that you could accept. As that was impossible—it always has been—and we could neither of us accept the other as we are, I am now taking steps to remedy those wrongs and, in keeping with the metaphor, bring down the curtain.

I am leaving, the moment I finish this, for Southampton and thence for America. We would both now be in a far better state if I had let you go on thinking that I was dead. My return was folly from start to finish. I hadn't meant to leave quite so abruptly, but my affairs are now in order and I choose to go before your brother (at your instigation?) corners me at last. Also, it would not be out of keeping to mention here that you need no longer concern yourself with our blackmailer. He has permanently retired from his dishonorable career. Considering that this is the last communication that I shall have with you, I feel almost compelled to extend my love or at least my affection, but I am not so great a hypocrite. Instead I shall be generous and wish you and Prescott well.

Yr. obedient servant,
R.

It was a cruel letter, a heartless letter, calculated to cut. Clarice read it again as though in doing so she could somehow change the words that were written there. She let her hands and the paper fall into her lap and looked up at her brother; but the only thing she saw was the empty, stretching years that lay ahead of her, denied what she had too late discovered was the one thing in the world that she truly coveted.

"I cannot bear it," she whispered with an anguish that went beyond tears.

"Well, I can understand that. It'll be damned hard to live down being deserted twice by the same man," he said, deliberately misunderstanding. "I hate to say I told you so, but I did, you know."

Clarice continued to stare as though she hadn't heard him, as indeed she scarcely had, and Peter took the letter from her nerveless fingers. He read it over again.

"Why the devil did you lie to me about giving him those letters?" he asked reprovingly. "You did tell him, didn't you? I can't see how else he could have known."

Clarice nodded mutely.

"Dammit, Clare, I warned you about that. Told you, didn't I, to sit back and wait. If you're unhappy, it's your own fault. When he realized that the game was up, he used your differences as a convenient excuse to get away before the whole thing broke over his head. Even you can't believe in his innocence now, can you?" When she didn't answer, he repeated his question.

"I'm sorry, Peter, I didn't hear you," she apologized, reluctantly breaking her train of thought.

"I said that you could hardly believe him innocent now," he repeated impatiently. "It wasn't what he believed of you and Prescott that made him leave, it was those letters that you gave him. What excuse did he offer when he saw them?"

"He burned them," Clarice replied absently.

"Dammit, Clare!" he said, smacking his fist down on a small table and causing the articles on it to jump. "I wish you'd told me this yesterday. You let me waltz into an empty house to go after a desperate man who, for all we know, has killed to cover his tracks."

"I will never believe that," Clarice said firmly, looking up at her brother.

Peter threw up his hands in exasperation. "I don't believe it! What more proof do you want? If it is only Prescott, why should he leave? Why not just divorce you as he said he would? The truth is plain. He doesn't dare stay to see it out."

"What would he have to fear?" she replied deliberately. "If you are right, if he has rid himself of Mme. Rouane and the blackmailer, if there is no Mr. Smith? He would not expect me to betray him. Or you."

"Me! You told him that I know?" With a groan Peter sank into a chair. "And I walked all over that great barn of a house without a care in the world! I suppose I should count my blessings that I did not share the end of Therese and our ineffectual blackmailer."

"I will not believe it of him," Clarice repeated doggedly.

"You'd better believe it," Peter said dryly. "This is no time to let past affections color your judgment." He sighed and stood up again. "There's only one thing to do. It won't be long before we have to let it come out that he's gone again, and who knows? Maybe the truth will come out. It will be better for you to be out of London when it comes. I was thinking on the way over here that it would be best for you to go to Lodin. I'll send Lyddy and the children after you and join you myself in a few days. I have a few things I have to take care of before I can get away."

"Peter—" she began, but he interrupted her.

"You can send to Creeley for Julia and the boys; it will be best, I think, if you have actual possession of them in case the Creeleys make any difficulties. If you pack now, you can be there by dark tomorrow, with only one night on the road."

"No, Peter," she said calmly and quite distinctly. "I know what I have to do. I am going to him. If there is any chance that I can see him before he leaves, I am going to take it." She got up and pulled the bell beside the mantel.

"What?" gasped Peter, incredulous. "Have you run mad?"

Before Clarice could reply, a footman answered her summons and Clarice told him to have the light travelling carriage readied and brought around in half an hour. When he bowed himself out of the room, Clarice prepared to follow him.

"Wait!" Peter shouted. "What the devil do you think you're doing?"

Clarice turned, her hand on the door. "I told you," she said in the same cool, calm voice as before. "I am going to Southampton to see Julian before he leaves, if I can get there in time." She turned again and walked out of the room.

Peter realized that short of dragging her physically back into the room he had little choice but to follow her. He caught up with her in her bedchamber and grabbed her arm roughly. "I think that letter of his must have disordered your brain," he said in a voice filled with amazement. "Don't you realize the danger you'll be putting yourself in? What do you hope to accomplish? Do you think you have any chance of convincing him that he is safe and should stay?"

Clarice pulled her arm out of his grasp and absently massaged the place where he had held her. "I don't for a moment believe that I am in any danger from him. I cannot, *cannot*, allow him to leave without speaking to him first. If there is any chance at all that I can persuade him to stay, I intend to try."

"And if you can't? What then, Clare?" he countered. "Are you going to abandon your children? Spend the rest of your life running all over the world with him? A fugitive?"

"Of course not," she answered coldly. "If I cannot convince him, if there is any chance at all that I am wrong and you are right . . . at least he will leave knowing that I love him and never betrayed him. With or to anyone." She turned her back on him, and going to the multiple glass doors of her wardrobe, drew them open and began hastily drawing out things that she felt would be necessary for her journey.

"Clare—" he began again.

"No, Peter," she forestalled him. "This may be the last chance I shall ever have of seeing him again. I will not let it pass. You need have no concern for my welfare."

At that moment Eddly came in, and with a gesture of disgust Peter left the room and went back to the library. He poured himself a rather stiff amount of brandy and drank it down with surprising speed and imprudence. He was about to repeat this action when he thought better of it and replaced the stopper on the decanter. He returned upstairs to stand in the hall across from the door of his sister's bedchamber. After a footman, carrying a portmanteau and accompanied by Eddly, who gave him instructions as they walked, came out of the room, Peter went in and shut the door with a bang.

Clarice looked up. "Go away, Peter," she said in an exasperated voice. "You are wasting your time, and more to the point, my time."

"I have no intention of letting you go on a mad chase after a man we both know to be a liar, a traitor, and probably a murderer," he said implacably.

"I don't know that he is any of those things," she replied coolly as she picked up several small items from her dressing table and tossed them into her reticule.

"Because you don't choose to know." He came up very close behind her. "This insane start of yours is not only dangerous, it is probably a fool's errand. As far as we know, he left last night and the odds are that he will be gone before you can get there. If he ever meant to go there at all," he added.

Clarice turned to him and said frostily, "He said that he was going there. There was no need to mention it if he was not."

"Don't be so damned naive, girl," Ardane replied waspishly. "Would a dangerous man like Rown take chances? There was, indeed, no reason to mention it. He probably put it in on the chance that should anyone try to follow him, they would be put off his scent."

The scorn in Clarice's expression showed what she thought of that idea. "If he has," she said coldly, "I shall discover it soon enough."

She pushed past him and he took hold of her wrist. At that moment there was a discreet knock at the door and at Clarice's bidding it opened and a footman entered to tell her that the carriage was at the door. Peter made a small exclamation of annoyance and dropped her hand.

Clarice thanked the footman and went out of the room,

leaving her brother standing amid the shambles of a hasty packing. In disgust and frustration Peter glanced about the room until his eyes fell on a small and, to his mind, sickeningly bucolic shepherdess figurine. He picked it up off the table on which it rested and dashed it to pieces against the hearth, unaware that Eddly, who was not accompanying her mistress, had reentered the room. He turned to catch her disapproving eye and cast her a look of such undisguised fury that the dresser's mouth fell open in surprise. He pushed her roughly out of his way and quitted the room and the house.

15

The light outside was fading fast and objects in the small, cramped room were beginning to lose their form and take on a shadowy appearance. Julian, sitting on a chair just out of sight of the room's single window, took out his watch and squinted to discern the time; it was extremely difficult, and he barely managed it.

"It's time you were leaving," he told Rodgers, who stood several feet away from him. From this position, he, like his master, could see out the window without being seen from the outside.

"I don't like it, my lord," observed Rodgers in a tone of voice that suggested it was an often repeated statement. "I think I should stay."

"And I think the time for that argument has passed. You'd better leave."

Rodgers shifted his weight from one foot to the other, the only sign he gave of his restlessness. "What if things don't happen as you expect?"

Julian permitted himself a half-smile. "Then we have nothing to worry about."

"That isn't what I mean."

"I know what you mean. Go, Simon, it will be fully dark soon."

With a disgruntled sigh, indicative of acquiescence, Rodgers turned and walked to the door. As he opened it, he paused and said, "One hour past dark, my lord. Not a moment more." He received no reply, but then, he hadn't expected one. He left.

For some time Julian continued where he was, listening until the sounds of his companion's departure had ceased. He waited until darkness surrounded him and he felt certain that his eyes were fully adjusted to it, and then he left the small room and went up the service stairs to the main part of the house.

He moved cautiously and quietly, but steadily and without hesitation, toward a pair of large double doors leading into a room on the ground floor. He had just reached for the handles when a minute sound from the front of the house checked him. He smiled with grim satisfaction, opened the door soundlessly, and went into the room. Just as silently he closed them again. He glanced around the room. The moon had just risen and it was flooded with moonlight from the two enormous windows from which the thick draperies had been drawn back. He crossed the room quickly toward the door of an adjoining room, entered, and again closed the door after him, but this time not completely. He left it just slightly ajar. He then felt for the table beside him and the loaded pistol he had placed there earlier in the day. He waited.

The person who had entered the house took no pains to hide his presence. Julian heard footsteps approach the room he had just left, and the doors open and shut. A man passed him, not noticing the crack in the door Julian stood behind. The bright moonlight revealed precisely the person Julian had expected to see. He waited.

There was the sound of the draperies being drawn shut, more footsteps, and then the scrape of a tinderbox. Bright light flared for a moment and then settled into a steady dim glow, that of a single candle. Julian opened the crack in the door wider, in time to see the other man seat himself at a small writing desk at the opposite end of the room, pull out papers from a side drawer, and begin to mend a pen. Julian carefully let himself into the room, taking care that his pistol was in clear sight.

"Good evening, Mr. Smith," he said softly.

The effect on the man at the desk was as though he had shouted. Ardane stood up abruptly, whirled to face him, and then instinctively reached toward the desk behind him. He checked the movement as he saw Julian's pistol. He collected himself and said in a voice as soft as the other had used, "Is that you, Julie? Come into the light where I can see you. Yes, that's better," he added as his cousin complied. "Do you really think there is a need for firearms between brothers? I had thought you more clever than this."

"As I had you, Peter. For a man of your resources—incidentally, I do compliment you on your resourcefulness—to fall so handily into my trap was almost more than I had dared hope. You've become greedy, Peter, and impatient."

Peter shrugged unconcernedly. "It was a bit overconfident of me to suppose that you had gone off again so conveniently, but then, I saw you leave yesterday."

"Yes," said Julian with a humorless smile. "And had me followed. To be abducted and . . . shall we say, silenced, at your leisure. Do I have that correctly, Peter? Never mind. I'm sure it is close enough to the truth. It is the greatest pity that the depth of your pocket does not equal the deviousness of your mind. Fortunately, mine does. The report you had of me this morning from your man was quite expensive; however, as you see, it has been worth it."

Ardane darted quick glances about the room, seeking a means of diversion, always returning his gaze, not to his brother-in-law's face but to the pistol he held in his hand. He could physically feel the presence of his own pistol on the desk behind him, and his fingers itched to touch it, but common sense prevailed. He was almost certain that Julian did not know of its existence, or at least its proximity, and that was ace enough to hold for now.

"The depth of your pocket brought you no succor four years ago," he sneered.

"Due indirectly to the shallowness of yours," Julian replied. He sighed wearily. "You really are the greatest fool in England, Peter. Why didn't you leave it alone? If I had had proof and meant to use it, I would have done so four years ago. You had nothing to fear from me. I tried to make that plain to you on that first night."

"And let you get away with being a traitor? I think not," he said with a fine show of outrage. "I now know you for what you are, and so does Clarice."

"You mean you've poisoned her mind against me," said Julian icily. "More effectively, I might add, than your attempt to poison me. Not that I believe that you meant me to die; an enquiry would hardly have suited you. You wanted to force my hand, Peter, and you have. Do the results please you?"

"I wanted you exposed for what you are," sneered Ardane.

"Is that for the benefit of whoever you think might be listening? Rest assured, we are completely alone. If it can be helped, if you are sensible, there is no need for anyone to share in your disgrace." Peter laughed shortly and Julian continued, "Don't be a fool, man. It may have been my clear duty to unmask you four years ago, but you know well enough why I did not. Nothing has changed. It is time we understood one another."

Peter laughed again and addressed his cousin with a series of expletives that were as obscene as they were descriptive. "Well, unburden your heart, damn you," he added. "I'm quite agog to hear what you've concocted."

With a slight sardonic smile, Julian obliged. "You are going to sit down again and write out a complete confession of all that you have done, and give it to me. You will then collect Lydia and your children and leave the country. I don't very much care where you go or what excuse you give for doing so, but it will be at once, and you will not come back. As long as you abide by these terms, you have my word that your treachery will never come to light through me."

"Your word!" Peter sneered. "And no doubt you will take mine that I will do so. I have always known that you were a weak fool, Julian. You'd best pull that trigger while you have the chance."

"I'm afraid I cannot bring myself to bloodletting as easily as you do," replied his cousin, unperturbed. "But don't you be the fool and make the mistake of believing that I will not if you force me to it."

Peter smiled slowly. "I should have killed you that first night when I found you like a specter in my bookroom. Everyone already believed you were dead. Perhaps I am the fool," he added in a self-mocking tone, seeking to deliberately digress. He knew that the longer he could keep Julian talking, the greater was the chance that some diversion would present itself to him, or that his cousin would make a mistake and give him the opportunity he needed to reach behind him for his pistol.

"With your butler and no doubt your entire household avid with curiosity about me, and unsure that no one else knew that I was back, you didn't dare," replied Julian, unwittingly playing into Peter's hands. "Besides, I was armed and you were not."

"Yes, I thought you might have been," said Ardane. "You aren't a complete fool, after all. Then you should have shot me. It would have saved us both a good deal of trouble. But not you. Not Julian the Good, Julian the Perfect." He raised his hands slightly in one of his characteristic gestures and brought them down again, this time ever so slightly behind him. "All these years, all my life, I've watched you, petted and sought after," he went on with biting contempt. "A rich man's cosseted heir who could do no wrong; buying friends and influence with your damned money. Even my own damn sister! It's easy for you to be self-righteous, isn't it? What have you ever known about tradesmen hounding you or not being able to go to Watier's with your friends because the play was too deep for you? When did your wife ever crave a trinket that you couldn't give her? When did she ever stay home from a ball that all her friends were going to rather than wear a gown that everyone had already seen a half-dozen times? Clare always had everything money could buy, didn't she? But what price did she pay for it? She knew what you were, but like a damn fool, she took you back every time."

His breathing had quickened, and he paused for breath. A cold smile spread over his features. "But not this time. This time her eyes are open and you've lost her forever. Nothing you can say or do will bring her back to you. Nothing you can do to me. So you see, that is just what it has all been for, nothing. You've sold out your honor and your country for nothing. You should have exposed me back then, Julie, or else stayed dead."

Julian listened calmly to this embittered speech, unsurprised by the violence with which it was delivered. Even when they had been closer as boys together, he had always been aware of Ardane's envy of him. Only the last reference to Clarice had affected him. "Where is Clarice?" he asked carefully.

"Out of your hands forever," spat Ardane. "No doubt by now she is in the arms, probably the bed, of Prescott. You'll never win her back, even if you still want her."

Julian relaxed perceptibly. "That I know for a lie. Prescott is in Devonshire courting a squinting heiress his mother has dug up for him."

Peter snorted. "You are behind the times, coz. Clare went after him. Do you think the squinting heiress had a chance against the charms of your beautiful wife? Especially since Prescott has already so liberally tasted of them. Damme, how

I laughed when she told me she'd given you your horns. That must have been quite a blow to your vanity, Clarice preferring the bed of her gentleman farmer to yours. I think I would have given almost anything to have seen your face that night."

Julian's breath began to quicken as well, as anger slowly overtook him. He understood perfectly that Peter was deliberately baiting him to catch him off his guard, but that spot on his pride, on his heart, was too sensitive for touch. He repeated with a calmness that cost him dearly, "Where is Clarice?"

But he had allowed himself to be more distracted than he realized. His agitation had been quickly checked, but Ardane, purposefully arousing it and closely on the watch for it, had used that moment to quickly snatch up the pistol behind him, and he now stood almost at his ease with his right hand, and the pistol it contained, slightly hidden in the tail of his coat. "She's gone, coz," he replied silkily. "Gone forever. Out of your hands, out of mine. My lovely sister was too clever by half, and she didn't have your nobility of spirit—which to my mind is just squeamishness—and meant to ruin me. I didn't have much taste for it, but I had no choice."

"I can't believe that, even of you," Julian said in a taut voice. "But if it's true, you're dead."

Peter laughed maliciously. "It is you who are dead!" His hand clutching the pistol flew from behind him and instantly fired. It happened so quickly, so unexpectedly, that Julian, without even a moment to curse himself for his laxness in letting down his guard, was forced to return fire.

The candle flame stirred, flickered, and almost went out in the draft caused by Peter's sudden movement. When the light was once again steady, only one man stood.

Ardane crossed the short distance to the inert form of his cousin and bent down to retrieve Julian's gun.

Clarice had instructed her coachman to spring the horses, although a day or two of intermittent storms had left the roads in deplorable condition, and now she was paying for this piece of folly. She held on to the straps, but even so she was tossed violently about the interior of the travelling carriage. It was luxuriously appointed with dark blue velvet squabs, but these were small comfort against holes in the road that threatened to loosen the wheels.

The jostling began to ease a bit as the carriage slowed in approach to an innyard to change the lathered horses. The coachman, aware of her ladyship's desire for haste, began to yell to the ostlers even before the carriage had come to a stop, but to his surprise, Lady Rown pushed down the window and asked that the steps be let down.

Clarice had decided after the last perfectly awful stretch of road that a moment of rest and a chance to stretch her legs and ease her battered bones would stand her in better stead for the search she would have to make when she reached Southampton than the few added minutes she would gain by going on directly. As it was, she was fairly pleased with the progress they had made. They would manage the coast easily before dark.

The landlord of the luxurious establishment catering to the quality was inclined to look askance at a young woman travelling with only the protection of male servants, but the obvious elegance and quality of both the lady and her crested equipage allayed his doubts, and the coachman, overheard addressing her as "my lady," put his concern to rest.

Clarice was immediately shown into a small, comfortable oak-panelled parlor, and her request for lemonade and biscuits was seen to with appropriate haste. She went at once to a mirror that hung on a wall near a window that faced onto the courtyard and removed her bonnet. What she saw caused her to giggle for the first time that grim day. What a fright I look, she thought, and wondered that the landlord had not sent her away. She set about tidying her hair, and when the maid entered with her refreshment, requested to be shown to a room where she might wash up before she began her light repast.

After she had eaten, she found it difficult to leave the luxury of comfortable seating to return to her bouncing ride. As much from habit as for an excuse for delay, she pulled Julian's brief letter out of her reticule and unfolded it. It was badly creased and even slightly torn in one spot, so many times had this action been repeated during her journey. She read it over again, though she already knew the words by heart. It troubled her immensely, and not just because of its cold cruelty or the fact that it announced his intention of leaving her again.

She reluctantly agreed with her brother that Julian would not be leaving the country merely to bring their life together to an end. He would have simply divorced her as he had said he would. Did that mean that Peter could be right? She was unable to accept this as the only logical answer, and perhaps because of this she was inclined to doubt the letter itself.

It seemed to her that the letter was not so much written in her husband's style as in parody of it. She had stared and strained her eyes looking at the writing until her head ached, but there was nothing in the bold strokes of the pen to convince her that it had been written by any other hand than his.

Reluctantly she folded the letter again after another unsuccessful perusal, stood up, and reached for her reticule, which she had left perched precariously on the edge of the table. As she did so, its balance was overset and she made a quick grab for it and caught at the bottom of it, succeeding in overturning it completely. The contents spilled out and scattered over the broad-planked floor. With an unladylike exclamation, Clarice stooped down to retrieve the small items which had gone this way and that, and began stuffing them back in her reticule in a jumble.

She took a step back to reach an item which had rolled under her skirts, and in doing so, unearthed a crumpled piece of paper. She was about to stuff the paper into her reticule when on impulse she smoothed it out and read it. It was a brief note from her husband written on his solicitor's stationery, informing her that he was detained and requesting that dinner be set back to accommodate him. She remembered quite well that she herself had been late returning that day several weeks ago, and she had arrived home at almost the same moment that the message had been delivered. She had read it in the hall, stuffed it into this very reticule, and then completely forgotten its existence. She crumpled it again and threw it into the grate.

Clarice stood up and took a quick survey about the floor to be certain she had missed nothing and then picked up Julian's letter again to put in her reticule. As she did so, a sudden idea, born of desperation, occurred to her. She went to the grate, thankful that the warmth of the day had not made a fire necessary, and picked up the paper she had thrown there.

She smoothed it out and carried it back to the table, where she took out and unfolded Julian's letter. She placed them side by side and sat down again.

After a few minutes she sighed unhappily; as far as she could tell, the same hand had penned both. She knew she was clutching at straws, but she continued staring at one and then at the other, comparing letters, and when she could, words. It began to seem to her, finally, that there were slight differences. The general slant of the *l*'s was not quite the same, and the loops of the *e*'s were for the most part narrower in one than in the other. Not, of course, that either specimen was totally consistent, but each showed a definite trend in the forming of the letters, and with a cry of triumph Clarice realized that the trend appeared to be different in each.

She was hardly an expert at handwriting, and she knew that the minute differences she perceived might mean nothing more than that one had been written with more haste than the other, but she now believed that it was just possible that the letter that Peter had found at the Curzon Street house was a forgery, for she could not, for even a moment, doubt the authenticity of the note she had found in her reticule.

If it was a forgery, then she could not believe anything that the letter said. Julian was not leaving her and the country, was probably not even in Southampton, but still in town. But who had written it if Julian had not? The would-be blackmailer who had written the other letter as well? How could such a person be conversant with the intimate details of her relationship with her husband? She pressed her fingers to her eyes and willed herself to reason calmly. She had to put together the pieces of this nightmare and make sense of them.

16

Lord Ardane kicked over the body of his cousin and surveyed it with satisfaction. A thin trickle of blood ran down the side of Julian's face, and when Peter saw it, he smiled and congratulated himself on his marksmanship under pressure. "Your riches didn't come to your aid this time, did they, coz?" he said aloud, and laughed again. He went back to the desk and examined the bullet hole in the wall behind it. He whistled under his breath as he realized that it had been a near miss. Well, Julian had always been a good shot, too, and for a few minutes he amused himself with the fantasy of he and Julian having managed to shoot each other and being found, both dead, in an empty house and with no explanation.

Ardane tossed up the tails of his coat and sat down again. He finished the task of mending his pen that Julian had interrupted and then went through the papers that he had pulled out of the drawer; papers that he had observed his cousin placing there on the previous morning, almost exactly as he had reported to Clarice.

As he had suspected, they were mostly legal documents, and several contained Julian's full signature, which pleased him very much. Up until now he had not dared to go beyond duplicating the distinctive initial signature of his cousin, because it was the only specimen he possessed, and he knew quite well that nothing would give away a forgery like a questionable signature. He opened another drawer and found some blank paper and proceeded to copy the signature for several minutes until he was quite satisfied with the result. He folded that paper along with one that had Julian's full name written out, put them into his pocket, put the rest back into the drawer, and stood up. He consulted his watch and walked over to where Julian lay stretched out on the floor. Even in the dim light he could tell that Julian had not moved. He bent to feel for the wound, but a faint sound in another part of the house reached his ears, and he checked the movement.

He had no reason to doubt Julian's statement that they had been completely alone, and surely the retort of the pistols would have brought anyone else concealed in the house immediately to Julian's aid. He supposed that the sound he had heard might be his imagination. An empty house set back from the street was uncommonly quiet, and even the natural sounds of settling and creaking floorboards could be deceptive. Peter cursed softly. He had much to do yet before this night was out, and he could afford no distractions. Especially, he thought, at this compromising moment. He reached into his pocket and took out a small sack; he reloaded his pistol and was pleased with himself for his forethought.

Ardane unbuttoned the front of his double-breasted coat, placed the freshly loaded pistol against his breast, and rebuttoned it partway. He left the room, carefully and silently closing the door behind him, and went out into the hall. He stood very still, ears pricked for any sound, and was almost instantly rewarded. He moved forward cautiously in the direction of the sound, and quickly found himself in the main front hall. The moonlight streaming in from the windows framing the door revealed no one. He was about to take a step backwards into the shadow of the side hall when a movement beside him caused him to wheel about. Instantly his hand went to his breast and closed about the butt of his pistol, but then he relaxed a little. Beside him stood Mr. Peregrine Rown, looking at him with as much surprise as he was sure his own expression registered. It would have been the work of a moment to dispatch Peregrine as he had his brother, but Ardane's successful treachery was based on his ability to think well quickly. Perry, too, carried a weapon, but it was not aimed at him. Clearly whatever the reason for his presence in the house, the quarry Peregrine sought was not him. Killing Peregrine would have added a complication to his plans that he had no wish to add. He knew it might still prove necessary, but if it was at all possible to avoid it, he meant to.

"What the devil are you doing here?" asked Peregrine in a hoarse whisper.

"The same thing you are," replied Peter. "Looking for Julian." It was a shrewd guess and a risk, but it paid off.

Peregrine knit his brow. "Rodgers told me that Julie was here and might be in trouble, but he didn't mention that you'd be here."

"He doesn't know. If it comes to that, I had no idea *you'd* be here," retorted Peter.

"What the devil is going on?" asked Peregrine, genuinely puzzled. "Rodgers wouldn't tell me anything; said Julie'd explain when he got the chance. But he made sure I brought this," he added, indicating his pistol, "and told me to be sure I had it ready."

"I don't know any more than you do. I found out accidentally that Julian was here, and even Clarice had no idea of it; she thought he was at Creeley. I think he lied to us when he told us he was through playing spy. *Something* damned odd is going on. I came by to see if I could find out what it was, for Clare's sake if not his," Peter lied glibly.

"Frankly," said Peregrine with an exasperated sigh, "I'm beginning to think the whole thing is all a hum. I've gone through nearly every room on this floor and in the basement, and the place is empty."

"I know," said Peter. "I went through those rooms over there, and there's not a soul about."

"Did you?" asked Peregrine, brightening. "Splendid. You've saved me the trouble. I don't suppose Rodgers has had any better luck, or we'd have heard by now," he added gloomily. He had been about to leave his lodgings to join a few friends at Watier's for the excellent dinner they served there, when Rodgers had accosted him. And, as he was rapidly coming to the conclusion that Rodgers was imagining things and that Julian, wherever he was, was perfectly able to take care of himself, he was anxious to get on with his revels. If Julian were here and in trouble, that would be one thing, but he clearly was not, and there was no trouble of any kind to be found.

"We might as well wait here for Rodgers to come down," he told Ardane. He walked across the checkered floor to the front of the main hall and cast himself onto a bench that rested against a side wall. He had an excellent view of the street from the large window beside him, and the street, he informed Peter, was as deserted as the house. So certain was

Peregrine that this was all a great waste of time that he did not even bother to lower his voice. This did not please Ardane in the least.

The news that Rodgers was in the house, though he might have expected it, was not welcome. He had crossed one fence in the shape of his cousin, and he feared a far more difficult one with Rodgers. His thoughts ran apace, selecting one plan and just as rapidly discarding it. Rodgers clearly knew things that Peregrine did not, but if Julian had intended that no one should know the truth about Mr. Smith, would he have confided in Simon Rodgers? Ardane decided that it was possible, but not probable. He smiled with grim irony. Julian dead was thwarting him as effectively as Julian alive.

So, another risk would have to be taken; but not until he had had a little time to think it out, and for that he had to keep Peregrine quiet. Voices on the ground floor would bring Rodgers upon them without a doubt. He went over and sat beside his cousin.

"Just the same," he was careful to whisper, "if we are mistaken and something is afoot, Julie won't thank us for making an uproar; we'd better keep our voices down."

Peregrine grunted agreement and turned back to look out on the empty street.

His disinclination for conversation suited the earl only too well. It gave him time to think of elaborations he might safely add to his story for Rodgers' benefit, and also to solve the problem of getting both him and Peregrine out of the house as quickly as possible without arousing the suspicions of either.

If anything, Clarice felt more bounced about the carriage on the return journey to town than on the one out. What had begun as an annoying drizzle shortly after their last change had turned into a full-fledged storm as they reached the outskirts of the city. The coachman was travelling forward relying more on instinct than on vision, which in the heavy rain and darkness was all but nonexistent. It was with a great sigh of relief that he spotted the feeble lights of the city and began to leave the encompassing blackness behind.

Clarice, too, sighed with relief. Not because her battered body received any relief from the constant jostling—the streets of the city were largely churning mud and in little better condition than their country counterparts—but because she knew she would soon be at her journey's end; though not nearly soon enough to please her. The day had been warm, and the rain brought with it an uncomfortable and oppressive humidity, and the slight throbbing at her temples that had begun shortly after leaving the inn was now a full-blown headache that made even thinking painful. But her thoughts would not be still.

Even now she could scarcely bring herself to completely accept the truth that had dawned on her at the inn. She had prayed for another explanation, though she knew it was unlikely that there could be any other. She had tried to push it out of her mind as too incredible, too horrible to contemplate, but in the end she had forced herself to look at her theory rationally and not emotionally.

The allusions to the private affairs between her and her husband in the letter Peter had brought her from Curzon Street could not have been known by anyone out of the family and at first seriously threatened to shake her assumption of its being a forgery; but then she had realized that there was one other person besides Julian and herself who was conversant with the intimate details of their relationship, and one person, and only one person, who also was aware of the existence of the blackmail letter.

Clarice had at once dismissed the possibility as absurd and motiveless, but little things crept into her mind: inconsistencies of behavior, snippets of conversation, obvious opportunities. Impossible as it was to accept, she hadn't been able to reject it out of hand; all of the jumbled pieces fit too neatly into place and led her again and again to the same conclusion. If Peter, her closest confidant since Julian's return, was not Mr. Smith, then he must be closely allied with whoever that person might be. There could be no other answer, and one possibility was as horrible as the other.

Clarice became convinced that the purpose of this last letter was to remove her from town, and eventually, no doubt, to account for Julian's disappearance, for which their marital difficulties would have unwittingly supplied the motive. She also realized that this could mean that Julian was in the gravest danger, and whether he was himself aware of it, she hadn't any idea. Her mouth dry, her heart pounding wildly, she had ordered her puzzled servants to return her to town as quickly as possible.

A foggy mist was now rising from the streets to compound the misery of the driving rain. Clarice ran her hand over the glass to remove the haze that had formed, but could still see nothing but the occasional spot of light from a streetlamp. Her nerves were on edge and her head ached abominably; she closed her eyes and leaned back against the squabs.

The carriage had been forced to slow to a walk some time ago, but now it stopped altogether. Clarice dimly perceived the front of the house that had once been her home and, more encouragingly, a faint reflection of light behind the hall windows.

As Peregrine and Peter sat on the bench in the front hall, the bright moonlight faded and then disappeared altogether, and a slow rain began that shortly turned into a steady downpour. Peregrine cursed softly and told Peter that if Rodgers did not come down in a few minutes, he, for one, intended to go after him. He felt the entire night was turning into a farce, and his usually equable temper was rapidly becoming exacerbated. Not only had he lost half an evening on a wild-goose chase, but now it was pouring rain, and not one of them with a carriage. At this time of night, and especially in this weather, finding a hack would be impossible. There would be no walking to Watier's in this mess, he would have no recourse except to return to his lodgings to change what would unquestionably be sodden clothing. He sighed aloud, partly in disgust, partly in resignment.

Ardane heard the young man beside him sigh and echoed it. He was in a quandary he had not bargained for. On the one hand, he was in no hurry to have Rodgers return and to have to face whatever that situation might bring, but on the other, every moment he had to sit there in the knowledge that precious time was ticking away and that Julian's body lay only a few rooms away caused in him a rising tension.

He still had no wish to harm either Peregrine or the valet, but he was beginning to fear very much that the choice would not be his to make. Not that he had any real scruples about doing so, should the danger to his safety necessitate it, but he knew that while he had already made plans to account for Julian's disappearance, no amount of cleverness would enable him to conceal three deaths or disappearances on a single night. The uproar that must necessarily ensue would probably endanger his security in a manner equal to or worse than any knowledge of him that Julian had possessed.

The rain pounding against the house and the windows hid the sound of Rodgers' approach, and only the light of the candle he carried as he came into view alerted the two men of his presence. Peregrine immediately rose and went over to him.

"You took the devil of a time about it," he said, not bothering to lower his voice. "I don't suppose you found Rown either, did you?"

"No," said Rodgers in a tight voice, "and I'm mortal concerned."

"Well, I'm not," said Peregrine roundly. "You're an old woman, Rodgers; there's nothing in this damned house but dust and holland covers. Very likely Rown is at Creeley House with his feet up before the fire, sipping brandy, and let me tell you, that's where I wish I was. How the devil are we to get home in this mess without half-drowning in the process?"

Just then a brilliant flash of light illuminated the room and was immediately followed by a loud clap of thunder.

"Oh, splendid!" exclaimed Peregrine in disgust. "Now it is storming as well."

But Rodgers was no longer paying attention to him. By the glow of his single candle he had not yet noticed Lord Ardane sitting in the shadows across the room, but the flash of lightning revealed his presence.

Realizing this, Ardane strolled toward the two men. "Good evening, Rodgers," he said casually. "I am inclined to agree with Mr. Rown; this has been a wild-goose chase. Save us, there is not another living person in this house." He smiled slightly at his own grim humor.

"What brings you here, my lord?" asked Rodgers levelly. He did not precisely aim his pistol, which he still carried in his other hand, at Lord Ardane, but he raised it slightly. Ardane noted the gesture.

"I have explained to Mr. Rown that I had accidentally discovered that Lord Rown was staying here, and not at Creeley House with my sister. I came to find out what was going on," the earl said easily in the manner of a man who has nothing to hide.

"How did you get into the house, my lord?" asked Rodgers in a monotone.

"That is a question I might better put to you," replied Ardane coolly. "*I* did not break in. I have a key."

"Given to you by his lordship?"

"No, by Lady Rown. I am here for her sake." Ardane was beginning to relax a little. He realized that Rodgers' questions proved that his suspicions were based on his own doubts and not on anything that Julian might have told him.

"Lord Ardane helped me search this floor," Peregrine said, not quite accurately. "There is no one here, and I think we would better apply our time to discovering how we are to get out of here without being soaked to the skin."

"Mr. Rown—" began Rodgers, but was interrupted by the clatter of a carriage drawing up to the door.

The three men exchanged surprised glances, and Peregrine said, "That is probably Rown now, come to tell you you are a damn fool, Rodgers. And a very good thing, too; now we shall be able to leave this infernal place."

"It can't be his lordship, sir," said Rodgers in an odd tone.

"Well, I don't see who else it can be," retorted Peregrine. "Who the devil else would know that there was anyone here?"

Privately, Ardane wondered the same thing, and he put his right hand inside his coat and closed his fingers over his pistol. He alone knew that the one person it could not be was Julian.

Peregrine crossed to the door. As he drew it open, a very wet Clarice almost fell into the hall. To the amazement of her servants, she had insisted on going to the door herself, but to them it was becoming all of a piece with her other odd actions of this very strange day, not the least of which had been her sudden request to return to town and to come to this dark house, leaving them miserable outside in the pelting rain.

As she stumbled into the room, she mistook Peregrine for Julian in the bad light, and threw herself into his arms.

"Clare?" he said, puzzled but momentarily returning her embrace. "What the devil are you doing here? Has the whole world run mad?"

When Clarice heard his voice, she realized her mistake. The moment she had seen him and thought him to be her husband, she had been overwhelmed with relief, but now apprehension returned.

"Where is he, Perry? Where is Julian?" she asked sharply, freeing herself from his arms. Peregrine replied that he had no idea, and Clarice looked across the room toward the source of the light and saw the two other men.

"Rodgers! Peter!" she exclaimed in surprise, and then added tensely, "Where is Julian, Peter?"

"I thought you knew," he replied noncommittally. He knew he could not bluff his way through with the story of Julian having gone to America in front of Rodgers and Peregrine. His mind raced frantically for some solution to the situation he now found himself in. All of the many alternate plans he had concocted while waiting in the hall for Rodgers had become as ashes the moment his sister had arrived. Nothing he could say to allay her suspicions would satisfy the two men, and the reverse was also true.

Three pairs of eyes regarded him, and Rodgers still held his pistol. He fingered the hilt of his own gun and came to the conclusion that the time had come to cut his losses after all; to get away from this house and from the country at least with his freedom. He had been living by his wits for far too long to doubt that with patience and a little luck an opportunity would come, as it had during his encounter with Julian.

"You know that letter was false," Clarice cried accusingly. "Where is he, Peter?" Rodgers walked over beside her, and she turned to him, noticing for the first time that in addition to the candle he held in one hand, he had a pistol in the other. Her alarm grew by leaps and bounds. "Do you know where my husband is, Rodgers?" she asked, almost crying in desperation. "Is he here? Is he safe?"

Before Rodgers could reply, Clarice turned again toward her brother and discovered that he had moved directly behind her. She took a step backward. "Where is he, Peter? Tell me now!" she demanded, her voice becoming shrill.

Ardane regarded her calmly. He had used the distraction of her questions to Rodgers to move up behind her and to remove his pistol from his coat. He stood at his ease, the pistol, as it had been earlier, hidden behind him.

"You are as likely to know the answer to that as I do," he replied evasively, biding his time.

Rodgers was an extremely puzzled man and had been since the arrival of Lady Rown. Lord Rown had kept him in the dark about his plans for this night as much as possible, but he found it hard to believe that her ladyship had had any part in them. The exchanges between brother and sister did nothing to enlighten him, but one thing was clear: Lady Rown expected her brother to know of her husband's whereabouts, and this circumstance sharpened his suspicions toward the earl.

"My lady, I think . . ." he began, and as Clarice turned toward him, Ardane moved swiftly.

In the space of a moment he had hold of Clarice and something hard was pressed firmly into her back. Rodgers reacted quickly, levelling his pistol, and Peregrine, who had stood apart from them, a bemused spectator, rushed to his side, cursing himself for leaving his pistol on the bench.

Ardane forestalled any further action. "I think," he said carefully, "that it would be wise to throw down your pistol, Rodgers. Mine has a hair trigger, and if I am nervous, my hand will be unsteady."

"Good God, man!" exclaimed Peregrine, shocked.

"I think it is you who had better put down your weapon, my lord," Rodgers said evenly. "We both know that you have no intention of using it on her ladyship, and I am sure we would all be more comfortable if you were to explain yourself without imperilling her."

"You are responsible for her safety now, Rodgers," Ardane said nastily. "Put it down."

Clarice was overwrought to a point near hysteria. "Don't do it, Rodgers," she cried. "He knows where Julian is. He forged a letter from him to get me out of the way and tricked me into giving him the key to this house. He means to harm him, I'm sure of it. He's Mr.—" She ended abruptly in a gasp of pain as Peter increased his grip on her.

But Clarice was not daunted. Fear for her husband's safety made her completely oblivious of the danger she stood in. She repeated yet again the question that had been so often asked that evening and never yet answered. "Where is Julian?"

Ardane laughed in such a way that Clarice could actually

feel her blood run cold. "Beyond your aid," he replied deliberately. "And precisely where he deserves to be. He has done his best to ruin me, and I have rid myself of him once and for all. He would have done himself much better to have remained dead, and you, dear sister, would have done him a better turn if you hadn't been fool enough to succumb to him again so easily. You have your share of blame in this. He might have gone back to America and left us all in peace.

"If this fool Rodgers puts down his pistol, I'll see you free once I'm away," he promised. "Then you can still pick up the pieces of your life. You can return to Prescott with good conscience: you are a free woman."

"No," Clarice burst out in an agonized cry. She twisted in his grip in a futile attempt to get away. "Shoot him, Rodgers, shoot him now. Never mind about me, you can't let him escape; he has murdered Julian."

In the stunned silence that followed this outburst, a cool, soft voice from the direction of the side hall behind them said, "Despite his determined efforts, he has not quite accomplished that yet."

The oddly assorted group in the main hall turned toward the sound with the motion of a single person. Ardane gave a strangled cry of rage and abruptly released her. Then the room, indeed the whole world, seemed filled with flashing light and a horrible booming sound that echoed again and again off the high ceiling and around the empty room. For a moment no one moved or spoke in shocked silence as the echoes died away. Time itself seemed suspended to Clarice. Then the lightning flashed again and she saw her brother sway and suddenly fall against her. She moved away from him, horrified, the acrid smell of powder searing her nostrils. By the light of the candle that Rodgers still held, she saw the dark smear on her dove-grey carriage dress. She reached down and touched it, and the stain transferred itself to her gloved fingers. She brought her hand to her face in disbelief, and the frayed thread of self-control snapped at last. As if from a great distance away, she heard herself screaming.

17

When Clarice opened her eyes, it was to a dimly lit room with the sound of rain slashing against the windows. For one frightened moment she thought she was still in that awful empty house with horror all around her. Then she realized that she was in bed, and not just in any bed, but her very own at Creeley House. She wondered if it had all been a terrible nightmare, but reality returned to her in a rush and she sat up and cried out, "Julian!"

At once Lady Gus was at her side, and taking Clarice's hand in hers, she murmured soft reassurances that everything was well.

It was not enough for Clarice. "Gussie! Why are you here?" she cried in alarm. "Is it Julie? *Is* he alive? Is he safe?"

Augusta pushed her gently but firmly back against her pillows. "Hush, Clare," she said softly. "You have had a dreadful shock and you must rest and not excite yourself. Julian is very much alive. I begin to agree with Perry that our dear brother is part cat, so many lives does he seem to have. And he is quite well, or at least he would be if anyone could persuade him to obey Sir Walter's orders and get the rest he is supposed to be having. The shot grazed his head, you know, and he has had a concussion, and should be on his bed this very moment; but he will insist on seeing a perfect troop of strange men that keep coming and going at all hours. And all of them so official-looking! Though that's hardly surprising under the circumstances. Perry told me that he and Rodgers had to practically use physical force to get him into bed at all last night, and of course he was up at some ungodly hour this morning and it began all over again.

"He is shockingly pale, and I am sure his head must be paining him dreadfully, but he will not allow anyone to deal with anything for him. He insists on doing everything himself." She paused for one of her infrequent breaths, and noticed Clarice's obvious concern.

"Oh, dear," she continued contritely. "I've done it again, haven't I? I only wanted to reassure you that Julie was safe and well, and now I've made you worry about him. There is truly no need. The concussion was not severe, and as soon as everything quiets down a bit and he knows that you are well, he will be sensible and behave as he ought. He has been in a great taking about you, though I've told him there was not the least need; you are not so fragile that you would fall into a decline just because you have had a shock. I shall send for him at once and ease both your minds at a single stroke. Then I shall endeavor to close my lips before I say anything else that will upset you." She picked up a small table bell and rang it. "Although my dearest George insists that when it comes to holding my tongue, both my hands are always tied behind my back," she added with a laugh.

The door leading into Clarice's sitting room opened and a housemaid entered and curtsied, and Lady Gus requested her to fetch Lord Rown.

Clarice had listened to her sister-in-law in silence, but now she asked, "Where is Eddly? Why didn't she answer the bell?"

"Oh, poor Eddly!" cried Augusta in doleful accents. "She is quite laid up. In bed on Sir Walter's orders, and it was really quite a good thing for everyone else that he did so. She was nearly hysterical and frightfully in the way. Even Julie lost his temper with her, and that, I must say, is a thing that I have never seen him do with a servant before. But he certainly had more cause to be distraught than she did, and he did apologize at once; very prettily, too, which I thought quite made up for it. Only, then that made her cry, whereas the rebuke had not, and Sir Walter—such an understanding man—took the matter to hand.

"Not, of course, that one can blame poor Eddly. What chaos there was here last night! Moreton told me he was quite flabbergasted when he opened the door to discover you unconscious in Perry's arms, and Julie, his head all bound up in the tattered remains of his neckcloth and blood all over that and his shirtfront, being supported by Rodgers; it would not at all be an exaggeration to say that hell quite broke loose, though of course, it *is* vulgar.

"Perry had the very good sense to send the footman that was with you to fetch me and the doctor at once, so I arrived almost on your heels, and everything was at sixes and sevens. It was such a good fortune that I was at home, though we did have guests which I abandoned to George's care, and what they must think of me, I can't imagine." She broke off at last to listen with a tilted head as footsteps approached in the outside hall. "Here is Julian now, I think. He mustn't stay long, though. You need to rest, you know, and I mean to convince him, if I can, to do the same."

Lady Gus was still speaking when Julian entered the room, and before she could regather sufficient breath to exclaim at it, Clarice had scrambled out of the bed and rushed across the room to meet him halfway. She cast herself into his arms, and he held her as tightly as he could without causing her discomfort. Neither spoke, but Clarice was sobbing softly on Julian's shoulder, and from where she stood, Lady Gus could see that, though her brother's eyes were closed, his lashes were matted and wet. She tactfully took herself into the sitting room and remained there for as long as she supposed they would need to regain their composure.

When she returned to the bedchamber, Clarice was back in bed propped up against her pillows, and Julian was sitting beside her on the edge of the bed. As she entered, they both looked up at her without any noticeable sign of pleasure, and Lady Gus, believing she understood, and very much in love with her husband herself, felt every kind of monster to have to break up the charming picture they presented. But Sir Walter had impressed upon her very sternly the need to see that her charge had complete rest and calm, and she walked up to them and said in a brisk, efficient voice, "Come, Julian, you must leave now. You should be lying down yourself. Clarice has seen that you are well, and you have seen that she is, and you must both be content now and rest, as you are supposed to be doing."

"Leave us, Augusta," said Julian, regarding her balefully.

"Leave you!" cried his sister. "Of course I will not. I am sure I am pleased that you have finally made it up between you," she added, assuming that this was so. "I rather thought that you had, but as no one ever tells me anything and—"

"No one ever tells you anything, Augusta, because you are never quiet long enough for them to have the chance," her brother said, breaking into what promised to be one of her usual long speeches.

"You may be as cross with me as you like," replied Lady Gus, not in the least perturbed. "I do not intend to be routed. You will have the rest of your lives to play at being young lovers, so you shall have no sympathy from me." She crossed her arms over her breast and looked so uncharacteristically stern that Clarice laughed.

"Please, Gussie," she said. "You will be doing me a far greater service if you permit Julian to stay. I have so many questions bouncing against each other in my head that I would never be able to rest until we have spoken."

"No, Clare," Julian said quickly. "Gussie is right. We will talk after you have rested."

"But I have rested!" Clarice said plaintively. "If it is dark again, I must have slept around the clock. I *must* know, Julian, truly I must."

Julian and his sister exchanged meaningful glances, and Augusta reluctantly left the room without further protest.

Julian watched her until the door closed, and then turned back to his wife. Clarice searched his eyes anxiously, but they held only the shuttered expression he assumed when he did not want anyone to know what he was feeling. "Peter . . ." she began tentatively, her voice catching.

"Is dead," replied her husband baldly. "Rodgers shot him when he pushed you away to get at me. He did not necessarily mean to kill him, but there was no time for niceties such as careful aim. He is almost beside himself that it had to happen at his hand, but he had absolutely no other choice." He paused and looked directly into her eyes and said carefully, "It was precisely what I meant him to do when I spoke. I knew that being confronted with my 'ghost' a second time would probably unnerve Peter sufficiently to cause him to forget about you, and the fact that Rodgers had a pistol aimed at him, in his desire to get at me. He was a very single-minded man, you know. It was a risk because I was unarmed, but if I had been, I would have shot him myself without a moment's hesitation."

"He meant to kill you. He thought he already had," Clarice said quietly, and reached up to gently touch the small bandage held in place by sticking plaster on the side of his head near his temple. It was nearly hidden by his hair, and as she touched it, she wondered that an injury which appeared outwardly so innocuous could have so easily been so deadly.

Julian took her hand from his face and held it in his. "It was horrible," she told him. "I told Rodgers to shoot him, Julian, but I didn't mean it, I truly didn't. At least, I don't now." She began to cry.

"Of course you did not," her husband soothed her. "You were hysterical, and no wonder. There is nothing I wouldn't have done to have spared you this grief, Clare."

"You already have, haven't you," Clarice composed herself enough to say. "You've always known that Peter was the traitor, I'm certain of it. You left four years ago because you knew that if you stayed you would be forced to expose him, and you wanted to spare me that."

Julian looked away from her face to her hand, which he still held in his. "No, Clare," he said. "I will not have you making me out a patterncard of noble sacrifice. I left precisely for the reasons I told you I did. Because I wanted to. When they told me to leave, I could have refused, but instead, I went along with everything they suggested, even allowing you to believe me dead and to grieve for me. It was entirely selfish and entirely unforgivable."

Clarice shook her head slowly. "I don't believe that. Our problems might have made it easier for you to take such a course, but I know you would not have done so for that reason alone. We have both of us had far too much time to dwell on our unhappiness and to give ourselves the blame. What was wrong in our marriage was not the sole fault of either; we are both to blame."

He raised his head to look at her, and his eyes were so sad that Clarice had to bite at her lip to keep from crying again. "You are far too generous, Clare. You know that isn't so," he said quietly.

"I know that it is," she replied, her voice catching a little, "and I wish you wouldn't try to convince me otherwise. I, too, have used the years that we have been apart to gain maturity, though I have given you little evidence of it since your return, especially in recent days."

He did not reply at once, and was then forestalled by the entrance into the room of his sister and Sir Walter Beamish, who at once castigated him for being up and dressed, and shooed him out of the room so that he could examine Clarice.

Clarice was so vexed that she could have cried again. Contrary to Lady Gus's belief, they had not made it up between them, or even begun to do so; but Clarice had felt that they had at least been on the point of it. Her last statement had been by way of a prelude to explaining to him the truth about the night he believed her to have spent with John Prescott, and she wanted him to know that she understood about Lady Susan, that it had been brought on by her refusal to be a wife to him, and that she forgave him entirely.

After that, if they were able to get through it, she had meant to tell him how very much she loved him and wanted to be his wife again. Now the opportunity was gone and she would have to find her courage again.

When Sir Walter left to see Julian, pronouncing himself pleased with the recovery she had made from her shock, Lady Gus went with him, leaving Clarice to her unprofitable regrets and the hope that Julian would return to her when the doctor had finished with him.

In a short while her sister-in-law returned, and Clarice immediately wanted to know if the doctor had left and what he had said of her husband.

Augusta came over to the bed and in the process of plumping the pillows and rearranging the covers forced Clarice back into a prone position. "Sir Walter is still with Julian, who is behaving himself very nicely now, as you must," she said in a conversational tone as she did this. "I gather that the wound is trifling in itself, merely a scratch, but it did bleed a lot and Julian lost consciousness for a time, so the doctor has prescribed a restorative diet, rest, and most important, sleep. Julian can be quite the most stubborn of men when he pleases, but he has at last listened to reason and has been persuaded to undress and get into bed, and if Rodgers or anyone dares to wake him before he does so of himself, he shall have me to deal with and I shall not be kind." As she said this, there was a discreet knock at the door leading into the hall, and with an annoyed exclamation Augusta crossed the room to answer it.

Clarice heard muted voices, and then Lady Gus stepped aside, saying, "Only five minutes," and Simon Rodgers stepped into the room.

He walked up to Clarice and began speaking at once. "My lady, I have come to beg your pardon for what I have done," he said in a formal, rehearsed voice. "I am very sorry that I should have been the instrument of causing you such pain. I know that it may be grievous for you to have me continue in his lordship's employ, and I understand and think myself that it would be the best thing if I left. I have already given Lord Rown my notice, and only wanted to stay to tell you how bad I feel over the way things came out. I know it isn't enough."

Clarice looked at the doleful figure of the little man who stood before her and smiled sadly. "You must not blame yourself, Rodgers," she said gently. "If you had not fired when you did, my brother would have killed Lord Rown. You saved his life, you know. And you did not kill the brother whom I loved and who was my friend and confidant; Peter did that himself when I realized what he had become. The man that you shot was a vicious, terrifying stranger, a heartless traitor and murderer; and the man that I once believed him to be, the good that was in him, that is in my memory and will die only when I do."

"I do not deserve this kindness, my lady," replied the valet with a catch in his voice.

"Yes, you do, Rodgers," said Clarice, "and my deepest gratitude as well. You preserved the life of my husband. Tell me, how was it that you came to be there with Mr. Rown?"

"I knew his lordship was there, my lady," Rodgers said quietly. "We did not go to Creeley, but only to the first change, and then returned to town at dusk. Lord Rown was laying a trap to flush the traitor, though he wouldn't tell me who that person was. By that time I had guessed for myself that it was someone he was close to and did not want brought to account if there was any way that could be managed, and his lordship took good care to leave me out of his arrangements as much as possible, so that I wouldn't learn the truth for myself.

"When the time came for his lordship to confront the man," Rodgers continued, "he insisted on doing it alone. But we had plans to meet an hour after dark if everything went well, and when Lord Rown failed, I sought out Mr. Rown, as I thought it would be a good thing to have help if anything had gone wrong."

"Rodgers!" said Clarice, shocked. "Were you a spy too? Was every person I know a spy?"

For the first time Rodgers permitted himself a hint of his usually cheerful smile. "I wouldn't know about *every* person, my lady, but I was in field intelligence for a time, and when I met his lordship, I was a recruiter. I am out of it now, as is his lordship."

"Rodgers, what did Lord Rown say when you gave him your notice?" asked Clarice suddenly.

Rodgers dropped his eyes to the floor. "He said that I should see you before he would accept it. But it is best if I leave, my lady."

"Do you want to, Rodgers?"

"I am very attached to his lordship, but it is not a question of what I want, my lady."

"It is very much that question," Clarice said firmly. "I know that my husband is very fond of you, and now more than ever I can see why. I think you would be doing both him and yourself a great disservice if you were to leave us for any other reason than that you no longer wished to be in our employ. Please go to him, Rodgers, and tell him for me that I wish you to stay."

Rodgers looked up at her and, not trusting himself to speak, deeply bowed his thanks and left.

Clarice, realizing that in spite of her long sleep she was still very tired, lay back against her pillows and closed her eyes.

18

When Clarice awoke early the next morning, it was at last to sunshine, and though she protested that she was quite well and completely restored, neither her sister-in-law nor Eddly, who had returned to her duties, would allow her to think of leaving her bed, at least until Sir Walter had come and delivered his verdict. Fortunately, he was in good time after breakfast, but he could not be prevailed upon to allow Clarice more than permission to leave her bed and to spend a quiet day in her rooms, and Clarice, though thinking it absurd and unnecessary, agreed to obey.

Shortly after Sir Walter had left, Anne arrived and Clarice was told for the first time of the story that was being given to the world to account for the events of that wretched night and her brother's death.

"And whether they or anyone else will ever completely believe it is more than I can tell," Anne said with a tired sigh. "With Julian's antics, and now this, the whole world must think we are a family of maniacs to whom dreadful things are forever happening." She paused to dab at the tears that intermittently coursed down her cheeks. "It is so awful, Clare! Peter! I cannot bear to think of it. But I know he never meant to hurt you. He could not; he loved you, Clare!" She burst into fresh sobs, and Clarice put her arms around her and began to comfort her.

Discussing their brother and his unhappy end with Anne had brought her to tears as well, but an underlying thought could not be erased: Clarice wondered, but did not speak aloud, whether Peter, in light of what they now knew about him, had ever truly cared for anyone but himself, and perhaps Lydia. Clarice asked Anne about their sister-in-law, feeling a little guilty that it was the first time she had thought of her.

"Oh, her!" Anne replied scornfully through her sobs. "You needn't trouble yourself about that one. I cannot but think that poor Peter was sadly deceived in her; though he was always very attached to her and never seemed to mind her grasping ways. Do you know the very first thing that she said when Fowle and I went to break the sad news to her? She wanted to know what would become of Peter's income, if she would be able to control it for little John until he came of age. She went on and on about the money and never a word of grief for the man who had loved her best in the world. I was so overset by her behavior that it was all I could do to keep my tongue to myself, and Fowle had to send for her mother and sisters to stay with her so that he might take me away from there. Oh, Clare!" she cried, and began sobbing again.

When she had recovered herself, she went on, "We needn't worry about them, though. Fowle is joint guardian with Lydia of the children, and Julian has insisted on assisting them financially so they will never want, except for a father, but, oh, Clare, if Peter *was* such a dreadful man and even we who were closest to him were so deceived in him, mightn't it be for the best?"

Clarice did her best to soothe her, and after a short while Anne left, and Clarice amused herself first with a book, and then with needlework to pass the time.

By late afternoon she still had not seen or had any word of her husband, which struck her as odd, but in the intervening hours since she had last seen Julian her thoughts had returned to the problems which still remained unresolved, and as time heightened them in her mind, she became diffident of asking for him.

As the hour for dinner approached, Clarice's thoughts took a different direction, and now she worried that perhaps Julian had not come to her because he was unwell. She asked Augusta if that were the case.

"Good heavens, no!" replied Lady Gus with a smile. "He was quite a good boy today and slept almost until noon, which just proves that he did need it, for you know what an early riser he is; and then Sir Walter returned early this afternoon and saw him again. His color is much better today, and he is much more himself, so even though I did tell him that I thought it unwise, I could not really object to his going out this afternoon, heaven knows where. He is not back yet, at least as far as I know; but did he not come to see you before he left? I thought from something he said that he meant to do so."

Clarice replied that he had not, and their conversation was brought to an end by the arrival of the man himself. He enquired solicitously after his wife's health, and listened with patience to his sister's ramblings on what he should and should not do for his own, and then, making no request or attempt to be private with Clarice, he excused himself to change and find his dinner. He made no mention of joining them or returning later to be with Clarice, and all her worst fears and apprehensions were renewed.

To Clarice his manner had seemed more withdrawn and certainly colder than it had been the previous night. More than ever she regretted the interruption that had prevented them from speaking of the things that concerned them most intimately. She began to believe that his earlier gentleness and affectionate demeanor had been assumed to comfort her grief over the loss of her brother, and not, as she had dared to hope, because he still loved her and wanted her. But he had been in a good frame of mind toward her then, and if she had been able to explain everything to him, he might have listened and they might by now have been happy.

Instead she made herself miserable with her worries, which only increased when he did not return to her that night. She slept badly and awoke the following morning with a headache.

Augusta, though anxious to return to her husband and new daughter, had made up her mind to spend another day with her sister-in-law. Though Clarice protested that she was now quite recovered from the shock of those grievous events and needed no further cosseting, Lady Gus could not but notice that she was dispirited and possessed of an underlying discomposure.

Late afternoon found them in the cheerful morning room engaged in needlework and from time to time taking part in a desultory conversation. As evening approached they were joined by Julian and Peregrine, and Clarice immediately began to express her gratitude for the part he had played.

He would have none of this, though, and quickly cut her off, saying, "I do not at all deserve your thanks. Quite the reverse. It is I who beg your pardon; if things had been left to me, we might have suffered an even unhappier outcome. I was so taken up with my own selfish wishes that I hadn't the least idea what was going forward, in spite of Rodgers' warnings."

Clarice insisted that he was too hard on himself, and Augusta, not so concerned to spare her younger brother's sensibilities, broke into their conversation to ask Peregrine when they might reasonably expect their father to arrive. An express message had been sent at once to Lord Creeley, informing him of what had occurred and requesting his immediate return to town.

"Later tonight, perhaps, or sometime tomorrow," replied Peregrine, "depending on how rapid are his stages and when he was able to get away."

They discussed this and went on to other topics, but Augusta observed that she and Peregrine carried most of the conversation. Clarice had little to say, and Julian, when he spoke at all, did so with restraint. She also noticed that Clarice from time to time directed quick, earnest glances at her husband, as though she were trying to gauge his feelings, and Lady Gus began to wonder if her surmise of the other day, that everything was at last well between them, was after all correct.

After a while Peregrine got up to take his leave of the others, but was diverted by the sound of a carriage being drawn up to the door. It drew him and his sister to the windows, where they recognized the carriage at once as belonging to their father, exclaiming at his being so quick. In a very few moments footsteps were heard in the hall and Lord Creeley appeared in the doorway. Augusta at once ran over to hug him and then drew him into the room. Clarice stood a little apart while he exchanged greetings with his children, but he quickly perceived her, crossed to where she was standing, and took her hands in his.

"My dear Clarice," he said gently. "I only wish that I had words to say that could properly console you."

"Beaupère . . ." she began, but emotion closed her throat. He guided her to a sofa and sat down beside her.

"I am so sorry," Clarice said emotionally. "I shall never be able to beg your pardon for the grief and disgrace that I and my family have brought to yours."

Lord Creeley was astonished. "My dear girl, whatever can you mean? Never, ever say such a thing to me! You are a part of our family and have brought us nothing but happiness and light; and gaiety and youth as well, in the form of three of the loveliest grandchildren that any man was every blessed with. You are not for a moment to take the sins of your brother on your shoulders. Is that clear?" Clarice nodded, unable to speak, and he continued, "I think I have much to be grateful to you for, as does your occasionally graceless husband. The finest act of his entire life was the day he took you to wife, and I have raised a fool if he does not know that."

This praise, which Clarice did not at all believe she deserved, instead of making her feel better, made her all the more depressed. The conviction which she had formed in the last hour, that Julian, when everything was more settled, fully intended to proceed with his plan to divorce her, would certainly prove to Lord Creeley that she was not worthy of his approbation.

Clarice looked so obviously unhappy that Lord Creeley, though he mistook the cause of her wretchedness, tried at once to lighten the mood of the conversation by telling her of the adventures and mischiefs the children had gotten into at Creeley Lodge during her absence. This succeeded very well for a short time, but Lady Gus, whose head was still full of the events of the past few days, turned the subject again as soon as a break in the conversation allowed her to do so.

"Papa, when Julian wrote to you, did he tell you the absurd story he and Perry and Rodgers made up to account for everything?" she asked with a reproving look at Peregrine. "Frankly, I think most of it was Perry's doing, for it sounds very like him, and whether or not it will answer, heaven only knows, but it is just like him not to consider *that*."

"Well, of all . . ." began Peregrine, affronted. "With all sorts of horrors happening at once and Clare's servants pounding on the door to know what had happened, it is a miracle that we managed anything at all in that space of a few minutes. I suppose you think you would have done better."

Augusta's face showed clearly that she did, but before she could speak, Lord Creeley said quickly in the interest of peace, "No, I hadn't heard. Julie just gave me the bare facts and told me to come at once. Why don't you explain it to me, Julian," he added, casting a concerned look in the direction of his elder son. He had been assured by Julian in his letter that his injury was of a trifling nature, but even in the short time that he had been present, he had noted his son's lack of animation and effacing behavior and was reasonably certain that, if not the injury, something was troubling him.

"We have let it be known that while there to go over the house, we surprised thieves, who turned out to be armed, which led to the results that we could not hide from the world. Unfortunately, the thieves escaped without injury and without a trace," replied Julian succinctly.

"Have you ever heard anything so paltry!" exclaimed Augusta. "The world is supposed to believe that Julian, having been away for a sennight, returned in the middle of the night and immediately got up a party consisting of Clare, Perry, Peter, and, goodness knows why, his valet, to tour an empty house in the dark! I know the servants have been paid well to forget that Julian did not first come to this house and that Clare had left that morning for Southampton and, nearly there, came rushing back to town, and I know that they are all very loyal to us, but honestly! It is all so fantastic! There is bound to be talk. And questions."

"It will have to serve," replied her father. "We could not for a moment think of telling the true story, and as Julian has said, there were certain results that could not be hidden. Of course there will be talk, but we can none of us do anything about that."

"But what on earth am I or any of us to say when everyone wants to know what happened?" persisted Augusta. "A complete refusal to discuss it will look as though we are trying to hush something up."

"So we are!" said the earl agreeably. "Your mother thinks, and I quite agree with her, that the best thing would be for all of us to retire to the country as soon as possible—our doing so will hardly be wondered at—and she wishes all of you at Creeley for at least a part of the summer. I'm afraid she has been in a bit of a pelter since Julian's letter arrived in that most dramatic fashion, and will not be reassured until she sees for herself that none of her chicks have come to harm."

He turned again to Clarice. "I know, of course, that you were present and forced to witness the dreadful things that occurred, but I knew nothing of your going to Southampton; Julian gave me the barest facts in his letter. I shall not ask it of you now, for I know how raw that wound must be, but someday, whenever you are ready, I hope we will be able to discuss it. There is much I do not understand in this affair."

Clarice smiled at him sadly. "It is not a wound precisely, Beaupère, but an uncomprehending sadness which I fear will always be with me when I think of Peter. I loved my brother, but I cannot, will not be blind to what he was, and I hope this will in some way console me for his loss. I shall certainly speak of it, and now if you like, for you, of all people, must have the truth in all of its details."

Lord Creeley objected that it was not necessary for her to put herself through this now, but Clarice insisted. She told him everything from the time she received the blackmail note until Julian had appeared in the shadows of the hallway of their former home, leaving out only the part of her discussion with her husband that had concerned his intention of divorcing her.

Lord Creeley then turned to Peregrine to enquire after his part in the affair, and when he had finished, tactfully bringing his story to a close at the point where Clarice had arrived, the earl said to Julian, "Was your brother right all along, then? Did you know that Peter was Mr. Smith?"

"Yes."

"And did you know it four years ago?"

"I suspected it, no more," replied his son. "I *knew* the night I came back; the moment that he looked at me, I was positive. But I wanted, rightly or wrongly, to let sleeping dogs lie. I didn't have an iota of evidence to prove my belief, and seeing him hang would no longer have served anyone except for revenge. I believed it would bring a tremendous amount of grief to a great many people if he were exposed, and at the time, I felt it to be the lesser of two very great evils to do nothing against him. Obviously, I was mistaken."

"I don't believe you were," said Lord Creeley. "You tried to act for the best, and in many ways I'm sure the course you took was the more difficult for you; certainly the more hazardous. I wish you will tell me how this confrontation came to take place in the Curzon Street house, and why you were living there by yourself without comfort or servants, when everyone believed you at Creeley."

"I did it to force the confrontation," Julian replied. "I understood perfectly from our first meeting that merely telling him outright that I knew what he was would never do. Tacitly, it was already understood between us that I did, and had I brought it out into the open, he would have denied it with his last breath, no doubt questioning my sanity as he did so. I had to force him into a position that was so obvious that even he would not have the audacity to brazen it out."

"But why in that house?" persisted his father.

"It was not part of my original plan to accomplish it there," said Julian quietly. "Certain circumstances, though, made it desirable for me to leave this house, but I couldn't leave town, and I decided that it would serve as well or even better for me to be there as a means of drawing him out."

Clarice had not been looking at her husband as he spoke, but at these words she did look up at him and momentarily caught his eyes, which told her nothing. Lord Creeley did not enquire after the nature of the circumstances that had made Julian's departure from Creeley House desirable, and for this Clarice was grateful. She looked at her hands in her lap and listened attentively to her husband. When he reached the point where Peter had produced his pistol and shot him, Clarice realized that he had not explained, at least to her satisfaction, what caused the distraction that had allowed Peter to gain the upper hand. She knew that her husband was not a man to be easily discomposed or unnerved, and seldom was he ever careless, and she drew her own conclusions as to the content of their discussion.

"I saw rather than heard it go off," Julian was telling his father, "and I suppose, as much as I was capable of thought, I believed that I was dead. I don't remember losing consciousness or regaining it, and I have no idea of the passage of time involved. The first thing I remember, after my amazement at still being alive, was concern for why I was. I knew Peter would not have shot at me and then run off leaving the business half-finished, even if he believed me dead. The obvious answer was that something had occurred to disturb him, and I had no doubt that that something had been Simon Rodgers."

"Did Rodgers know the truth about Ardane as well?" interposed the earl.

"No. Because I did not want Peter brought to public disgrace, I had done everything in my power to shield Simon from the truth, and I realized that in doing so I had probably placed him in the gravest danger. If Peter discovered that Simon was my confederate, and it was likely that he would if he found him in the house, he would be forced to act against him as well, and Simon would not even have the advantage of knowing him as the enemy."

Julian paused to thank his brother for a glass of wine he had poured out for him, and then continued, "I couldn't stay in that room and wait to see what might or might not happen, but the graze had stunned me and my progress was so damnably slow that I doubted my ability to be of aid to anyone, even myself. Added to that, Peter had apparently taken my pistol, and I was unarmed.

"Eventually I reached the door and went into the hall. I heard voices coming from the direction of the main hall, and as they became more distinct, I realized that one of them belonged to Clarice. By the time I reached them, Peter had taken hold of Clarice and was threatening her. Whether or not he actually would harm her, I hadn't any idea; I had long ago learned not to assume him incapable of any behavior." He turned to Clarice and addressed her for the first time. "I am sorry, Clare, but it was so."

Clarice nodded unhappy agreement, but he had already returned his attention to his father. "When he first saw me in his library the night I returned, Peter was nearly beside himself with horror, and for a time at least, fear. I hoped that a second 'ghostly' encounter would have a similar effect, and as Rodgers by now knew him for what he was, I knew I could place complete faith in his ability to back me up. He did."

"Do you mean to say that you exposed yourself, unarmed, to a desperate man with a pistol; a man, moreover, whom you knew wished you dead?" asked his father, horrified. But, recollecting that Clarice sat beside him, he added, "Just so. Well, it would be very wrong of me to say that things turned out for the best, for I always liked Peter and I am saddened by what has happened. But you, my dear," he said, addressing Clarice, "must feel it very much for all your composure. You, I think, will be very glad to come away from town and stay at Creeley."

Clarice gave him a half-smile, looked up at him quickly and then down at her hands again. "It shall be as Julian wishes," she said softly. "Though I own I would as lief not stay in town."

Lord Creeley looked toward his elder son, but he was not attending and gave the appearance of being completely absorbed in the appearance of his fingernails. Lord Creeley formed his own conclusions and sighed sadly. "Well," he said, standing, "I think it is time that I got rid of my dirt. Perry, will you escort me upstairs? And, Gussie, if you mean to leave with George tonight, you had better attend to your packing."

Lord Creeley hardly needed an escort in his own home, but Peregrine readily obliged, and Lady Gus, although she had packed her few things to return to her own house hours ago, quickly took their lead. Lord Creeley then turned to Julian. "Later, after I have made myself presentable, I hope you will come to me if you can spare the time. There is something I would like to discuss with you."

Julian agreed, and the earl turned to his daughter-in-law and gave her a reassuring smile, which she just managed to return. He held the door open for his two younger children to pass out of the room and then left it himself, careful to close the door behind him.

Almost the moment this was accomplished, Julian stood up and walked slowly to the windows. Clarice watched him, knowing that he had remained to speak to her, and fearing the worst.

"Julian," she began, determined to speak first, "I was wondering if . . . if you had seen Mr. Bolt again."

"No."

"But you will be seeing him again, won't you? Soon?" she persisted, taut in anticipation of his answer.

"I haven't seen him at all since my father first returned to Creeley."

Clarice looked her astonishment. "But you said—"

"Clarice, did you know that Prescott was in Devonshire? Paying his addresses, I've been told, to someone else?" he interrupted her. His voice was level; he might have been asking her opinion of the weather.

Clarice almost gasped at this. "Yes. But I so hoped that you had not," she blurted out artlessly. "How could you have discovered it?"

"I didn't. Rodgers heard word of it, servants' gossip when

he was out provisioning us at Curzon Street. He let it slip to me, no doubt meaning it as a kindness. It might have been so."

"I . . . I don't understand."

"Of course you do," he responded caustically. "Your sudden change of affections has already betrayed that you understand very well."

He was turned away from her, his profile etched sharply against the late-afternoon sun coming through the panes. He gave the appearance of being perfectly at his ease, but Clarice knew he was not. Tears welled into her eyes and spilled silently onto her face. "Oh, Julian!" she cried in a small choked voice.

"It doesn't signify," he said brusquely, and turned to her. "There is certainly nothing to cry about."

"Oh, Julian," she repeated with better control of her emotions. "You think . . . I . . . I wanted to explain everything to you myself, after . . . When you came to my room the night before last, I threw myself in your arms and behaved as though I never wanted to be out of them. I would have served us both better if I had been more circumspect. But I didn't think . . . it didn't occur to me . . . You thought . . . you think that it is cream-pot love, expediency, that I . . . that I am cutting my losses."

"Aren't you?" he asked softly.

Clarice shook her head slowly, having again lost command of her voice, but he had turned back to the window and didn't see the gesture.

"I admit that for a time I flattered myself that you were not so indifferent to me as you would have had me think. I suppose you *do* like me." He laughed in a self-mocking way. "I must learn to be grateful for that. Heaven knows there are any number of married people who get along well enough on less than that. We shall manage."

Clarice crossed the room to stand beside him. "You told me that morning in your father's study that you had seen Mr. Bolt and were bringing an action against me to divorce me. Wasn't that true?"

"No," he said shortly, and then added in an easier tone, "You would please me very much if you would forget everything I said to you that day, and the night before."

"I cannot, Julian. Not even to please you, at least not yet," she said unhappily. "That wretched night! I am the greatest of all possible fools!" He in no way responded to her, and she went on, "You must listen to me, Julian. I must explain that night to you."

He did not look at her but stared sightlessly out the window. "There is no need," he said quietly but coldly.

"There is every need!" Clarice cried. "Julian, you must and will hear me!" In her urgency she grabbed the lapels of his coat, and at this he did turn to her.

"I do not wish to know. Not now or ever," he said in a flintlike voice. "Your folly next to my many pales to nonexistence. I understood for the first time that night the pain that I had caused you. Believe that I will not deliberately hurt you again and, please, be charitable enough to let the subject drop."

"You don't know what it is I'm going to say."

"Perhaps I do. I know I have many faults, but self-delusion, I trust, is not among them. Do me the kindness, Clare, of not thinking me a fool."

This was certainly very daunting, and his eyes, so cold, so black and impenetrable, nearly made her despair, but the fear of what their life together would be like if she did not go on, if she did not make him understand, was greater.

"You did not flatter yourself," she said quickly before he could stop her. "So far from being indifferent to you, I was in the way of being as much in love with you as I have ever been, if indeed I ever had stopped loving you. Then I saw you with that . . . with Lady Susan and, well, it was not much to see, I suppose, and by absolutely refusing to be a wife to you I must have forgone my claim to your fidelity. It wasn't reasonable to expect you to adhere to nine months of celibacy while I sought to know my mind, but I didn't think of that then. I did not choose to think of it. I was wild with anger and hurt and self-pity. I wanted to punish you, to hurt you in the worst way I could manage. You were exactly right that night when you said that I had done it to pay you out. I taunted you and went with John not for love of him, but for revenge against you."

"Clare . . ." he interrupted, a warning edge to his voice.

She ignored him and went on, afraid that if she stopped he would never again permit her tell him the truth. "I went with John to his lodgings that night fully intent on becoming his mistress, and if intent *is* as good as the act, then I am guilty, but, Julie, I swear to you, on all that I hold sacred, on the love that we have had for each other, that in fact I was not. When it came to the point, I simply could not go through with it. I don't know why; because I loved you; because I didn't love John. I think it must be the former, because I cannot bear to think of another man touching me."

He roughly removed her hands from his coat and turned away from her completely toward the window. He leaned his weight on his hands, which were on the sill, and bowed his head, hiding from her the emotions which he was otherwise incapable of disguising.

Clarice, observing him, said tonelessly, "You don't believe me."

It was a full minute before he answered her. "I don't know," he replied in a voice absolutely devoid of his usual composure.

Clarice, unable to bear it, placed her hand on his shoulder and bowed her head against him. "I swear with all my heart that this is not expediency," she said with low vehemence. "I love you, Julian."

After several minutes he straightened, and Clarice moved a little away from him. He turned to her and said in more his usual tone, "I have never in my life wanted to believe anything more."

She gave him a watery smile and reached up to caress his face. "Then believe it, my dearest love. Believe that I love you deeply and wholeheartedly, and know that, though I may never have the power to convince you of it, I would give everything in the world to possess it."

He enfolded her in his arms and kissed her in a way that would have made her laugh for joy had she not been so busily engaged. Long after the kiss had ended, they stood before the window, the afternoon light fading and casting long shadows behind them, each simply content to be holding the other.

When they had at last sat down, Clarice, though she was loath to introduce anything that might dispel their happiness, asked a question to which she felt she had to know the answer.

"Do you believe me, Julie?" she asked diffidently. "About John?"

"Yes," he replied without hesitation, "and not just because I so very much want to. If I believe that you love me, and I do, then I must believe the other as well. Betrayal is not in your nature, Clare."

"How can you say so?" she said unhappily. "I *meant* to betray you, to wound you."

"But your loving heart would not let you," he said gently. "And it wouldn't matter now if you had. You have forgiven me crimes far greater than any you could commit against me. I love you and know how little I deserve that you should still love me." Clarice cried out against this, but he went on, "There is another reason that I believe you. I know, none better, how easy it is for one's behavior to be other than it seems. Will you do me the favor now of listening to me and trying to believe that I am telling the truth?"

Clarice nodded, her heart pounding a little faster.

"What you saw occur between Lady Susan and me was an act of imprudence on my part and nothing more. We are on very easy terms . . . though I won't pain you with recollections that are best forgotten. I should have had the good sense to know that even a mere friendship rekindled in that quarter would be a mistake. I kissed her as I would kiss Gussie or Anne, but you, my poor lovely wife, with so much bad experience of my behavior, could hardly help but think what you did." He paused and lifted her face to look into her eyes. "I beg your pardon, though I know it is not enough," he continued. "I swear to you, on everything that *I* hold sacred, that I have not been unfaithful to you with Lady Susan. Since I have returned, I have been with no woman, save you, or even wanted to be."

The Clarice of four or five years ago would not have believed her husband of the same period and would have scorned his declaration with bitterness, but they were neither of them the same people they had been then, and she did not hesitate to express her belief in him.

They talked quietly for a while of their future together, and he presently said, "I think we will do as Father has suggested and, as soon as everything is settled, we'll go to Creeley for the rest of the summer. I know there are three beautiful young people there who miss their mother very much."

Clarice smiled happily. "And their father too," she just

managed to say before he kissed her again. They were so engaged for several minutes, until she gently pushed him away, laughing. "You must not, Julian! We can't make love on the sofa. Anyone could walk in on us!"

"We won't," he agreed. "We'll go upstairs in a moment." Then he kissed her again in a way that made her doubt their ability to accomplish this.

At that moment the door opened, but neither of them heard Moreton, who, believing the room empty and wishing to clear away the wine tray and glasses had not bothered to knock, but simply entered the room. Nor did they hear his hasty but quiet retreat, nor the click of the latch as he closed the door after him, and if they had, neither of them, at that moment, would have cared a rush.

About the Author

Originally from Pennsylvania, Elizabeth Hewitt lives in New Jersey with her dog, Maxim, named after a famous romantic hero. She enjoys reading history and is a fervent Anglophile. Music is also an important part of her life; she studies voice and sings with her church choir and with the New Jersey Choral Society. All of her novels for Signet's Regency line were written to a background of baroque and classical music.